It Ain't So Awful, Falafel

It Ain't So Awful, Falafel

BY FIROOZEH DUMAS

HOUGHTON MIFFLIN HARCOURT

BOSTON   NEW YORK

www.hmhco.com

Text was set in 10.5 Minister Std.

Design by Christine Kettner

Cover photographs: © 2016 Courtesy of General Motors (Chevy Impala); copyright ©2016 by otsphoto/Shutterstock (hamster); copyright © 2016 by bluestocking/Getty Images (apple pie); copyright © 2016 by IvonneW/istock Getty Images (inflatable palm tree)

The Library of Congress has cataloged the hardcover edition as follows:

Dumas, Firoozeh, author.
Title: It ain't so awful, falafel / by Firoozeh Dumas.
Description: Boston : Clarion Books/Houghton Mifflin Harcourt, [2016] |
Summary: "Eleven-year-old Zomorod, originally from Iran, tells her story
of growing up Iranian in Southern California during the Iranian Revolution and
hostage crisis of the late 1970s."—Provided by publisher.
Identifiers: LCCN 2015034779
Subjects: | CYAC: Iranian Americans—Fiction. | Iran Hostage Crisis, 1979–1981—
Fiction. | California, Southern—Fiction. | United States—History—20th century—
Fiction. | BISAC: JUVENILE FICTION / Humorous Stories. | JUVENILE
FICTION / People & Places / Middle East. | JUVENILE FICTION / Social Issues
/ Emigration & Immigration. | JUVENILE FICTION / Family / General (see also
headings under Social Issues). | JUVENILE FICTION / Social Issues / Friendship. |
JUVENILE FICTION / Social Issues / Prejudice & Racism. | JUVENILE FICTION
/ Social Issues / Adolescence. | JUVENILE FICTION / Historical / United States /
20th Century. Classification: LCC PZ7.D89332 It 2016 | DDC [Fic]—dc23
LC record available at http://lccn.loc.gov/2015034779

ISBN: 978-0-544-61231-0 hardcover

ISBN: 978-1-328-74096-0 paperback

Printed in the United States of America

DOC 15 14 13 12

4500792800

To all the kids who don't belong,
for whatever reason.
This one's for you.

NUMBER FOUR

Today's Sunday and we're moving, again. Not everything fit in the moving truck, so our huge light blue Chevrolet Impala, or "land yacht," as the used-car salesman called it, is filled to the brim with boxes, pillows, and kitchen appliances. The back window's rolled down so the vacuum cleaner handle can stick out.

I am eleven years old, and this is my fourth move. I haven't met anyone who has moved so many times before sixth grade. Normal families move once or twice because they find a house with a swimming pool or more closet space, *in the same town.* Every time we move, it's to a new city or a new country.

I was born in Abadan, Iran. When I was in second grade, we moved to Compton, California. We stayed two years. For fourth grade, we moved back to Iran. Fifth grade, back to Compton. Now we're moving to Newport Beach. The two cities are only an hour apart, but they might as well be in different galaxies. In Newport Beach, there's no graffiti on the walls or overturned shopping carts on the sides of freeways. You don't see any stores with broken windows. There are trees everywhere and the city looks like it has just come back from a visit to a beauty salon. Where are the rusty cars with missing tires? Not in Newport Beach. There are a lot of those in Compton, usually on people's front lawns.

If our crazy nomadic life has taught us one thing, it's this: Don't buy stuff that breaks easily. Everything has to be packed sooner or later. Even our plants are made of plastic. Wherever we live, we have our fake red roses in the living room and the fake yellow daisies in our kitchen. They're ugly and don't look real at all; they look like those plants in horror movies that come to life and eat people. But they're one of the few constants in my life. At least they're always there.

The only time a kid came to my house after school in Compton, we were walking to my room when she suddenly stopped in front of the plants and asked what they were for. I thought that was a stupid question. I mean, how many possible uses could there be? They're just plastic flowers. But later, I realized that they are so big and ugly that they look like they *should* do something, maybe catch flies or squirt air freshener.

As we pull up to our new home in Newport Beach, I cannot believe my eyes. Our house has two stories and is surrounded by a huge lawn made of *real* grass.

"Do we have to take care of the whole lawn, *Baba*?" I ask, trying to figure out where our part of the grass begins and ends. There is no chainlink fence between the houses, so it looks like everyone's living in a huge park.

"No," my dad says. "There are gardeners."

I look at my mom to see how relieved she must be to hear this, but she's busy using the mirror on the side of the car to reapply her pink lipstick.

Our house in Compton had a small patch of grass in the front and back. By the time we figured out how often we were supposed to water it, it was all dead. Some of our neighbors had fake lawns. From far away, they looked good—better than our real, dead lawn, anyway.

As we get out of the car, I see an older lady standing in the driveway, and she seems way overdressed for daytime. She reminds me of Mrs. Thurston Howell III on *Gilligan's Island*. My mother introduces herself as my dad tries to unload the vacuum cleaner, which by now is sticking so far out the window that it almost hit the tree next to the driveway when we pulled in.

"I am Nastaran Yousefzadeh," she says, making the whole sentence sound like one word. "Dees eez Zomorod Yousefzadeh," she adds, pointing to me.

I smile. I can tell the lady's getting nervous. She has no idea what my mother just said. She has this strained expression, like she's trying to smile but only half her face is cooperating. My father, holding the vacuum cleaner, joins us, and the lady finally says, "I'm Mrs. Mavis, your landlady. Hello, Mr. You—You—Yous . . ." Her voice trails off, which is fine, since we never expect anyone to get past the first syllable of our last name. Two points for trying, Lady Mavis.

Then she gives him a key and shouts, "DO NOT LOSE THIS POOL KEY!" She pauses, looks at each of us, and continues, "If you do, you must pay fifty dollars, that's FIFTY DOLLARS, for a replacement." Then, for reasons I cannot understand, she repeats herself, but this time, loudly *and* slowly, "DO. NOT. LOSE. THIS. POOL. KEY."

I so badly want to ask her, "ARE. WE. ALLOWED. TO. LOSE. THIS. POOL. KEY?" but I don't. My mom stands there smiling like a statue. My dad, still clutching the vacuum cleaner, keeps nodding his head and repeating, "Yes, yes." He does that when he's nervous, which is often. I just roll my eyes and walk through our new front door.

Our home is a "condo," short for *condominium*. I figure this out when the landlady gives us a binder, *Rules for Condominium Living*, which we also have to return when we move out. Apparently there is no fine for losing the binder.

"Zomorod," my dad says to me, "read this and tell your mom what it says." My mom hasn't learned much English. I always encourage her to try, but she says, "*Az man gozashteh.*"

It's too late for me.

That's the most ridiculous thing I have ever heard, and I

tell her so. This always makes her mad. She says I should be a nicer daughter. But I am a nice daughter! I just don't want to be her translator for the rest of my life.

The rulebook begins with a "Welcome to Condominium Living!" page that shows a happy, good-looking blond family standing with another happy, good-looking blond family next to a barbecue, the fathers holding trays of hamburgers and hot dogs. We do not look anything like the people in the picture, but for once it doesn't matter. If there is one thing the Yousefzadehs love, it's grilling. My dad calls himself the King of Kebabs. I can almost imagine having a party with our new neighbors, just like in the picture—except that one of the families will be standing apart, holding a tray of bright orange, almost glow-in-the-dark chicken that everyone looks at but no one tries. This is what happens when you use saffron marinade instead of barbecue sauce.

In a condominium, there are rules for everything.

Chapter three, "Waste Management," is all about trash. You have to leave your trash out on Wednesday night for the trucks to pick up on Thursday morning. You can't leave the empty bins out; you have to put them back in your garage before the end of the day. You also have to put your garbage in proper trash cans with lids that fit; you can't just willy-nilly leave garbage by the curb like some sort of trash sculpture. There's even a drawing of the right and wrong way to put out your garbage. The wrong way looks like our trash in Compton.

I translate all that for my mom. She looks frazzled. "Why do they have rules for trash? I hope the landlady doesn't get mad at us," she says.

"Don't worry, *Maman*," I tell her. "I'll make sure we do it right."

I know that my mom has found something new to worry about, something else to make her want to go back to Iran, where houses do not come with rulebooks and landladies do not yell at us about losing pool keys.

I am going to have to read the rules to my mom many more times until she learns them. I don't want us to be "penalized for inappropriate waste receptacles." There is a whole section on penalties, too.

I sleep on the floor that night, because we donated my bed to the Salvation Army. Most of our furniture in Compton had come from an auction of seized goods. I didn't know what that meant until I asked Mrs. Semba, the librarian at my old school, Marian Anderson Elementary. Mrs. Semba said that seized goods means the stuff belonged to criminals and it's sold for cheap by the police because the criminals are probably in jail. When I told my mom this, she said it made her sick to think that she was eating off a table that belonged to a murderer. But my dad told her that none of our stuff belonged to murderers, only to people who had committed minor crimes like stealing apples from the grocery store. When I asked him how he knew that, he said he just did and told me not to ask so many questions.

All I know is that my mismatched bedroom furniture was really ugly and had six-digit numbers carved in the desk, bedpost, and chair. My dad said those were the serial numbers used by the auction house. I wish they had used pencil, but I guess people dealing with the criminal world usually have knives in their pockets anyway. Or they just don't care.

I hated my furniture and really want to buy a canopy

bed. I know exactly which one I want. It's on page 453 in the Sears catalog. I've looked at it so many times that the page is worn out. It's the most beautiful bed I have ever seen.

I also really, really want a beanbag chair. Every time I see a popular kid on TV, she's in her room, lounging on her beanbag chair. There is something cool about all the different ways that you can sit in it. You can sink in low; you can lie on your stomach; you can lie on your side; you can do whatever you want. It's a chair with no rules. I imagine myself sitting on my beanbag chair reading a Nancy Drew book; I imagine myself sitting on my beanbag chair sipping chocolate milk through one of those bendy straws. I think about my imaginary beanbag chair every single day and how much more fun my life would be if I had one. But best of all, I imagine inviting a friend over. The minute she sees the beanbag chair, she knows that even if my parents speak a different language and I do not have a pet and we have no snack foods, I am still cool.

I just have to convince my dad to buy one. I know that my family isn't poor—at least not compared to some of my classmates back in Compton—but when it comes to spending money, my dad's head and wallet are still in Iran. Before he buys anything, he multiplies the price by seven to see how much it costs back home. That's because one dollar is equal to seven *tumons,* which is the money in Iran. The problem is that everything in America costs more than it does in Abadan. This is obvious to me, and I'm only eleven.

Still, as I drift off to sleep on the soft avocado green shag carpet of my new room, I dare to hope that my next set of furniture has no criminal past.

The next day, my dad surprises me. We go to Sears and he says, "Zomorod, pick whatever furniture you want."

"Are you sure?" I ask.

"Yes," he says. "Go!"

"This is the one," I say about a minute later, pointing to the white canopy bed of my dreams. It looks even more beautiful in real life than it does on page 453.

"What about those?" my dad suggests, pointing to the matching nightstand, desk, chair, and dresser.

"I can get *all that*?" I ask, wondering if someone has replaced my father with a very generous long-lost twin. I want to ask him if he's sure, but I'm afraid that if he thinks about it, he'll realize he's spending too much money, especially after he multiplies it by seven.

My dad is still smiling.

"What do you think, *Maman*?"

"If it makes you happy, it's good for me, too," she says.

Ladies and gentlemen, that's about as much enthusiasm as I am ever going to get from my mom.

This is the nicest bedroom set I have ever had! All white, all matching, all brand-new. No numbers carved anywhere.

I am also allowed to get the yellow ruffled sheet and pillow set, plus the canopy cover with its lace border.

"I hope we stay in Newport Beach a long time and you can use this furniture until you graduate from high school," my dad says, patting my head. My mom doesn't look too pleased to hear that.

Since my dad is in such a generous mood, I seize the moment.

"Can I get a beanbag chair, too?"

"A bean chair?" he asks. I point to the one on display. The salesman who has been helping us asks if we want to try sitting on it. "No," my dad says. "We eat beans, not sit on them."

That is when I notice a girl my age standing with her parents, waiting for the salesman. I want to go back in time and leave before my dad started talking about eating the beanbag chair.

The salesman tells my dad that the chair just happens to be on sale today. "Normally, it costs twenty-six ninety-five, but for our back-to-school sale, it's only nineteen ninety-nine."

"In my country," my dad says, "a bag of beans is two dollars."

"Wow, where you folks from?"

"Iran," my dad replies proudly. "As you know, we are very famous for our oil industry. Let me tell you about it."

"I would love to hear all about it, but these customers are waiting," the salesman says, pointing to the other family.

I smile at the girl. She glares at me. My excitement about the furniture disappears and I suddenly remember that I am about to start at a new school again.

It's the third night in our condo and my mom and dad and I are doing what we do every night: sitting on the sofa, eating dinner and watching a comedy. We know the shows are comedies because whenever one of the actors says something, people laugh. Of course we don't understand why half the stuff is funny, and that's where I come in. My job is to look up the words in *Webster's Dictionary*. Lucky me.

But why is it hilarious if someone calls you a turkey? In Iran, if you want to make fun of someone, you call him a donkey. Now, that's funny! We're lucky if we understand three or four funny lines out of an entire show in America. Sometimes we just laugh along with the audience for the sake of it.

We're at the end of *Three's Company* when someone knocks on our door. Counting our landlady, the movers, and the two nice women who wanted to help us find the Lord, it's only the fourth time anyone has come to our new house. All three of us scramble to answer it.

As soon as I look through the peephole and see that it's somebody my age, I tell my parents to go back to the sofa. There is nothing that can come out of their mouths that would not be embarrassing.

I open the door and a girl says, "Hi, I'm Cindy. We're neighbors."

I freeze. Of all the names in the United States of America, her name has to be Cindy. What are the chances? I mean, that's *my* name.

Let me explain.

Zomorod is not a good name here. It translates to "emerald" in Persian, but does anyone care? No. My dad wanted to name me Sara, which would have made my life a million times easier. I mean, whose name starts with a Z? Nobody on this planet who counts. It's clunky and loopy and ever since second grade when Bill Garrett* made the o's in my name into eyeballs, I realized that having *three* o's in one name is possibly even weirder than having it start with a Z.

But my problems don't stop there. Ever since third grade, I have wanted one of those Wild West belt buckles at Knott's Berry Farm with my name on it. Of course they don't have Zomorod. I always look anyway, just in case. Sure, they have Zelda, Zelena, and Zoe. But no Zomorod. Ever. They have Sara *and* Sarah. In my third grade class, Heather had one; so did Connie, Karen, and Holly. (Holly had the belt buckle, bracelet, *and* keychain.) My dad says I should

---

* Note to Bill Garrett: You are a dork, forever and always. And your first name means "shovel" in Persian.

just get one that says "Foxy Lady" on it. I am one hundred percent sure he doesn't know what *foxy* means.

Then, on the first day of gym in fifth grade, Mr. Knoff said my name was like an alphabet train that keeps going and going and going. Everyone laughed and the boys started chanting, "choo choo, choo choo." They continued to do this whenever they saw me, *for the whole year.* Mr. Knoff* asked if I had a nickname. Iranians don't have nicknames. Bobby Henderson makes everyone call him Scooter. How do you get Scooter from Bobby? And why would anybody want to be called a scooter?

Mr. Knoff's PE class of horrors is just a small sample of my misery. Anytime I meet a new kid, it's a nightmare. This is how it goes:

Cool person: "Hi, what's your name?"

Me: "Zomorod Yousefzadeh."

Cool person (stepping back, looking scared): "What kind of name is *that?*"

Me (being extra cheerful and not scary): "I'm from Iran."

Cool person (looking more scared): "Where is *that?*"

Me (having to be Miss History and Geography Teacher, which I hate): "You might know Iran as Persia, its name until 1935. It's right between Iraq and Afghanistan." (It would be

---

* Note to Mr. Knoff: Your name means "bellybutton" in Persian. Every time you made a stupid comment about my name, I was thinking, "Okay, Mr. Bellybutton."

so much cooler to say, "It's near the Norwegian fjords," or anywhere near Italy or France. Or Japan. Or Africa.)

Cool person (looking scared *and* confused): "Where is *that?*"

Ad nauseam.*

So when I found out we were moving to Newport Beach, I knew this was my chance to break the cycle of embarrassment. I decided to change my name. I mean, what is a name, anyway? In English, you say "table." In Persian, I say *"meez."* They're the same thing. If I were being logical, I guess I could've called myself "Emerald," but that would just be switching one weird Persian name for one weird American name.

So I chose the most normal American name I knew, Cindy. Like Cindy Brady from *The Brady Bunch.*

It's not like I'm trying to pretend that I'm not Iranian. I just want people to ask questions about *me* when we meet, not about where I'm from. Why does that matter, anyway? Yes, there are a few differences between me and any other kid in America, but these are the main ones:

1. I speak Persian at home.

2. The only pet I have ever owned is a goldfish.

---

* Note to God: Next time, please make me be from one of those places I just mentioned.

I realize that goldfish are a sad excuse for a pet, since you cannot hold them, walk them, train them, or do anything fun at all. Worst of all, they never act like they like you, no matter what you do for them.

3. *My mom does not know how to make oatmeal raisin cookies.*

4. *All my friends are in books.*

So now you see why I am standing frozen at the door as Cindy introduces herself. Why does the first person my age that I meet in Newport Beach have to have my new name? I consider saying my name is something else, but it took me a long time to think of Cindy and frankly, I have not thought of a backup name. Also, when someone tells you her name, you only have a few seconds to tell her yours.

So I smile and say, "Nice to meet you. I'm Cindy too."

"Oh my God!" she says. "We're both Cindy! That's so cool!"

"So cool!" I repeat.

"You wanna come over and hang out?" she asks. "I live right next door."

Even though it's getting late, I cannot pass up this opportunity to make a friend. "Yeah," I say.

(I never say "yes"—just "yeah," all drawn out and slow like molasses, as Mrs. Semba, the librarian, described it.

That's one reason I sound so American. That, and I know a lot of slang.)

When I tell my parents I'm going to the neighbor's house, they say, "Zomorod, wait. Why is it funny to throw a pie in someone's face?"

"Look it up," I tell them, and I walk out the door.

Original Cindy's condo is just like ours, except they have matching furniture and real plants, so it looks much better. Her parents must be in their room because I don't see them. We go straight up to her room, which is red and white with tons of photos of her horse, Magic. This is the first time I have ever seen framed pictures of a horse all over someone's house. People usually have framed photos of *other people*. Baby photos, wedding photos, Disneyland photos, all with humans—that's what I expect to see. In Iran, we also frame pictures of elderly relatives who have died. It's usually not a photo from when they were really, really old and didn't look as good, but old enough so you know they were old.

"I'm really into horseback riding," Original Cindy explains.

I have never been horseback riding, so I don't know what to say. I nod. That's the good thing about nodding. It lets you say nothing while still staying in the conversation.

"I also have an older brother, two kittens, a lizard, and a dog. My kittens are Captain and Tennille," she says. "They're named after my favorite band that plays my favorite song,

19 ★

'Love Will Keep Us Together.' Do you like that song?" she asks.

A nod is no longer enough.

"Oh, yeah," I say.

I have never heard that song.

"My lizard's name is Eddie. My dog's name is Mick Jagger. My brother, Mark, named him that because he loves Mick Jagger. You should see his room. There's like four huge posters of Mick on the wall."

"Who's Mick Jagger?" I ask.

"You don't know who Mick Jagger is?" Original Cindy exclaims, acting like I just asked her who Mickey Mouse is—who I am pretty sure is the more famous Mick of the two.

"Hello? *Hello?* Have you *heard* of the Rolling Stones? And their lead singer, *Mick Jagger?* He is really, really famous, maybe *the* most famous singer in the world," she says, stretching her arms out, trying to show me how big the world really is.

Since I now have a normal name, I don't worry that she thinks it's odd that I don't know the world's most popular singer. Plus, we have already agreed that we have the same favorite song. If I were using my real, clunky name *and* I didn't know who Mick Jagger was, that would be strange. Being Cindy makes me so much more normal.

The next day, Original Cindy and I go to the condo pool. I take the key, which is now attached to a keychain with two bulldogs sitting in a boat holding fishing rods and drinking beer. On the side of the boat, it says, "A Bad Day Fishing Is Better Than a Good Day at the Office." We don't fish, own a dog, or drink beer, but the keychain was on sale at Sav-On Drugstore.

That's also why we have four rolls of blue wrapping paper decorated with pacifiers and "It's a Boy!" all over it. Buy three, get one free.

As I'm leaving, my mom yells from the living room, *"Keleedeh estakhr ra gom nakoni!"*

Don't lose the pool key!

The pool is pretty big, and even has a twisty slide. All around it, there are chairs with backs that go up and down so you can choose whether to lie down and get a tan or sit up and talk while you get a tan. There are also tables and chairs, an outdoor shower, a changing area, and a barbecue. But there aren't that many people at the pool. Original Cindy says that a lot of our neighbors use the private pool at the

Newport Beach Tennis Club, which is for paying members only. I don't understand why anyone would pay to go to a pool when there is already a free one here. That's what my dad calls flushing money down the toilet.

"Right here is good," Original Cindy says, choosing one of the lounge chairs. "We can get maximum sun exposure." I lie on my back, just like she does, facing the sun. Immediately, my eyeballs feel like they're burning.

A few minutes pass and then Original Cindy starts telling me stories about her horse. If I didn't know Magic was an animal, I'd think she was talking about a person.

"The first time I saw Magic," she begins, "I knew she was the one."

She goes on to tell me, in detail, how she and Magic learned to become friends, what happened the first time she cried in front of Magic, and how they practically speak a secret language.

After an hour of horse stories, Original Cindy finally stops. "I miss Magic so much," she sighs.

"When did you last visit her?" I ask.

"Yesterday," she replies. "Magic is always so happy to see me."

"Do you feed her?"

"Of course. I always have treats."

"Maybe that's why she's so happy to see you," I suggest, trying to be helpful. "You know the dancing seals at

Sea World? It's not like they *want* to wear a tutu and hop around in circles, but they do it for the fish. Animals will do anything for food."

"No! That's not it at all!" Original Cindy suddenly sits up. "Please do not compare my horse to a stinky seal. Magic and I have a bond, a connection. Maybe it's hard for you to understand because you've never loved a horse."

I panic. My one and only friend in Newport Beach is mad at me. I have to say something meaningful.

"I do know about humans and horses being friends. I absolutely love Pippi Longstocking."

"Who?" she asks, lying back down.

"You know, that book about the little girl who lives alone while her father is lost at sea, and she has a horse and a monkey and—"

"Is this a true story?" Original Cindy asks before I can finish.

"No, not at all. Pippi is an imaginary character. She's like ten years old and lives alone and she can lift up her horse with one hand." As I am saying this, I realize that this conversation is not helping me connect with my only friend. "It's a stupid story," I say. "Never mind."

"Yeah," Original Cindy agrees. "Sounds stupid."

"But you know what is not stupid? *Black Beauty.* Now, that is a touching story told by a horse and not at all stupid."

"What's it about?"

"It's about this horse who tells you his life story, first as a colt and then as a workhorse, which is really hard because he lives in London a long time ago when they didn't treat them very well."

"A talking horse who wrote a book?" she says. "No, thank you."

"No, that's not it," I reply. But it doesn't matter, since it's obvious that talking about books with Original Cindy is not a good idea.

"Hey," I begin, trying to change the subject, "wanna go swim?"

"Swim?" she says, as if I have suggested something totally unacceptable to do in a pool.

"Well. Yeah. I mean. If you want."

"You mean get our hair wet?" she asks. "No."

"How about we swim without getting our hair wet?" I suggest, not even sure why I'm saying that.

"I guess." She sits up and ties her hair into a bun so it doesn't touch the water. My hair is short, not that I would care if it got wet.

We go in the pool up to our necks and walk from one side to the other, then back again, chins held up high, straining to keep our heads out of the water.

"Hey, you know what we look like?" I ask.

"What?"

"You know those African women in *National Geographic* who wear stacks of neck rings so their necks get really long?"

"No." She climbs out of the pool, bringing our time spent in the water to a total of five minutes.

Apparently, pools in Newport Beach are used only as tanning destinations.

We reapply coconut-scented suntan lotion and turn our lounge chairs a few degrees, for maximum sun exposure, like human sunflowers. After a while, Original Cindy suggests we lie on our stomachs to even out our color on both sides.

"Great idea," I say, realizing with a growing horror that no matter how many times I blink, I have no moisture left in my eyes. All of a sudden, I remember my dad's warning about staring into the sun during eclipses and going instantly blind. Is this the same thing? I close my eyes and try to think sad thoughts so I might cry and get some tears in my eyes. But I can't concentrate because Original Cindy is going on and on with another stupid horse story.

After what feels like five lifetimes, I hear her say the glorious words: "We should go now."

"Yeah," I say, jumping up—but trying not to seem too excited.

"And you know what? We should totally work on our tans a lot," she suggests as she folds her towel, which—surprise, surprise—has a picture of a horse on it.

I've never heard the phrase, "work on our tans." I puzzle over it for a minute. Where's the work in that? You just lie there like a steak on a grill.

"Yeah, we totally should," I finally say.

In Compton, I went to a pool party once and there was a sign that read WE DON'T SWIM IN YOUR TOILET; PLEASE DON'T PEE IN OUR POOL. I translated the sign for my mom and she said it was rude to have a sign with the word "pee" on it. I told her that's what made it funny. She insisted it wasn't funny at all.

That's the hard part about translating. Saying what words mean is easy, but trying to make my mom understand why something is funny is much harder. Getting my mom to laugh in America is nearly impossible.

WHAT HAVE YOU DONE?" my mom yells at me as soon as I walk through the door.

"What do you mean?"

"You look like a radish!"

"I was at the pool," I remind her.

"How did you get so sunburned swimming?"

"We didn't swim."

"What did you do?"

"We tanned," I confess. I know what's coming next.

"That is the stupidest thing a girl can do. Why would you do that?"

So here's one more thing that's different about me. In Iran, pale skin is considered beautiful. Nobody tans. If any-thing, women avoid the sun. But what am I supposed to do? I live in California, where pale skin means you *need* a tan.

"The only reason I let you go to the pool with your friend is because I thought you were swimming, and you know that makes you tall," my mom says.

My parents actually believe that swimming or riding a bicycle makes a person grow more. That's why the first thing they bought me when we moved to America was a bike. That's also why I took swim lessons at the YWCA in Compton—to swim and get tall. My mom thinks she's short because she didn't swim or bike when she was a kid.

"I'm sorry, *Maman*," I say.

That's a total lie. I'm not sorry at all. My mom does not understand that sometimes there is a price for friendship. This is why she has no friends in America. She doesn't try doing anything that American moms do. She wants to have the same life she did in Iran, and even I know that is not possible. So she just watches TV. And frankly, I don't think TV counts as a friend.

I may be sunburned and in pain, but I now have a friend.

The next day, someone knocks on our door and my dad answers. I hear Original Cindy asking if I'm home, then my dad's voice: "Wait, please. Zomorod! ZOOO-MOOO-ROOOD!"

I run down the stairs as fast as I can. Why does my dad have to yell loud enough for all of North America to hear? Now I'm going to have to explain my name change to Original Cindy.

Thankfully, she doesn't seem fazed by the strange sounds coming out of my dad's mouth.

We walk to her house, and when we get there I'm ready to say hello to her parents, like I'm supposed to. It's very quiet. "Where are your parents?" I ask.

"They're not home," she says casually, like this is a normal thing.

"What happened to them?" I ask, trying not to sound too scared.

"They're at work."

Oh, boy. This is not good. There is no way my parents would allow me to be here if they knew. This is much worse than tanning. I start making a list in my head of everything that could go wrong, starting with fires, burglaries, and earthquakes. Right when I get to kidnappings, Original Cindy suggests we go upstairs. *I'll just stay for a little bit,* I tell myself.

We sit on the floor in her room, on the red shag carpet. She puts on the cassette of "Love Will Keep Us Together" and starts singing along. She knows all the words. Since I claimed that it's also my favorite song, I move my head from side to side, repeating the words, "love will keep us together" whenever they come up, which is often. For the rest of the lyrics, I just close my eyes and hum quietly, pretending like I'm singing in my head.

After rewinding the cassette and listening to the song three times in a row, Original Cindy decides it's time to go play with the kittens, Captain and Tennille. They're fluffy and tiny, but unfortunately not very friendly. As soon as I start playing with them, Captain scratches my hand.

"Ouch!" I yell, covering the wound with my other hand. "I need a Band-Aid. And some Neosporin."

"For *that?*" She points to my hand.

"Yes. It hurts. And I don't want to get an infection."

Original Cindy starts to laugh. "That's nothing."

"Can I just have some Neosporin?" I ask again.

"What is that?" she asks.

I can't believe she basically lives in a zoo and has never heard of Neosporin.

"It keeps you from getting infections so you don't need penicillin," I tell her.

"Well, we don't have any, and I don't know what the other—pencil whatever—is either."

"Penicillin," I say. I don't even bother explaining what it is, especially since I had learned about it in a book. It was a story about a Belgian family who moved to Africa and the father got sick. That's also how I learned about tsetse flies, which I'm also not going to bring up.

"Whatever," she says, letting Tennille lick her face. "I guess you've never owned a cat."

"Nope."

"That's too bad. My parents are barely ever home, so they let me have as many pets as I want. I go to the stables after school, do my homework, and then ride Magic."

I have never, in my entire life, been home alone. "Where are your parents?" I ask, still covering my wound.

"They have an insurance business," she says. "It's all about prevention and planning ahead. My parents would be happy to talk to your parents about all their insurance needs."

I almost choke! Her parents can*not* meet my parents until I've known her long enough to tell her that I'm from Iran and my name isn't really Cindy. If they meet before that, her parents will hear my parents' accents and ask where we're from. Then my dad will start talking about the oil industry and my mom will say something that makes no sense.

I guess I just don't like people to meet my parents. I know that sounds bad. It's not like I don't love them. I just want to hide them until they stop being embarrassing.

"Thank you," I say, "but we don't have any insurance needs."

"Everyone has insurance needs," she says.

"Not us," I reply.

I'm trying to figure out her next question before she asks it, but then she says, "Let me show you Mark's room. He'll be starting at a boarding school in Hawaii soon, so you can sleep in his bed if you ever want to stay over."

That's one thing I like about Original Cindy. Just when I think, *How am I going to answer her next question?* she moves on to something else.

Mark's room is indeed filled with posters of Mick Jagger. I imagined Mick Jagger to be handsome, but he's not handsome at all. He looks like a girl, and not even a cute one. But I'm glad I know who he is now, just like every other kid in America.

What happened to your hand?" my dad asks when he comes home that night. I knew this was coming.

"Cindy's kitten scratched it," I say.

He takes a deep breath. "Zomorod, you are lucky it was your hand and not your eyeball. I have known many people whose eyeballs were scratched out by cats. They are now learning to read with their fingers, and they walk with canes, regretting that they ever tried to pet a cat."

He pauses, as if to let his words sink in. Then he continues, "You should never play with cats, only look at them, from a distance."

"What are the names of these people?" I ask skeptically.

"It doesn't matter. Also, you should never let dogs lick you because you can get one of those diseases that comes from being licked by dogs."

"Everyone in Compton got licked by dogs and nobody caught any diseases," I remind him.

"I know *many* people who did."

"Who?"

"That's not the point," he says, a bit flustered.

You don't find a lot of people in Iran who have pets in

their homes. You would never find anyone with a big dog *in* the house. Dogs are kept outside.

The first time we went into an American supermarket in Compton, we were going up and down the aisles and all of a sudden, whoa! A whole aisle of food for cats and dogs! In Iran, most cats and dogs live on the streets and they're lucky if someone throws a scrap at them now and then. Most of the time, they're on their own. In America, there's dog food for young dogs, old dogs, fat dogs, small dogs, active dogs, and lazy dogs. And cats have choices like salmon-, beef-, or chicken-flavored meals.

I always thought cats would eat any food. Then I saw the cat food commercials on TV that show cats that are insulted when they're served food that isn't moist enough. You see the cat turning around and walking away, tail in the air, disgusted. Meanwhile, the owner is going nuts because of his pouting cat, so he buys the juicy and delicious chicken liver cat food in the can that he should have bought in the first place instead of the cheaper, dry cat food. The animal is *finally* happy, and the owner breathes a sigh of relief.

I have never seen a cat in Iran walk away from food. Even if their meal is not their first choice, they eat it because who knows when the next meal will come? Plus, if they don't eat their food, some other cat will for sure.

My dad says that the dogs and cats in America are luckier than most people in the world.

Original Cindy has decided that for the entire month before school starts, we will work on our tans every other day. This puts me in an awkward position. I have always been a kid who tells the truth, and now I don't know what to do. If I listen to my mom and refuse to tan, I will lose my only friend. So I lie to my mom and tell her I will be doing laps. She mentions that when I get tired of doing laps, I should hold on to the side of the pool and just kick. That will also lengthen my legs, she says. I feel terrible lying to her.

On the way to the pool that afternoon, I ask Original Cindy, "Did you know I moved here from Compton, but I'm originally from Iran? I speak Persian at home. And did you know we write from right to left?"

"No, but one of the trainers at the stable, Scott, is from Compton," she says. "You wouldn't believe what happened to his horse last year." And just like that, she launches into another story about horses.

I can't believe she doesn't ask me a single question about Iran or about writing from right to left. In Compton, I wrote my name in Persian on the chalkboard

35   ★

for Show and Tell, and Bill Garrett yelled, "You write backwards!"*

Instead of listening to Original Cindy, I pray silently, *Dear God, this is such a small matter compared to everything going on in the world, but can you please stop these horse stories?*

And just like that, the story ends. *Thank you, God!* This is my chance to change the topic.

"We should call ourselves the Sultans of Suntan," I suggest.

"What's a sultan?" she asks.

"A sultan is like a ruler in Arabia."

"I love Arabian horses!" she exclaims. "Some people think Magic is an Arabian, but she's not."

Even God can't stop these stories. I realize that Original Cindy is a compass, but instead of pointing north, she points to "horse story." As boring as she is, though, she's my only friend, so I listen, and listen, and listen. Plus, I figure someday she will ask me a question about *me.* I mean, how many horse stories can one person have? I don't think even horses have that many stories about other horses.

Two weeks into our tanning sessions, which my mom thinks are my swimming sessions, Original Cindy comes to pick

---

* Note to Shovel: No, *you* write backwards. Persian is older than English.

me up as usual. I go to the kitchen, where we keep the precious pool key in a drawer. I rifle through all the stuff in there—the mini-flashlight, paper clips, rubber bands, extra batteries of all sizes, a yellow highlighter, a measuring tape, a glue stick, soy sauce packets, and matches. My heart starts to beat real fast. "*Maman*," I yell, "did you put the pool key somewhere else?"

My mother flies down the stairs faster than I thought she was capable of moving. "*Chi?*" she screams. "*Keleedeh estakhr ro gom kardi?*"

What? Did you lose the pool key?

Usually in mystery novels, there are six possible suspects and you have to wait until the last chapter to find out who is the guilty one. This novel, *The Girl Who Lost the Pool Key*, is very short, with only one chapter.

Original Cindy, who has been standing quietly beside me, speaks up. She's very brave, since my mom's face is turning a dark shade of red, the shade that the guidebook to my mood ring describes as "passionate." I know that my friend's presence is the only thing keeping my mother from fully exploding.

"We can go look for it. We can put up signs," Original Cindy says, in a positive tone that does not exist in the world of angry Iranian parents—at least not my mother's.

Then, before my mom can say anything or strangle me, we say goodbye and run next door.

It's been three days since I lost the pool key, and my mom is now permanently mad at me. I am sure she has a superpower that allows her to stay angry without a break whenever I do anything wrong, which is why I try never to do anything wrong. I wish she could just forget for one minute, but all day long, it's as if there is a flashing neon sign on my forehead: HORRIBLE, TERRIBLE, GOOD-FOR-NOTHING KID WHO LOST THE POOL KEY. $50 DOWN THE DRAIN!

I remind her that Cindy and I put twenty flyers all over the greenbelt, and that I know that fifty dollars is three hundred and fifty *tomans* in Iran, which is a lot of money, especially to flush down the toilet, which is what it will feel like if we have to pay the landlady just because I was not careful and lost the pool key. My mom's silent glare doesn't change.

I feel so frustrated! This is totally unfair. I don't think she realizes that I'm actually a really good kid. My teachers are always telling me that.

When my dad comes home from work, he notices that my mom is still not talking to me. "Why don't you look in the clothes dryer and in all your pockets?" he suggests.

Of course! Why hadn't I thought of that? I am suddenly filled with hope. I look in all my clothes, in the washer and dryer, and in the vacuum cleaner bag. I even look in between the sofa cushions and find twelve cents. In the upstairs shag carpet, I discover two bobby pins, a paper clip, and a still-wrapped piece of Dentyne gum, cinnamon flavored.

No pool key.

The next day, my dad comes home from the office and says that one of his coworkers, Bob, told him that whenever his wife loses something, she prays to Saint An-tony and it always works.

"Saint *Anthony*, you mean?" I say.

"No matter," my father replies. "I'm sure however you pronounce his name, he knows it's him."

My mom suggests that instead of praying to him, we ask him to come over and look for the key.

"He's a saint, so he's been dead for a long time," I explain.

"If you think a dead man is going to help you find the key, good luck," she says.

I know more about saints than my parents. Our next-door neighbor in Compton, Mrs. Popkins, had a fountain with a statue of a man surrounded by birds. She told me that it was Saint Francis of Assisi, the patron saint of animals. She said that he could communicate with animals and that birds gathered around him when he preached. How cool is that? Helping people find lost things is very cool too, and very practical. When it comes to my favorite saints, there's now a tie for first place.

We don't have saints in Islam, just a prophet with twelve imams, and they don't preach to animals or help find lost items. My family, like most Iranians, is Muslim, but we never do anything religious. I've never even been in a mosque, which is like a church. My dad always says that kindness is our religion and if we treat everybody the way we would like to be treated, the world would be a better place. I agree with that—but it would be so cool to have a bird audience.

I spit out the piece of cinnamon Dentyne gum and go to my room. I kneel on the shag carpet, clasp my hands, and close my eyes, just like they do on *Little House on the Prairie*.

"Saint Anthony," I pray, "I am Zomorod Yousefzadeh, originally from Iran."

I do not feel the need to explain where Iran is, since I assume saints automatically know geography, being able to fly and all.

"I am now living in Newport Beach and I recently lost our pool key. I am a very careful kid, good at all subjects in school except PE. I do not understand how I lost the key. Our landlady, whom you may already know, will charge us fifty dollars if we don't find it. That's a lot of money, and I am sure it was even more when you were alive. If you can please help me find the key, I promise to . . ."

I can't think of anything to promise. What kind of favor can a saint possibly need? So I say, "I promise that I will do something really nice for someone, and when I do, I will think of you."

CINEMA REX

We turn on the TV that evening and the first news segment is about Iran. My mom, dad, and I watch in silence. Cinema Rex, the biggest and most famous movie theater in Abadan, was set on fire. The doors had all been locked from the outside. About five hundred people burned to death.

Cinema Rex! We used to go there all the time. Who would do this? The reporter says that the shah—our king—and his secret police are being blamed.

Then they show mobs of angry Iranians marching in the streets of the capital, demonstrating against the shah. "Death to the shah! Death to the shah!"

I'm scared watching this, even though I'm on the other side of the world.

"How can *anyone* do something so horrible?" My dad keeps shaking his head.

"I wonder if we knew someone in there," my mom says.

"Abadan is so small. There must have been," my dad replies. My parents sit in silence, staring at the TV.

Then the reporter moves on to the next news segment,

about Proposition 13 and lower taxes. But we're still thinking about Cinema Rex, even though we're not saying anything. That's how we are. When we're really scared about
something, we don't talk about it.

As soon as I hear the knock on our door the next day, I'm sure it's someone who has found the key.

Instead, it's our next-door neighbor on the other side. I have seen her many times, and we always wave and say hello. That's what you do in America. You're walking down the street and a complete stranger coming toward you smiles and says hello. You say hello back, and sometimes you add, "How are you?" Then they say, "Fine, thank you." They might make a comment like, "Lovely day, isn't it?" Suddenly, you feel like you have a friend and the world is a better place.

I am particularly good at making comments about the weather, and grownups always appreciate it. My selection includes "What a sunny day!," "Another sunny day!," and "Love this sunny day!" Every once in a while, I am able to say, "Where's the sun today?" But here in Southern California, I don't use that one very often.

It's not like that where I come from. In Iran, you chat with people you know or people you do business with, like the baker or the shoe repairman. You do not exchange friendly greetings with complete strangers walking toward you. We spent the first few months in America wondering, *Who was that who just said hello? Where do we know him from?*

I was the one who finally figured it out. Whenever we went on Brownie field trips to the park, I noticed our leader, Mrs. Batson, said hello to everybody on the way. I asked her if she knew all these people. "Oh, honey, no. I'm just spreading a little cheer," she said. And that's how I solved the Mystery of the Friendly Americans. I felt a little bit like my idol, Nancy Drew.

"Is your mother home?" the neighbor lady asks when I open the door.

"Yes," I say, "but she doesn't speak English. Can I help you?"

Right then, my mom shows up. "Hello. Tank you," she says. When my mother doesn't know what to say in America, she thanks people.

"My mom means to say, 'Nice to meet you,'" I add, translating her English into English that makes sense. "And I'm Cindy."

"Nice to meet you both. My name is Rhonda Klein, and I would like to welcome you to the neighborhood," she says, handing my mom a chocolate cake and *The Ladies League of Newport Beach Cookbook*.

"Tank you," my mother says, correctly this time. She's smiling, and so am I because my mother just said something that I do not need to translate.

The conversation has clearly reached a dead end. After a moment of silence, all of us holding frozen smiles, Mrs. Klein turns to me. "Cindy, do you babysit?"

"Yes," I say.

"Great! I have a seven-year-old son named David and a daughter, Anna, who just left for college. Since Anna's no longer around, I'm looking for a babysitter. Do you like to play Go Fish? That's David's favorite game."

"Yes!" I have never played Go Fish, but I am one hundred percent sure I will like it.

"That sounds good. I'll get back to you. And by the way, your mother's English is fine, honey." She smiles and turns around to leave.

"Tank you," my mother says again, closing the door.

The next day, Mrs. Klein asks me to babysit for three hours in the afternoon while she plays tennis. "Is one dollar per hour fine with you?" she asks.

"More than fine!" I answer.

I've never babysat or had a babysitter, but I have lots of experience playing with younger cousins. Nobody in Iran would ask a neighbor's *kid* to babysit. You can always find a relative, or an adult who needs a job.

My cousin Bahram's family has a live-in maid, who also takes care of him when my aunt and uncle go out at night. My parents have never left me to go anywhere by themselves.

They always take me with them. My dad always says, "Early to bed, early to rise makes a man healthy, wealthy, and wise." When this is your motto, you do not need a babysitter.

That evening, as soon as I hear the garage door open, I run to meet my dad. "*Baba,* you know how much I miss my cousins?"

"Yes," he says, getting out of the car. "What made you suddenly think of them?"

"The lady next door asked me if I can babysit. Her son, David, is the same age as Hamid. And guess what? I get paid for playing! One dollar an hour! That's seven *tumons*! Can I pleeease?"

"I don't know."

I'm sure he's thinking of everything that could possibly go wrong.

"It's right next door. If I need anything, I can just come over. Pleeease?"

"Fine. We'll try it once."

I give him a big hug.

When I arrive the next afternoon, Mrs. Klein has a list of phone numbers on the refrigerator to call in case of an emergency, plus a list of medications for David's asthma. She also gives me the number of the Newport Beach Tennis Club. "You can call the front desk if you need to reach me."

As soon as she leaves, David tells me he wants to play

The Six Million Dollar Man, which is a really popular TV show. He tells me the rules, which I am one hundred percent sure he has made up, since there is no point to the game. First I have to say, "We can rebuild him. We have the technology." Then David starts moving his arms and legs in slow motion like a robot while I squeak, *"Eee, eee, eee, eee."*

"That is the sound of electronic technology," explains David. Then he jumps on the living room sofa, then to the floor, then to the other sofa, all in slow motion while I squeak *"Eee, eee, eee, eee"* the entire time. I'm not sure if he's allowed to play in the living room, but every time I try to say something, he yells, "Sound effects!" so I have to start going *"Eee, eee, eee"* again. Then he runs up the stairs, down the stairs, in and out of all the rooms, and jumps on all the beds s-l-o-w-l-y. He ends up back in the living room. We do this many, many times.

After what seems like an eternity, my throat starts getting scratchy and sore, so I stop squeaking.

"Sound effects!" David yells.

"Wait a minute, David. Do you know what is even cooler than the Six Million Dollar Man?" I ask.

He stops suddenly. "What?"

"Oh-ree-gah-mee," I say, stretching out the syllables so it sounds like something exotic in a Bruce Lee movie.

"What's that?" he asks.

Every kid in Iran can count on receiving at least one

book on origami before her tenth birthday. I have about a dozen.

"It's the Japanese art of making things out of paper by folding," I explain. "Watch this."

I make a boat out of an advertising flyer from El Rancho Market.

"Whoa," he says. "Can you make another one?"

I make another one.

"Can you make another one?" he asks.

I make another one.

"Can you make another one?" he asks.

I make a crane instead.

"Can you make another boat?" David asks.

"Okay, but it's the last one," I say. "What are you going to do with all these boats?"

"I'm making a flotilla," he explains.

I don't know what that means, but I'm not going to ask him. He's younger than I am and I should know this. I make a mental note to look it up in *Webster's Dictionary* when I get home.

"Hey, you wanna see something cool?" David asks.

"Sure."

He goes into his dad's office and comes back holding a giant eyeball.

"Look at this," he says, opening it up and pointing. "This is the cornea, this is the retina, and these are blood vessels.

My dad's an ophthalmologist," he explains. "That means eye doctor."

I am happy to hear this, because I was wondering what kind of creepy family owns a huge eyeball.

David adds, "I want to be one too when I grow up, and invent a bionic eye."

"When you become a doctor," I say, "I will come to you whenever I have an eye problem."

"You'll have to make me some more origami boats first," he says.

So I do.

When Mrs. Klein comes home, David shows her all the origami boats. She gives me three dollars and asks, "Are you available on weekend nights?"

"I am available all the time, except when I'm at school," I tell her. She seems pleased to hear that.

"Oh, just one thing," she adds. "Please keep David out of the living room next time."

TUNA

The next day, I see Mrs. Klein in her driveway. "Hello, Mrs. Klein," I say. "What a sunny day!"

"It certainly is, Cindy. And thank you again for babysitting."

"Anytime," I answer.

"You know, I'm just so happy to have found you, Cindy. It's so important for me to spend time with my friends. Sure, we play tennis, but it's just an excuse to chitchat and vent a little bit, if you know what I mean."

I don't know what she means by "vent," but the image of her chatting with her friends gives me an idea.

"Mrs. Klein," I begin, "my mom does not have any friends in Newport Beach, and I was wondering if you could please help her meet some people."

"Honey," she says, "I'd be happy to organize a doubles match and then lunch at the tennis club. The restaurant there makes *the* most fantastic tuna fish salad with cashews."

"My mom doesn't play tennis," I say.

"How about a round of golf?" Mrs. Klein suggests.

"She doesn't play golf."

"How about an easy hike?"

"My mom likes tuna fish salad with cashews."

"I'll try to think of something," Mrs. Klein says, somewhat hesitantly.

I feel completely stupid for asking.

Original Cindy and I did not reach our tanning goal. During the second week of our month-long project, she got sick and missed a week. Then I started babysitting David a lot, so I missed the last week. I was actually relieved. Tanning bores me to tears, even though it leaves me without tears. But since school starts tomorrow, I've decided to connect with her again. After all, she's my one and only friend at Lincoln Junior High.

I knock on her door. "Hi, Cindy," I say when she answers.

"Hi," she says, with her hands on her hips.

"I was wondering if you want to walk together tomorrow. We can be two tan gals going to school, even though the color on my legs is totally peeling," I say, pointing to the pink patches on my calves that look like the Hawaiian Islands.

"Well," she says, shifting her weight from one leg to another, "I don't know how to say this in a nice way, so I'm just gonna come out with it. I don't want to walk to school with you."

"What?"

"I don't want to hurt your feelings, but I'm just gonna

53   ★

be honest. You have nothing to say. When we're together, I have to talk all the time. Plus you called Magic a unicorn, and Captain doesn't like you. I feel like that's a sign."

It's true that I don't say much when we're together, but that's because Cindy never stops talking.

"I only called Magic a unicorn because you said you danced together to imaginary music," I explain. "Don't you think that's unicorn-ish?"

"That's disrespectful," she says. "I'm pretty sure Magic wouldn't like you, just like Captain doesn't."

I want nothing more than to be invisible and disappear. I turn around to leave.

"Um, one more thing," Original Cindy adds. "You don't know the words to 'Love Will Keep Us Together.' I could totally tell."

She's right. I don't know the words to the coolest song ever. I have no friends, and apparently horses and kittens don't like me either. I may have changed my name, but my life is still the same.

LiFE AS A TURTLE

I set my alarm for six but wake up at five with a stomachache. I lie there hoping and praying that I will not have a class with Original Cindy. I wish I could be like Pippi Longstocking and not go to school and have a pet monkey who loves me.

My dad offers to drive me, which is good, since I do not want to walk alone. On the way there, he asks me if I'm nervous.

"I'm fine," I tell him.

"Now that you have an American name, things should be easier. Plus, Susan is a beautiful name," he says.

"It's Cindy," I remind him.

I told my parents about my name change yesterday. My dad thought it was a great idea. He understands my problem, because whenever someone asks his name, he starts sweating. My mom said it made no sense. I didn't expect her to understand.

My dad drops me off in the front parking lot. "Have a good day," he says. I think he's hoping his cheerfulness will somehow make this terrible experience better. I watch him drive away in the Impala. All I hear around me are squeals of excitement from kids who haven't seen their friends all summer. "Oh my God! It's so good to see you! Who do you have first period?"

This is not just a terrible day. It's a terrible, horrible, very bad day. I'm used to being the new kid, but this time it feels worse. Maybe it's because the school is so big. Lincoln Junior High is *huge*. It's like an airport—loud, crowded, and confusing, but without helpful people in uniforms telling you where to go. I have six classes each day, and each day has a different schedule. That's a lot to remember. Elementary school was so much easier.

I walk around looking for my locker, but all I notice is how big the eighth-graders are. The girls are wearing makeup and fancy clothes. You can definitely tell the sixth-graders from the eighth-graders. I avoid eye contact with everyone, especially the boys, who are not just big, but mean-looking.

I have ten minutes to find my first class, so I decide to look for my locker later. If only they had signs telling us where to go, like on freeways.

As soon as I find Room 23, I go in.

"You're early," the teacher says, looking up from a stack of papers. The classroom is empty.

"I know. I just wanted to tell you that I have a different name from what is on your roll call."

"What's your name?" she asks, holding up the attendance sheet.

"It's right there," I say, pointing to it. "But just call me Cindy." I don't bother pronouncing my real name. No need to go there.

"All righty, then," she says, crossing out "Zomorod" and writing in "Cindy." "Thanks for letting me know."

"Can I stay here until the bell rings, or do I have to leave?" I ask.

"You can stay," she says. "Sit anywhere."

I sit in the front row, in the seat closest to the wall, hoping I will blend in with the poster next to me. It shows a dog jumping high for a Frisbee on a sunny day. Across the blue sky, it says: "Attitudes Are Contagious!"

The bell rings and kids start streaming in. I take out my binder and pretend to be reading something. A few minutes later, a second bell rings. Every seat fills up except front row center. No one wants to sit right in front of the teacher.

When everyone is settled in, the teacher stands in front of the classroom. "Hello, I am Ms. Masatani. Welcome to homeroom and to Social Studies. Before I make announcements and hand out books," she says, pointing to a stack of books next to her, "I'm going to quickly take roll."

For the first time ever in America, I am not dreading this moment.

Elizabeth Anderson, Michael Avis, Matthew Brown. She goes down the list and when she gets to my name, she looks up and says, "And Cindy. I know you're here."

Brilliant! Not only do I have a normal name, but the teacher already knows me.

"Starting next week," Ms. Masatani announces, "I'm going to assign helpers to take the roll sheet to the attendance office. For today, I will take it myself. While I'm gone, I want you to grab one of these textbooks and start reading chapter one."

As soon as she leaves, someone says, "Move!" I look up to see a boy standing over me. "Move! Quick!" He pushes me aside. With a thick black marker, he writes something on the poster under the words "Attitudes Are Contagious!"

He runs back to his seat while a bunch of kids giggle. I hate this class already.

A few minutes later, Ms. Masatani returns and takes a seat. A bunch of kids are still giggling.

"Settle down," she says. "Now let's open up our books and see what's in store for us.

"Cindy, can you please tell us—" That's as far as she gets.

"Okay, who did that?" she asks, pointing to the poster, which now also has the words "So is Venireal Disease!" written in the blue sky.

No one says anything.

"Is anybody going to tell me who did that, or do I have to punish all of you?"

No one makes a peep.

"All righty, then. Here's what's gonna happen. Instead of having our first test in two weeks, we're going to have it on Friday. That means you will have twice the amount of reading this week. You can start chapter one now. I want complete silence. If you make a sound, you will go to the principal's office. And by the way, if you are going to deface private property, you should at least learn to spell correctly." She turns around and writes "venereal disease" on the blackboard.

I have to look it up in *Webster's Dictionary* when I get home.

PASTA

I can't find my next class. There are only five minutes in between classes and I'm frantically rushing all over the place. I realize eventually that I have been running in circles in the wrong part of the school, like those hamsters in the pet shop, running on a wheel, going nowhere fast. I am panicking. *Finally,* I find the room, but dear God, it's too late. The teacher, Miss DeAngelo, has started taking attendance, even though the class is still pretty rowdy and loud. I take the first empty seat I see. I'm all out of breath.

When Miss DeAngelo gets to my name, she pauses. I recognize her look of sheer panic. It's that face you make if you bite into a lemon instead of an orange.

Before she begins the many embarrassing attempts to pronounce it, I interject, "You can call me Cindy."

"Thank you, because I needed help with *that* name!" she says. Then the class becomes very quiet while everyone stares at me. Miss DeAngelo asks me how to pronounce my real name. Why can't she just move on? Isn't there a lesson plan today?

"Zo-mo-rod," I say, real quietly. A bunch of kids go,

"Whooooaaaaaa." She asks me what kind of name that is. I think, *Dear God, please make this the last question.*

"I'm from Iran," I say.

"That's lovely," she says. "My family is from Italy."

Being from Italy is very different than being from Iran. Everyone knows about Italy; it's shaped like a boot and they eat pasta and have nice purses. Being from Iran is like being from Mars. Aside from Iranians, pretty much no one has been there.

Right when I think the detour into questions about my life is over, some kid yells, "Did you, like, bring your camel with you?" Everyone laughs. I look to see who said that. It's a boy with blond, feathered bangs that need a trim.

I want to say something but I cannot think of anything clever. I want to yell back, "I have never owned a camel!" I don't, though. I just keep quiet while everyone laughs. Finally, Miss DeAngelo says, "Okay, everyone. Enough." I can't believe the boy doesn't get in trouble for being so rude.

I manage to find my next class pretty easily. I tell the teacher my new name before she calls attendance. Smooth sailing. No drama. Phew!

In the middle of the lesson, there is a giggly announcement on the loudspeaker. "Um, apologies for this interruption. Don't miss the Welcome Rally in the Quad at lunch!

And for all you sixth-graders who don't know where the Quad is, it's the center of campus near the flagpoles. Just listen for the marching band! Go, Lincoln Lancers, go!"

At least I know where I will *not* be eating lunch. Original Cindy will probably be there, so I will not.

Then, toward the end of the period, there is another announcement. This time, it's an older woman talking slowly. "Attention, all students. Starting Friday, the library will be open during lunch. Please note that no food or drinks are allowed. Thank you, and keep reading."

That is the best news I've heard all day!

A minute later the bell rings and everyone rushes out the door. I'm in no hurry. I take my time gathering my back-pack, which is getting heavier with each textbook. I need to find my locker.

Turns out the sixth grade lockers are behind the science building. I can barely hear the marching band. It's the per-fect spot to have lunch. I sit on the ground against the lock-ers, unwrap my bologna sandwich, and eat it slowly. Then I stay there, reading my Social Studies book, waiting for the bell to ring. Only three more days until the library opens! I can't wait.

I didn't have that many friends in Compton. For the first few months we lived there, I didn't speak English. Even after I learned English, my parents didn't want me going to other people's houses, since they didn't know them. Our next-door neighbor was in my class, but she had a big dog that always growled at us. They also had a sign on the chain-link fence that said: WARNING: GUARD DOG ON DUTY. It was the opposite of a welcome mat.

This is why I love books so much. They've always been there for me, and I can take them wherever I go. But still, when I found out that we were moving to Newport Beach, I was hoping to start a different chapter in my life. I will always love books, but it would be nice to have some living, breathing friends.

As I walk home that day with my heavy backpack, I know one thing. All the kids already have friends and there's no room for newcomers.

In fifth grade, Mrs. Goodspeed asked us to write what animal we are most like. I said I'm like a turtle because when I need to, I go into my own shell. She taped the stories to the wall and guess what? I was the only kid who picked turtle. Most of the other kids picked dogs, cats, and horses. Everyone thought being like a turtle was "totally weird." That seems to be my talent in America, doing things that other people think are weird.

I still think I'm like a turtle.

On Wednesdays and Fridays I have PE first period. It's Wednesday, so I wake up in a bad mood. I already hate the day.

And who do I see as I walk into the gym? Original Cindy, standing next to the bleachers with a group of girls. I walk quickly, trying to glide past them as fast as I can. As soon as I get close, they stop talking and turn around to look at me. I panic and say, "Hi, Cindy." She glares at me, then whispers something to the other girls, and they all start laughing.

What is so funny? I know my stretchy gym shorts are not flattering and my tennis shoes are a weird pink color (fifty-percent-off sale), but neither of those things is laugh-out-loud funny.

On second thought, I don't even want to know why they're giggling.

I go up to the gym coach, who has a whistle on a rope around her neck and is holding a clipboard.

"Hi, I want to let you know that I have a different name from what is on the attendance sheet."

"Okey-dokey. Which one's yours?" she asks, showing me the list of names.

"Right there," I say, pointing to the longest name on the list. "Please call me Cindy."

"Okey-dokey," she says again. "*Muchas gracias.*"

As soon as the class bell rings, she blows a whistle. It's earsplittingly loud in the gym, thanks to the echo.

"Hello, ladies. I am Coach McAndrew and it's my job to get you in shape this semester. As you know, boys and girls have separate PE classes, but I don't want you to think that girls' PE is some kind of social hour. It's not teatime, ladies! The motto is simple: No pain, no gain! For the next two months, we're going to rotate through different activities every two weeks, starting with tumbling, then dodge ball, then . . ."

Tumbling and dodge ball? I don't hear anything after that. *Dear God, this is the only time I will ask for a broken arm. Please make it the left one so I can still do homework.*

Coach McAndrew blows her whistle four more times, pointing each time to one of the four mats on the floor. "Line up behind these mats. We're gonna start with forward rolls, then backward somersaults, then cartwheels, then repeat." She blows her whistle again.

I go up to her. "Excuse me, I don't know how to do any of those things. Can I please go to the library?"

"No can do, *amiga*. Just watch what the other kids are doing. You'll learn. It's not hard. No pain, no gain!"

I stand way in the back of the line, letting everyone go ahead of me. All the kids do the forward rolls effortlessly. How am I supposed to learn by watching them? It's like telling someone to learn how to swim by watching a fish.

It's finally my turn. I kneel down and put the top of my head on the mat. That's as far as I get. I don't know what to do next. I hear giggling. The coach walks over.

"Just roll," she says.

Can she possibly be less helpful?

I close my eyes and push myself forward. I roll sideways off the mat—*splat*—onto the wooden gym floor. I hear more giggling.

"Okay, why don't you sit this one out and just watch?" Coach McAndrew suggests.

"Thank you," I say, walking toward the bleachers with my head down. I hate PE more than ever.

All pain, no gain.

At lunch, I'm sitting in the usual spot against my locker when I hear someone say, "Excuse me, are you the one from Iran?"

"Um, yeah," I say hesitantly, looking up to see a girl smiling at me.

"That's so cool! I'm Carolyn. I heard you say that in Miss DeAngelo's class. I'm from Norway," she says, sitting down on the ground next to me.

I'm so happy that someone is talking to me, but then I think, *What if she turns out to be mean like Original Cindy?* I'm willing to take a chance.

"When did you move here?" I ask.

"My grandparents came here. Not me."

"So you were born here?"

"I was. When you said you were from Iran, I thought you meant your grandparents were from Iran. So do you speak any other languages?" she asks.

"I speak Persian."

"That's really cool. My grandparents still speak Norwegian, but my parents and I only speak English. My grandparents wanted their kids to speak only English so they would have a better chance in America," she explains. "Too bad, huh?"

"It's different for us, because we're going back to Iran when my father's assignment is finished, so I can't forget Persian," I say.

"Can you say something in your language?" Carolyn asks.

"What do you want me to say?"

"Anything," she says. "I just want to hear what it sounds like."

"*Man shotor nadaram.*"

"What does that mean?"

"I don't own a camel," I translate.

Carolyn laughs. "Brock Vitter is an idiot. You know, he's the guy who asked about your camel the first day of school. Ignore him always."

"I'll try," I say.

"I think you're going to like living in Newport Beach. I've lived here my whole life. Here's all you need to know: When the weather is in the sixties or low seventies, we call that sweater weather. Anything else is just called weather."

"I'll remember that."

"And if you want to meet nice people, you should join the Girl Scout troop," Carolyn suggests. "We do fun things and the leaders, Mrs. Stahr and Mrs. Woods, are super nice."

"That would be great!" I say.

"And you know what? We should meet for lunch every day, but let's eat on the benches near Miss DeAngelo's class."

"Okey-dokey."

"And on Friday we should go check out the library," she suggests.

"We totally should do that!" Unlike my fake enthusiasm for tanning, this is real.

"I'm what you call a bookworm," Carolyn says as the bell rings, and we get up to leave.

"Me too!"

When I get home, my mom is watching TV.

"Guess what? I met the nicest girl today named Carolyn, and I am going to join Girl Scouts. And guess what again? She's a bookworm."

"That's nice."

I know that my mom knows what Girl Scouts is, because I was in Brownies in Compton. She just never gets excited over stuff. She's probably thinking about her sisters in Iran. She spends a lot of time doing that. Plus, she's not a bookworm—and only bookworms get excited over other bookworms.

Carolyn's last name is Williams, which means that our lockers are near each other. I've only had one conversation with her, but I've already decided that she's the coolest person in Newport Beach.

We meet at the bench, as planned. It's much nicer than sitting on the ground.

"So what's going on with the demonstrations in Iran?" she asks.

"You know about them?" I almost choke on a mouthful of cucumber.

"Well, yeah. It's all over the news," she replies.

"I know that, but I didn't know American kids watch the news too."

"I watch every day. I want to be a journalist when I grow up," she says. "So what is going on over there?"

"It's a big deal because we normally don't have demonstrations. We don't have freedom of speech, so people can't complain about the shah, which is what we call our king," I say.

"You can't complain *at all*?" she asks.

"Not at all."

"Whoa, that's hard to imagine. We're allowed to complain about anything and everything," Carolyn says. "If you don't like something the president does, you can put a bumper sticker on your car telling everyone behind you how you feel. You can start a petition. My mom started a petition once when they were going to cut an after-school program for kids who need extra help."

I think about that for a second and try to imagine my mom starting a petition. There's no way in a million years.

"You can't do that in Iran," I tell her.

"That's not all," Carolyn goes on, getting revved up. "You can write letters to the newspaper. You can organize a rally. Or, if you just can't wait to be heard, all you need is a posterboard, a marker, a street corner, and your voice."

"You guys are so lucky. Iranians can't do any of those things. The shah's military stops all demonstrations," I say.

"Why hasn't the shah stopped them?"

"He's tried. Some protesters have gotten killed, but the people keep protesting."

"What exactly are they protesting?" she asks, offering me some of her barbecue potato chips.

"Lots of things. In the early fifties, Iran had a really popular prime minister, Mohammad Mossadegh. He was actually elected by the people. But the U.S. and British governments got together and got rid of him."

"Wait! Why did they do that?" Carolyn asks.

"They wanted to make a profit from Iran's oil, and Mossadegh wouldn't let them. He said the Iranians should profit from the oil, not foreigners."

"That makes sense to me."

"Me too, but the shah was willing to let Western powers profit from Iran's oil, so the U.S. and the British made him the leader. Iranians are still mad about this."

"So people are protesting because of what happened thirty years ago?"

"There's other stuff too. Some people don't like the ways that the shah is trying to make Iran modern. Other people are angry that the shah and his friends are getting all the oil money and not sharing it with the rest of the country. There's a ton of other stuff too. It's not like it's just one or two things."

"How come you know so much about that Mohammad guy? The fifties was so long ago."

"He's a huge hero in Iran. Everyone knows the story."

"I see. So tell me more about Iran," Carolyn says. I can tell that she's going to be an excellent journalist some day.

"Everything is so different."

"Like what?"

"Where to begin? We don't have barbecue potato chips," I offer. "These are so good!"

"You can have the rest. But seriously, tell me," she pleads.

Just as I open my mouth to say something, the bell rings.

"Meet me here again tomorrow," Carolyn instructs me. "I want to hear part two of this story."

"For sure!" I answer, wiping the bright orange barbecue spices from my fingers onto my jeans.

TGIF

On Friday, I wake up with a smile on my face, even though I must endure the medieval torture known as PE class. I have someone to eat lunch with! Then we're going to check out the library.

Sure enough, when I get to the bench by Miss DeAngelo's room, Carolyn is already there.

"I thought about your question yesterday, and I have a bunch of stuff to tell you."

"Let's hear it," Carolyn says.

"My name's not really Cindy."

"I know. You told us that in Miss DeAngelo's class. Why did you change it?"

"It's such a pain! No one remembers my name and it's too long. You should see my old library card. Half my last name goes down the side, like a waterfall."

Carolyn laughs. "Do you want me to call you by your real name?"

"No, thanks."

"So what else is there, Cindy?" she asks.

"In Iran, we speak a different language and eat different foods, but those are not the big differences for me."

"What do you mean?"

"Ever since we moved to America, I have to go everywhere with my mom so I can translate. It's like I'm the mom now."

"Why doesn't she learn English?"

"She stays home all day, so her only English teacher is the TV. She knows things like, 'Hurry! Sale ends Monday!' and 'Kellogg's Frosted Flakes. They're gr-r-reat!'"

Carolyn laughs again. I can't believe how wonderful it is to have a friend who is genuinely interested in what I have to say and who is not obsessed with horses. It is the best feeling!

"There are things that are hard here that are easy in Iran. Like the first time I went to the doctor here with my mom, the receptionist asked for her first name. I said, 'Nastaran.' So the receptionist said, 'Oh, goodness gracious. I'll have to call her something else. Let's see. We can shorten this to Nas, Nasty. Oh, no, that won't work. Not Nasty.' Then she started to giggle."

"That's terrible," Carolyn interjects.

"It gets worse. Unfortunately, at that moment, my mother decided to practice speaking English. 'Yes, yes. I am Nasty,' she said, which made the receptionist laugh even harder. So I told my mom to please be quiet. 'Nasty is not a nice word,' I whispered. But how was she supposed to know? That was pretty much the last time she tried to speak English."

"That's tough," Carolyn agrees, nodding her head. I appreciate that she's not laughing at my mom. "At least your mom has someone in her family who can help her."

"Yes, families are very close in Iran," I continue. "They usually have an older person living with them, maybe a grandparent or a widowed aunt. I don't see that here. Where are the old people?"

"Most grandparents live on their own, and when they can't, they move into senior homes, like Leisure Land," she says. "My Aunt Tilly lives there."

"We don't have those in Iran. People just make room in their houses. There's always room for one more person, especially for an old person."

"That's really nice."

I can't believe Carolyn is so interested in my country! Her enthusiasm encourages me.

"We also don't have weekends," I continue. "Fridays are the only day off, and most kids spend the whole day doing schoolwork. We have homework starting in first grade, and lots of it. School is *a lot* harder in Iran."

"You go to school on *Saturdays* and *Sundays*?" she asks.

"Sad but true. But the strangest thing is that being smart in America is not cool. In fifth grade, I got a perfect score on the math test at the beginning of the year that we're supposed to take at the *end* of fifth grade. It's not like I sud- denly expected to be popular, but I thought the kids would at least congratulate me. Instead they kept calling me Brain. They said it like it was a bad thing. I was used to Iran, where it's really, really cool to be good at math."

"*I* think it's very cool to be good at math," says Carolyn. "And so do my parents."

"I don't know. It seems like most people only think you're cool in America if you're pretty or good at sports. I don't look like anybody who is considered pretty here, and I don't know how to play basketball, or how to do the monkey bars. And please do not say the word *tumbling* around me or I will have an allergic reaction. *And* I hate dodge ball. How is that even a game?"

"I hate it too. It should be called here's-your-chance-to-be-mean-and-get-points-for-it."

"My cousins get all kinds of awards in Iran for being good at math and chemistry. I've always wanted to be just like them. They've even had their names in the paper a bunch of times, and my aunts and uncles brag about it to everyone. I guess the kids here would call them dorks too," I add.

"I'd like to meet your cousins," Carolyn says. "So what college do you want to go to?"

"I don't know." I'm at a loss. I've never thought about that.

"I want to go to either Stanford or Occidental and study journalism," she says. "I want to report the news on TV. You know, like on *Sixty Minutes*."

"You'd be good at that," I tell her.

I have never met anyone who has asked me so many good questions about Iran. Usually people ask me about camels, which, for the record, I have only seen once—in the zoo.

GEORGE

Friday after school, I find a note slipped in my locker from Carolyn. *Do you want to come to my house on Saturday at noon? We can swim and have lunch. Call me.* Below that is her number.

When I get home, my mom is watching *The Phil Donahue Show,* which means her mood could go either way, depending on the show's topic. I can't risk asking her and getting a no. I decide to wait and ask my dad.

As soon as I hear the garage door opening, I rush to meet him.

"*Baba,* can I *please* go to a friend's house tomorrow? Her name is Carolyn. She likes math and for sure wants to go to college."

"Sounds great," he says.

"But you have to drive me. She lives in Harbor View Hills. I don't know where that is."

"I'll look it up on the map."

I go back in the house. "*Maman!*" I yell. "I won't be here for lunch tomorrow. I'm going to a friend's house. Remember the one I mentioned?"

"That's nice," she says.

• • •

On the way over to Carolyn's the next day, my dad prac-tices his English. This is what his accent sounds like: "Good morning Mee-sees Veel-yahms. My name eez Mohsen Yousefzadeh from ee-ron and eet eez nice to meet you."

I try to help him say "Williams" instead of "Veel-yahms," but he claims his mouth does not work that way. "Maybe I'll introduce myself as Mo," he says. Before I can tell him no, he asks, "What about George? That's an easy name, and eve-ryone has heard of George Vasheeng-tone." By then, we are almost at Carolyn's, and I'm getting worried.

"Just say your real name slowly and don't mention being from Iran. They already know that. And don't talk about the oil industry, unless Mrs. Williams says, 'Tell me about the oil industry.'"

That will never happen.

Harbor View Hills is very pretty. It's full of big trees, flowers, and real houses, not condos. I know this because a condo usually shares at least one wall with a neighbor. Thanks to the *Rules for Condominium Living* binder, I now know a whole bunch of facts about a second useless, boring topic: condos. The oil industry being the first.

Carolyn's front door has a wreath on it decorated with real flowers and lemons. I have never seen lemons used as decoration, but it looks nice. I wonder if the Williamses will eat them at some point. It would be a waste not to.

We ring the bell. I can tell my dad is practicing in his head. When Carolyn's mom opens the door, he says, "Hello, Mee-sees V-v-v-veel-yahms. Hello. I am Mohsen Yousefzadeh. Please call me Mo or George."

Carolyn's mom pretends that my dad has just made perfect sense.

"I'm so happy to meet you," she says. "Carolyn has told me many nice things about Cindy."

My dad nods his head a few times, turns around, and leaves. He doesn't even say goodbye to me. I think he's embarrassed. All that practice did not help.

Carolyn runs up to the door. "Welcome! Come in! Let me show you around."

"You have a lovely house, Mrs. Williams," I say as Carolyn pulls me inside.

"Thank you, Cindy. I hope you have fun today. Carolyn's told me so much about you."

"This is our pool," Carolyn says, taking me outside. "I hope you brought your bathing suit."

Before I can tell her that I am wearing it under my clothes, ready to go, a big dog bounds up to us and starts licking me. I turn around so he can't lick my face.

"This is Sam. Down, Sam, down! I don't know where our cat, Elizabeth, is. She's probably sleeping someplace. Come, I'll show you my room. Get down, Sam!"

As soon as we walk into her room, what do I see? A beanbag chair. And not just any beanbag chair, but an extra-cool one covered with orange shag. She also has a parakeet named Tweety, plus all the Nancy Drew books, the Boxcar Children series, *and* the complete set of *Encyclopedia Britannica*. How lucky is she?

"I love your room," I say as I scan her bookshelf. "Hey, you've read *Black Beauty*?"

"It's one of my favorites. That copy was my mom's when she was our age. I'll show you her books later. But let's eat first. I'm starving."

We go to the kitchen and sit down at the table underneath a huge sign that reads IF YOU CAN DREAM IT, YOU CAN BE IT. We have a sign at our house too, by the front door. It says PLEASE TAKE OFF YOUR SHOES.

We eat tuna sandwiches and chocolate chip cookies and chat about school. During lunch, Mrs. Williams calls, "Matt, come and say hello to Carolyn's new friend."

"My brother's in high school and he's a straight-A student," Carolyn tells me.

A tall, skinny boy shows up. "Nice to meet you," he says, shaking my hand.

"Nice to meet you, too."

He reminds me of my favorite cousin in Iran, Mehrdad.

As he turns around to leave, Carolyn whispers, "We can bug him later."

After lunch, we play a game of Yahtzee, which Carolyn teaches me, and then we go in her room so she can change into her suit. I'm already wearing mine, so I take off my clothes and fold them neatly on her bed. As soon as Carolyn is ready, we run to the pool and jump in! Carolyn knows how to dive. She can also touch the bottom of the deep end with her hand. We spend two hours swimming, doing cannonballs, and chatting about school and our teachers.

It was a great day, but the best part was when Carolyn said that she'd told her mom about my perfect score on the math test at the beginning of fifth grade, and that her mother had said, "Bravo!" It's my first *bravo* ever.

I love this family.

ZENITH

I have English, Social Studies, and Pre-Algebra with Carolyn, so I go to her house after school a couple times a week to do homework with her. We're taking a break, sitting in their family room in front of their huge twenty-inch color Zenith TV while Mrs. Williams irons a pile of shirts. My family has a black-and-white Zenith at home, but it's a thirteen-inch tabletop with an antenna, which we constantly have to get up and adjust. Sometimes we tape a wire hanger to the antenna and somehow that makes the picture clearer. Color TV is so much better! My dad wants to buy one, but he says there's no point, since we can't take it back to Iran with us. The electricity current is different there. Whenever we go to Sears, we have to go to the TV section so my dad can see what the newest Zenith models that we can't have look like. He always likes to stand there and say the slogan from the commercials: "Zenith. The quality goes in before the name goes on."

A report about the protests in Iran starts, complete with full-color footage of crowds in Tehran. During the commercial, Carolyn turns to me and asks, "What's the shah like?"

I think for a minute about how to describe the shah to

an American. "You don't have anyone like him in America. He's like someone in a fairy tale. He and his family live in a palace and have the fanciest and most expensive of everything, including jewelry straight out of Aladdin's tales."

"Whoa," Carolyn exclaims, a little surprised.

"You never see the president and Mrs. Carter wearing crowns, but the shah and his wife wear them—and they also have thrones, capes, imperial swords, and belts, all covered with emeralds, diamonds, and rubies. They don't do stuff with ordinary people, ever. I guess when you own a belt with a huge emerald instead of a buckle, you don't mingle with the baker or the plumber. I bet he's never talked to a taxidriver."

"Is that the main problem?"

"Yes, but it's more than that. If you're friends with the shah, you have all the advantages in the world: education, a high-paying job, and a nice house. Even if you commit a crime, you don't get punished. Rules do not apply to the rich and well connected. You are guaranteed a life of privilege. You don't have to try."

A perfect comparison pops into my head. "It's like those cars at Disneyland that are on tracks so you don't need to steer. Rich people are on a good track from birth—they can just sit back and enjoy the ride. Poor people are on a bad track and they can't change anything no matter how much they try to steer in a different direction. Their life is set, just like those tracks."

"It's different here. Abraham Lincoln started out poor and then he became president," Carolyn points out.

"Things like that don't happen in Iran."

"Sounds like classic corruption," Mrs. Williams chimes in. "The president of the United States is an ordinary human being who wins an election. He doesn't have a throne or a bejeweled sword, but that would be great for photos." She laughs at the idea.

"And people don't curtsy to him," I say.

"I don't even think Americans know how to curtsy," Carolyn adds, "except at the ballet."

"And the shah never retires. He rules until he dies."

"Our president serves for eight years, max," interjects Mrs. Williams. She walks over to the TV and turns it off. "Get back to work, ladies."

"One more second, Mom!" Carolyn turns to face me, cross-legged on the sofa. "Your shah almost sounds like some kind of god," she concludes.

"I guess. I've never really thought about it. He has always been there for as long as I've been alive. His picture is everywhere. If you go in a bank, there he is, above the doorway. If you go to the hardware store, there's his picture, above the cash register. If you open your textbook, there he is, right before the first chapter. His face is like wallpaper."

"That would never happen here because the picture

would have to change after every election," Carolyn explains, offering me the bowl of pretzels that was on the coffee table.

"I know." I take a handful of the salty snacks. "I've already been here for three presidents. When I first came to Compton in second grade, the president was Nixon. Then it switched to Ford. Then we went back to Iran, same old shah. Then we came back to America for this assignment and you have President Carter now. My dad says it's amazing how American presidents change without any fighting or wars. For my whole life, it has always been the shah. When the shah dies, it will be his oldest son. We don't get to vote on that."

"So if the shah is so powerful and he doesn't allow free speech, why hasn't he stopped the demonstrations?" Carolyn asks, in between bites of pretzels.

"Whenever there were demonstrations before, the secret police, SAVAK, would take the protesters to jail and torture them. This always scared others away from protesting, but apparently it isn't working anymore. Protesters are actually getting killed, but people keep demonstrating."

"Wow. That's huge." She wipes crumbs off her shirt.

"The shah likes to scare people. He buys the most modern weapons in the world for his military and shows them off during parades. My dad says you don't see tanks and guns on parade in America because democracy keeps the country together, not fear of the military."

Carolyn looks at me thoughtfully. "Now that I think about it, that's true. I've never seen a tank in a Fourth of July parade, just marching bands, dogs wearing tutus, and people dressed like Uncle Sam. Once, I even saw a dog dressed like Uncle Sam!"

I nod, relieved that she understands. "You're lucky that people can do that kind of stuff in America and no one ends up in jail."

We each grab another handful of pretzels and get up from the sofa. Our homework still awaits us in the dining room.

MEXICAN HEAVEN

On the way to our first Girl Scout meeting a few weeks later, I start telling Carolyn stories about babysitting David.

"He's such an interesting boy," I say. "We have an expression in Persian, *ghoor o maveez*. *Ghoor* is an unripe grape and *maveez* is a type of raisin. That's David. He's both young and old at the same time."

"I love that expression," Carolyn says. "By the way, how much do you get paid?"

"A dollar an hour."

"Is that it?" She sounds shocked.

"What do you mean?" I ask.

"Who came up with that amount?"

"Mrs. Klein said, 'How about a dollar an hour?' and I said that would be great."

"First of all, you should never answer right away," Carolyn says, clearly annoyed. "Secondly, you should have asked for a dollar and a quarter. If she asks you to do dishes or take care of any pets, that's an extra twenty-five cents *for each chore*. You need to ask for more next time. I make one fifty an hour, sometimes two dollars with add-ons."

"I don't know. She's really nice and I don't think I can ask for more now. I've already babysat a bunch of times. That seems kinda rude," I say.

"Rude?" repeats Carolyn. "That's called business. Plus, there's college. You *are* saving for college, aren't you?"

"No."

"Well, you'd better start! You have six years. Tick tock, tick tock. It's gonna be here before you know it."

I've never thought about paying for college, but Carolyn's right! There is no way I am going to ask for more money from Mrs. Klein, though. I'll just save everything I earn from now on.

The Girl Scout troop in Newport Beach is huge, with about eighty girls. Thankfully, Original Cindy is not one of them. It's bad enough that I have PE with her twice a week, where she now pretends I don't exist. It's better than that first day when she laughed at me, but I still can't believe I spent six weeks listening to her horse tales and shedding an entire layer of skin for nothing.

When I told the story to Carolyn, she said, "You shed that friendship like you shed your skin."

I liked that. It made the whole sorry episode seem less pathetic, and more poetic.

During the break, I start talking to a girl named Rachel, whom I recognize from two of my classes. "I heard you're new this year. So how do you like Newport Beach so far?" she asks.

"I like it," I answer. "It's getting more fun as I make friends."

"I moved here in third grade and I remember how hard it is to be the new kid. We should do something sometime," she suggests.

"We should," I agree, and we exchange phone numbers.

The Girl Scout leaders, Mrs. Stahr and Mrs. Woods, seem really nice. They tell us all about the Girl Scout Jamboree, camping trips, and a place called the Goodwill, where we will be volunteering. I have never been camping, so I am more excited about that than anything else.

Carolyn knows a lot of the girls at the meeting, since she was born and raised in Newport Beach. I can't help but think how much easier it is to live in one place your whole life. I will never know that feeling.

Before she drives me home, Mrs. Williams asks if I would like to have dinner with them. "It's make-your-own-taco night," she says.

"Yes!" I answer. My parents and I love the tacos at Taco Bell. "I just have to call my mom from your house."

When we arrive, Mrs. Williams sets up the dinner table while I call my mom. I'm one hundred percent sure she's going to say yes, because I am one hundred percent sure that dinner at our house is something cold and out of a box.

Somehow my mom has decided that breakfast food works just as well for dinner, so now our pantry looks like the cereal aisle at El Rancho Market. I definitely prefer tacos.

She says yes, and reminds me to thank the Williamses—as if I would forget.

Make-your-own-taco night is basically Mexican heaven and a million times better than Taco Bell. Carolyn, Matt, and their parents and I sit around the dining room table, which is covered with all kinds of ingredients. Matt starts telling us about his latest debate tournament as we pass the plates around. Mr. Williams is asking Matt all kinds of questions—he was also on the debate team when he was in high school. I'm trying to listen to the questions but I'm also trying not to miss any of the ingredients. This meal definitely requires concentration, because you have to add the fillings in the right order.

I put meat, lettuce, tomatoes, cheese, onions, salsa, guacamole, extra cheese, and extra salsa in my taco shell. It is the messiest and tastiest meal I have had in a long time. But for some reason, tacos don't fill me up. Mine were more stuffed than anyone else's, but I'm still hungry.

In Iran, eating a lot of food at someone's house is the polite thing to do. The hostess keeps insisting you eat more even after the top button of your pants has popped and you're lying on the floor, regretting the fourth helping. My dad had told me that in America, hosts don't push food on you. Still, I'm hoping Mrs. Williams will say, "Have another! You barely ate anything." She doesn't.

After my third taco, I ask Mrs. Williams how she made this dinner.

"Oh, goodness, I can't even call this cooking. It's really just assembling, except for the ground beef, which you just cook in a pan," she says. "You can buy all the ingredients at El Rancho Market, right near your house."

"My mom loves these 'make-it-yourself' meals," Matt explains. "If you stick around long enough, you'll see that she has a whole menu of meals where *we* actually have to do all the work, but she gets all the credit."

"Excuse me, Matthew," Mr. Williams interjects. "Would you like to cook dinner from now on? Then you'll be allowed to complain about your mother's dinners."

Matt doesn't say anything.

"So how do you bend the taco shells without breaking them?" I ask.

They all laugh. It's the first time I have made them laugh and it feels nice, not at all embarrassing. But I don't know what's so funny.

"The shells come in a box, already bent," Carolyn says. "Isn't it obvious?"

"No," I say. "It's like grasshopper pie."

"Like what?" she asks.

"One time, I asked my fifth grade teacher, Mrs. Good-speed, if there are any grasshoppers in grasshopper pie. She laughed too. But there are apples in apple pie, and pecans in pecan pie, so why not grasshoppers in grasshopper pie?"

"Good point," says Mrs. Williams.

After we finish eating, she stands up and starts to clear the table. "It just so happens that we have make-your-own sundaes for dessert," she announces.

"No complaints here!" exclaims Matt.

"Didn't think so," quips Mrs. Williams, with a chuckle.

She sets up a round tray on the table. "Now, Cindy, here's something you might not have seen yet. This tray, which turns like this, is called a Lazy Susan." She starts setting up little bowls of chopped nuts, candy topping, and chocolate sauce.

"Lazy Susan?" I repeat.

"I wonder who Susan was," says Matt.

"Probably the inventor's wife," says Mr. Williams.

"Who then became his ex-wife," adds Mrs. Williams. Everyone laughs again.

So much happiness in this house! I wish my mom laughed. I have a sudden thought.

"Mrs. Williams, there are no Iranians here, and my mother doesn't have any friends. Do you think you can do something with her? You need to know that she does not speak English, play tennis, or golf, and she does not hike."

"Of course!" Mrs. Williams says, handing each of us a napkin. "I'll invite her to the next PTA meeting. She'll meet lots of nice people volunteering and she'll pick up some English, too."

I'm so glad I asked her.

PISTACHiO

As soon as the Williamses drop me off, I tell my mom the good news. But I can tell from the frown on her face that she doesn't think it's such good news. She says she doesn't want to do anything with anyone until she learns English. Plus, she's still mad at me about the pool key.

"But you can learn English by talking with Americans. It's better practice than just watching people win coffeemakers and dining room sets on *Let's Make a Deal*," I say.

"I need to learn English first," she repeats.

"That makes no sense."

"It makes sense to me," she insists.

"The adults that you would meet are really nice. They don't care if your English isn't perfect," I assure her.

"I'm not interested," my mother says, and leaves the room.

"You have to learn English, *Maman*!" I yell after her. "I don't want to be your translator anymore."

I hear her bedroom door slam.

I don't know what to do. My mother is so difficult, and whenever I try to help her, she doesn't listen. I know her life would be so much better if she made a little effort. And now

I have to tell Mrs. Williams, who has been so nice to me, to forget our conversation.

I call Carolyn. "Can you please tell your mom that my mom is too busy to go to PTA meetings but thank you very much for the offer?"

"How does your mother know that she'll be busy for PTA meetings when she doesn't even know the dates yet?" Carolyn asks.

"Well," I say, trying to think of how to explain this, "in Iran, we studied plants. We learned that some plants grow in certain places but not in others. That's why Iran has the world's best pistachios but no pineapples. You could say my mom is like a pistachio."

"Pistachios also grow in California," Carolyn points out.

"Not my mom."

Right then and there, I give up trying to find a friend for my mother.

The day before we left Compton, when my dad and I were taping shut the packed boxes, I said, *"Baba,* do you think *Maman* will be happier in Newport Beach?"

He didn't answer right away.

Ever since we moved to America, my mom spends a lot of time being sad. She didn't want to move here the first time, even though it was only for two years. For months before we left, her three sisters would come over every day and they would just sit together, drink tea, and cry, and cry, and cry. I didn't understand why, since we were going to come back. The whole two years in Compton, my mom was sad. She didn't even try to like it. My dad planned fun weekends for us like going to the Gilroy Garlic Festival, the Cloverdale Citrus Fair, and the Palm Springs Date Festival, but nothing really worked. My mom didn't even try the garlic ice cream or the date shakes! I loved seeing all those places, but it didn't make a difference for her. My dad told her she could get whatever clothes she wanted from the Sears catalog. Not even *that* worked. Then we went back to Iran and she was a little happier. But after a year, my dad got another assignment, so we moved back to Compton. And it was the same old thing. My mom watched TV all day and didn't have any friends. But when we were moving to Newport Beach, I still hoped maybe things would change.

After a long pause, my dad finally said, "You have to be patient and understand that it will take time for your mother to adjust to living here. It's much easier being American in Iran right now than being Iranian in America."

"What do you mean?" I asked.

"In Iran, there are fifty thousand Americans."

"What are they doing there?"

"They work for oil and gas companies, the military, the universities, you name it. Plus, there's about two thousand American students at the Tehran American School."

"I'm the only Iranian at my school!"

"It's not lonely for Americans in Iran. They can see movies in English. Can you imagine if we could see movies in Persian in California? And there are lots of clubs for people who speak their language. It's so much easier. They have a community."

In the total of three years we have lived in America, we ran into other Iranians only once. We were at a mall and suddenly we heard people speaking Persian. That had never happened before. Speaking Persian in America is like speaking a super-secret language that no one understands. It's handy, except that my mom is always telling me, in front of everyone, to stand up straight, don't have a third cookie, and other generally annoying stuff.

So we went up to the people at the mall and asked them, in Persian, if they were Iranian. They were so shocked! It was like two polar bears running into each other in Hawaii. *You are like me! How did you end up here, so far away from home?*

I was so relieved, because I'd thought this meant my mom would *finally* have a friend, but they said they were just visiting California on vacation. We invited them to our house the next weekend anyway.

I hadn't seen my mom that happy in a long time! She made kebabs and rice. I told her we should serve Kentucky Fried Chicken with biscuits and coleslaw, since that would be more special for them. My mom said that was the most ridiculous thing she had ever heard. I know why she thought that—if you are Iranian and you invite someone to your house, your food must be homemade, Persian, and perfect. Food is the most important part of every Iranian's life. Let's say you're invited to someone's house for dinner, and let's say this person shelters orphans and also discovered the cure for malaria, but the rice is not good. The next day, everyone will be talking.

"The rice was terrible."

"The rice was horrible."

"How can she live with herself?"

And Iranians never forget. You can't say my Aunt Jila's name without someone saying, "You mean the one who burned her rice?" That happened before I was born and even I know about it.

I also told my mom that instead of fruit for dessert, we should serve Chips Ahoy chocolate chip cookies and Baskin Robbins ice cream, genuine American foods. But my mom gave them watermelon, which is the most common dessert where I come from. I was certain they would have liked my idea better. Everyone in the world has tried watermelon, but Baskin Robbins rainbow sherbet—that's something they would have remembered forever.

My mom never listens to me.

Twice a week, I have drama class. We read plays, which are basically books written as if people are talking. It's my first time ever reading plays, and I love it. It feels like I'm an invisible visitor in someone's life.

The first play we read is *A Streetcar Named Desire* by Tennessee Williams. Our teacher, Mrs. Crockett, gave us two weeks to read it and write an essay, but I started it on Friday and now it's Sunday and I'm almost done reading. It's a very sad story but I can't put it down. Tennessee Williams makes you think you are *right there,* in New Orleans. I can practically feel the humid weather.

I get to the end of the book and the main character, Blanche DuBois, is being taken away to a hospital, and it's a really, really sad scene. She looks at the doctor and says, "I have always depended on the kindness of strangers." I go back and read it again. And again. That is the best sentence ever.

I could say the same thing about myself. When you move to another country, you always depend on strangers. You're so alone. I thought about all the kind people who had helped us in Compton and how without them, my life would be so different.

I bet when Tennessee Williams wrote that line for Blanche DuBois, he didn't think that a girl from Abadan, Iran, would tape it to her wall. But that's just what I do.

Two weeks later, we have to listen to everyone's report on the play. The first person called is Mary Howard. I recognize her from the Girl Scout meeting. She's the tallest girl in the troop, so she's hard to miss. She walks slowly to the front of the room, and I can tell she's nervous. Before she begins, Mrs. Crockett says, "All right, class, I want you on your best behavior."

Mrs. Crockett is a sweet-looking older lady, the exact type of teacher that certain kids don't listen to. That's one thing I quickly figured out about middle school. The kids are so much ruder than in elementary school.

Mary starts speaking with a shaky voice. "I am doing my report on the main characters in *A Streetcar Named Desire*." She pronounces it "Desiree" instead of "desire." A boy in the front row turns around and says, "Desiree! She called it Desiree! What an idiot!" He says it so loudly that the whole class hears. Then a couple other kids start laughing and saying, "Desiree!" Mary looks like she is about to cry.

Maybe this is why my mom resists learning English. She's afraid people will make fun of her if she makes a mistake.

It takes a while for Mrs. Crockett to calm everyone down. She's not very good at that.

Mary starts again, but she keeps forgetting her speech and saying "um, um" all the time. After class, I run up to her. "Hey, I thought that it was pronounced 'Desiree' too," I say.

That is not true.

"I'm so embarrassed," she says. "And my speech was horrible."

"Not at all," I insist. "Those kids are just mean, and mean people are always louder than the rest of us. Hey, weren't you at the Girl Scout meeting?"

"I was. Were you there too?"

"Yes. I'm Cindy. I just moved here."

"Nice to meet you." She holds out her hand and I shake it. "Everyone calls me Howie. There are a lot of Marys in our class."

"All right, Howie," I say, smiling.

And just like that, with a little help from Tennessee Williams, I make another friend.

We're almost finished with dinner when David's dad stops by. His name is also David, but my dad calls him Davood, which is the Persian version. They met a couple weeks ago when he came over and asked to borrow our ladder. My dad was so happy! He actually gave a short lecture on the oil industry during the time it took him to get the ladder out of our garage and into theirs. Dr. Klein didn't seem to mind.

My father opens the door and invites him in.

"Thank you, but I just wanted to return the ladder. I was able to do a lot of projects around the house for Rhonda."

"Anytime, Davood. And would you like dinner or something to drink?" my dad asks.

"I just ate, thank you," says Dr. Klein.

"Are you *shoor*, no dinner, Doktor Davood?" my mother asks, popping in from the kitchen.

"Yes, thank you," says Dr. Klein.

"Just a *leetel*?" my mom presses on.

"I'm good," says Dr. Klein, smiling at my mom. "I only have a few minutes before I gotta get back home, but thank you. Maybe next time."

I appreciate that he is not annoyed, since some people would be.

"Next time," my mom repeats, stopping the *taarof*, the custom of nonstop offerings of food to guests. It's an Iranian way of being polite, but it doesn't translate in America. Here, it seems pushy. In this case, Dr. Klein was lucky. My mom gave up pretty quickly.

"I open the garage door for you," my dad says. I follow him.

"So, Mo," Dr. Klein says as he sets down the ladder by the washing machine. "I'm curious about something. Jimmy Carter is always talking about human rights. What's your take on the subject?"

I can tell my dad is excited to give another mini lecture to Dr. Klein. He gets this look on his face when he can't wait to say something.

"I imagine it is very hard for Americans to understand the value of human rights and free speech. How can you appreciate something you have always had?" He pauses for a moment. "Perhaps it's like gravity. No one ever says, 'Thank goodness for gravity,' but if it suddenly went away, we would all appreciate it."

My dad is such an engineer! Who uses gravity as an example of anything?

"That's true," Dr. Klein says, looking thoughtful.

"American comedians are still making fun of when

President Nixon said, 'I am not a crook!'" My dad shakes his head in disbelief. "No one could ever do that in Iran! If they did, they would end up in prison. And when President Ford bumped his head getting out of a helicopter, they kept showing it on TV, over and over again. People made fun of him and called him a bad name."

"Klutz," says Dr. Klein, with a chuckle.

"I could not believe this!" my dad exclaims, throwing both hands in the air. "If the shah ever bumped his head, no one would ever hear about it. Instead, there would be news reports about how he has never bumped his head. We would never call him that word."

Dr. Klein laughs. "Our presidents would probably appreciate not being the punch line of jokes." He starts to leave.

"Yes," my father says, "and some of the jokes are very funny. I just wish your comedians talked more slowly."

"I agree. And I wish I could stay longer, but I have promised to help David with his science project. I'd love to continue this conversation later." Dr. Klein shakes my dad's hand before walking out of the garage. "Thanks, Mo, for helping me understand this crazy world a little bit better."

"Anytime," my dad says. "I have much more to tell you."

Dr. Klein smiles.

"Nice to see you, too, Cindy." He pats me on the head. "And, Mo, if you ever want to play a round of golf, let me know."

"Yes, yes!" my dad says quickly, even though he really means, *No, thank you. I have no idea how to play golf.*

SKIP

The following Sunday, as I'm searching my dad's closet for a Halloween costume, someone knocks on our door. My mom and I answer, and standing there is a human kaleidoscope: a man wearing a green and pink striped polo shirt with the collar up, light and dark green plaid pants, and shiny white shoes.

"Hello, neighbors! I think this belongs to you," he says, holding up our pool key.

My mom and I are shocked. We'd thought the key was lost forever. Before I can say anything, my mom whispers, *"In chi pooshideh?"*

What is he wearing?

There is no time to explain golf attire to my mom, so I say, "My mother wants to thank you."

"No need to thank me, neighbor. I'm Skip," he says. "I saw your flyers a while ago and found your key behind the bushes while walking my dog this morning. I said to myself, 'Skipper, whoever owns this keychain is a friend of yours.' You see, I love fishing, I love bulldogs, and I love beer. So here you go." He hands the keychain to my mom. "I live in the house around the corner, the one with the sign in the front yard that says 'An Old Sailor Lives Here.' Please tell your husband that the next time he wants to go fishing, I'll bring the beer."

"Tank you," my mother says.

"Thank you very much," I add.

As soon as I shut the door, my mom says she wants to make some Persian food for "Eskeep," to thank him. I suggest buying him a box of See's assorted chocolates instead. My mom thinks that is a very bad idea, of course.

Before I know it, she has opened one of her precious jars of grape leaves from Iran and is busy cutting off the stems. The onions and ground beef are in the pan, and the smell of cilantro and turmeric fills the house.

That night, my mom hands me a paper plate of stuffed grape leaves arranged in two circles, with a sprig of mint like a tiny tree in the middle. It looks nice, but I'm sure Skip is a hamburger-and-fries kind of guy. He might never return another lost item again.

Americans drink grape juice and moisturize their lips with grape-flavored Lip Smackers, but I know that eating grape leaves probably seems as wrong to them as eating the garden hose. On my way to Skip's house, I throw away the plate in the greenbelt trash can. I immediately feel bad. It's the first time I have ever thrown away a plate of food. I decide to go to Skip's house anyway.

I turn the corner and look for the sailor sign. His house

is easy to find, and when he opens the door, I say, "Hi, I'm Cindy, and I just want to thank you again for returning our pool key. I'm the one who lost it."

Skip smiles and says, "How sweet of you to come by. You know, I always say that a stranger is a friend I haven't met yet, so I'm glad your lost key made me make a new friend. And you look like you might be the same age as my son. Do you go to Lincoln Junior High?"

"Yes," I answer.

Skip turn around and yells, "Brock, get down here!"

As soon as I hear the name Brock, I feel sick. *Dear God, please tell me Brock is a common name in Newport Beach and this isn't that same jerk from English class.*

A few seconds later, Brock shows up. It's the same jerk from English class.

"Brock, this is Cindy, our neighbor. She's at Lincoln too."

Brock just stands there, one of his eyes hidden under his side-swept bangs.

"What do you say, Brock?" Skip asks, sounding slightly annoyed.

"Um, nice to meet you," he says, clearly not meaning it.

I want to say, "We already met on the first day of school. Remember how you made fun of me in front of the whole class?"

Instead I say, "Nice to meet you, too." But I don't mean it either.

Sensing that there is not going to be any more conversation between me and Brock, Skip jumps in. "Well, this has certainly been a terrific evening!"

"Thank you again," I say.

As I turn around to leave, Skip adds, "See you later, alligator. Or as Brock likes to say, 'See you soon, raccoon!'"

I can hear Brock's voice as I walk away. "Stop saying that, Dad. I never say that!"

I'm glad he's embarrassed. *I* am horrified. What are the chances? Now I have *two* people to avoid in my neighborhood, Brock and Original Cindy.

When I get home, I tell my mom that Skip thanked her.

"See," my mom says, "everyone loves stuffed grape leaves."

HALLOWEEN

Before I know it, it's Halloween, my favorite holiday in the whole world. This will only be my third one. I am so bummed that I have missed celebrating at least four Halloweens in my life because we didn't live in America. The closest thing we have in Iran is the one night during the Persian New Year when we go door to door and people give out *ajil,* which is a mix of nuts and dried fruits. That's it. Nuts and dried fruit at every house. I used to think it was fun until I experienced Halloween. It's like thinking seesaws are fun until you go on a roller coaster. Kids in Iran would *love* Halloween. Actually, every kid in every country in the world would love it. If you're a kid and you don't like Halloween . . . well, that's just not possible.

Carolyn has asked me to go trick-or-treating in her neighborhood. Rachel is invited too.

Rachel's going to be a cat, and Carolyn says her costume is a surprise. I'm going to be a hobo and wear my dad's old jacket and put brown makeup on my cheeks to make them look dirty. I will also tie a scarf on a broomstick, fill it with socks, and swing that over my shoulder. It's supposed to hold all my worldly belongings, since I don't have a home, just like the hobos in the American movies I saw in Iran.

I make the mistake of telling my mom about my costume. Now that she isn't giving me the silent treatment because of the pool key, she won't stop bossing me around. I wish Skip had waited until after Halloween to find it.

My mom says I should wear a nice dress and she will put makeup on me like "Ree-tah Hay-vort." That's my mom's favorite American actress, even though she's from a thousand years ago. My mom does not comprehend that it is now 1978, and hobos are way more popular than Rita Hayworth.

When they were teenagers, my mom and her sisters collected black-and-white photos of American movie stars. They thought these actresses were the most glamorous women in the world and they wanted to be just like them. My mom still has the photos in her top drawer.

Unfortunately, my mom does not understand that a) I will never look like Rita Hayworth no matter how much makeup she puts on me, and b) that is possibly the worst costume in the history of Halloween.

She says, "Why would a girl want to dress up like a beggar?"

I tell her that everyone here tries to have funny or scary costumes, and dressing as a hobo in Newport Beach is not the same thing as being a beggar in Iran. "*Maman*," I say, trying to explain the difference, "living like a hobo is a life-style. A hobo hangs out near the train tracks, sharing his one can of beans with his hobo friends, while another strums the banjo, singing sad songs from the heart. Hobos hop on the train without paying, going from town to town looking for work, and they don't mind having grime on their faces because they have each other and their dreams."

"*Gedahayeh deevaneh*," she says, shaking her head.

Crazy beggars.

"It's just a Halloween costume," I remind her.

My mother looks very disappointed. It's as if she's confusing Halloween with Career Day.

I finally realize there is nothing that will make her understand. She's upset, but what can I do? I'm going as a hobo anyway.

I ask my parents if they are planning to give out candy or keep the lights off and pretend to not be home. My dad says they're leaving the lights on, but that he bought miniature boxes of raisins, since kids in America eat too much candy. I certainly hope no one figures out where I live! I don't want to be remembered as the girl whose family handed out dried fruit.

In second grade, my first year in America, all the kids came to school on Halloween wearing their costumes except me. The class was filled with cowboys, ghosts, and princesses. I felt so bad being the only one who didn't know about this.

When you move here, no one gives you an instruction sheet on what happens during holidays.

I liked the costumes, especially the ghosts, but there was no way my mom would have ever let me make holes in bedsheets for the eyes. Plus, all our sheets had flowers on them, and who's ever heard of a floral ghost? Then right before lunch, Mrs. Henseley, who was a really nice mom who also helped in the classroom, told me to go outside in the hall with her for a minute. She tied a handkerchief around my head, gave me a bunch of bracelets, wrapped a long skirt around me, and said I was a "hippie." I didn't know what a hippie was, but I was so happy that I had a costume, because after lunch the whole school paraded around the basketball court. That's what Tennessee Williams meant when he wrote about the kindness of strangers. If Mrs. Henseley hadn't brought me that outfit, my costume would have been "sad kid from foreign country."

I thought the costume parade at school was all there was to Halloween. We had only been in America for a couple months and had no clue about trick-or-treating. My English wasn't great back then, so even if the kids had been talking about it, I wouldn't have understood. That night, when the first group of kids rang our doorbell, we had no idea what they wanted. My parents just told them their costumes were cute. But the kids stood there staring at us, and finally one of them said, "Where's the candy?"

We didn't have any candy, so we gave out all the apples, oranges, and bananas we had. When we ran out of fruit, we gave out pickling cucumbers. Iranians always have massive amounts of little cucumbers in their houses. If there is ever an emergency that requires huge amounts of small cucumbers, Iranians will be instant heroes.

But I don't want to think about our first, sad Halloween anymore. Tonight, my father is going to drive me to Carolyn's house. I go upstairs to get ready. I put on my dad's coat, roll up my jeans a little bit, grab my stick with the bundle attached to it, and spread some of my mom's brown eye shadow on my cheeks. I know she wouldn't want me to touch her makeup, so I only use a little bit.

I go to the garage as fast as I can to avoid my mom, but she still sees me. "There's something on your face," she yells as I run past her.

"Okay," I answer.

That's practically the most important part of my costume. Hobos' faces are always dirty in the movies.

"Nice costume," my dad says as I get in the car. He's been sitting there listening to the radio. "Are you dressed as a father? And there's something on your face."

"No. I'm a hobo, like in the movies."

Thankfully, he goes back to listening to the news, so our conversation stops. That's all he's been doing since the president of Egypt and the prime minister of Israel won the

Nobel Peace Prize. On the way there, he says, "What a year! Egypt and Israel found peace, although Jimmy Carter should have won the Nobel too. Anyone can destroy a bridge, but it takes great people to build one. Zomorod, always remember 1978. This is a great year."

As soon as we enter the gates of Harbor View Hills, I am one hundred percent sure that I *will* always remember 1978. This is a great year indeed! The neighborhood looks like the Haunted House ride at Disneyland! Every house is decorated to the max. Some people have set up entire grave-yards on their front lawns. There are life-size monsters on porches, and ghosts and skeletons hanging from trees. And carved pumpkins everywhere, and not just one per house!

When we arrive at Carolyn's, I jump out of the car, say-ing goodbye as I slam the door. Thankfully, my dad likes Carolyn, so he's letting me go trick-or-treating without him for the first time.

The Williamses' front door is now decorated with a wreath of orange flowers. Two seconds after I ring the bell, Carolyn answers, takes one look at my plastic pumpkin-shaped bag that I just bought at Sav-On, and hands me a pillowcase. "I knew you'd have one of those useless pumpkin bags. They're way too small for heavy-duty trick-or-treating," she explains.

In Compton, I went trick-or-treating for the first time in third grade. I didn't have a costume, so I put on an apron, grabbed a big spoon, and went as a mom. It was stupid. But that wasn't even the worst part. I was only allowed to go trick-or-treating on our street with my dad, and after every house, he'd say, "I think that's enough." He just wasn't comfortable with the idea of going to strangers' houses and asking for candy. I was.

After Carolyn gives me the pillowcase, she shows me her costume, which she hasn't put on yet. It's a box of Arm and Hammer baking soda. I don't know what that is, but it looks real and all the lettering is even and perfect. Her mom and dad made it with her. She tells me, "Every year, we try to do something unprecedented, which means something that no one else has done."

"Next year," I suggest, "you should dress like a dictionary, because you are one."

"That's a good idea," she says.

Rachel arrives right after me, and her costume is really cute. She has a black leotard, cat makeup, ears, and a tail.

Carolyn has already planned our route. We start trick-or-treating on her side of the street, then go across. We walk as fast as we can; sometimes we run. Carolyn was right. This is heavy-duty! An hour into trick-or-treating, I have, among my treasure trove, nine *full-size* candy bars. I had never gotten even *one* full-size candy bar in Compton. I didn't even know people handed those out.

The neighborhood is full of kids, mostly dressed as

masked monsters and vampires, running from house to house. The little ones have parents with them and even the parents are dressed up. It's really exciting being without an adult. It's not scary, even after it gets dark. We trick-or-treat for two hours! Our pillowcases are completely full by the time we stop.

At almost every house we visited, someone said, "Arm and Hammer baking soda! *That* is the best costume! And such a cute cat!" Then they'd turn to me: "And what are you dressed as?"

"I'm just a hobo, down on my luck, livin' by the train tracks, sleepin' under the bridge," I explained.

They just looked confused.

"You know, like in the movies."

"That's nice," they said, looking even more confused. Maybe the American hobo movies I saw in Iran weren't all that popular here.

My mom was right—I should've gone as Rita Hayworth. Or maybe a floral ghost.

POO POO

When I wake up the next morning, I realize that Newport Beach is really starting to feel like home. I think about all the fun I had with Carolyn and Rachel and can't believe that for the first time since we came to the U.S., I have friends. I like all my classes at Lincoln—even PE isn't too bad anymore. We're getting ready for something called the Presidential Physical Fitness Test.* We run, hang from bars, and do sit-ups while Coach McAndrew blows her whistle a lot. Everyone hates it except me. We don't have to pick teams, and there is no tumbling or dodge ball.

Then, boom, just like that, my dad bursts my happy bubble. He tells me that the sons of his former coworker Mr. Shooshtari are coming to stay with us for two weeks. They want to go to college in America and their father has asked us to host them. He's an engineer, like my dad, except that he's rich. Mr. Shooshtari owns two vacation homes in the South of France and an apartment in London. Everyone knows that people like him take bribes, but that's just a part of life in Iran. Accepting bribes is a job skill, like knowing

---

* Note to the president: Thank you for this fine idea.

how to type or use a copy machine. My dad says that Mr. Shooshtari really knows how to work the system.

I wish the two brothers weren't coming to stay in our house. It's going to be a lot of extra work for my mom, and of course for me, too, since I have to help her. I don't get any say in that. I never have a say in anything. My parents are not like Mr. and Mrs. Brady on TV, who constantly talk to their kids about their feelings. Even their maid, Alice, is always asking, "So, dear, how do you feel about this?" My parents just tell me what to do. How I feel about something doesn't matter.

My dad says the boys, Pooya and Pooyan, are nineteen and twenty and have never been to America, but they speak some English. That's good, because I do not want to be a translator for any more people, especially two strange boys whom I already dislike.

As soon as I see Carolyn at lunch, I tell her about their impending visit.

"Two complete strangers for *two* weeks? That's a long time!"

"That's how it is with Iranians. Guests stay for as long as they want. It's part of something called *taarof*. If someone asks you for a favor, you can't say no. You always say yes to be polite, even if you don't mean it."

"That's crazy," Carolyn says, unwrapping her sandwich.

"When we lived in Compton, my uncle Fattolah came to

see Disneyland and stayed for a year and a half. That wasn't *taarof,* because we were happy to have him, but that's the tricky part. You can't tell when an offer is *taarof* or when it's real. Someone might invite you and not mean it. You have to figure out what the person really means."

"It sounds like a riddle," says Carolyn.

"It kind of is."

On the day they arrive, my dad and I drive to the Los Angeles airport to pick up Pooya and Pooyan. The airport is an hour away, but that doesn't bother my dad. He loves driving on American freeways. "No potholes and lots of signs," he always says. But even though there are signs, we get lost. All the freeways have east and west and north and south, so while we get the number right, we still manage to go in the wrong direction. By the time we figure out how to get back on the right freeway, we're an extra half-hour away from the airport, at least. This happens every time we go somewhere. My dad says, "We get to see more of America that way." My mom hates the freeways. She thinks they're too confusing and the cars go too fast.

Luckily, my dad always leaves an hour earlier than we need to, so I'm not worried about getting to the airport on time. Eventually, we are at the gate waiting, watching all the passengers. I notice two guys wearing really tight jeans and shiny gold necklaces. Right when I think, *Dear God, I hope that's not them,* they come up to my dad and say, "*Salam,* Mr. Yousefzadeh."

Ugh.

They're tired from their long flight, so they don't say much during the drive home, which is fine with me. What is not fine with me is that they stink! Their cologne smells like the water from my goldfish bowl mixed with that smell in the doctor's office before you get a shot. I roll down my window so I can breathe.

When we get home, they give us a bunch of gifts, all of which smell like them. They give my mom a Persian miniature painting, a package of dried limes for stews, and a box of pistachios. The pistachios on top are really big and all the rest underneath are tiny. All packages of pistachios from Iran are like that.

Pooya and Pooyan give me a traditional Persian villager costume. It's a shiny purple, blue, and red skirt and blouse with tiny coins sewn all over it. There's also a little beanie that has lace with more sparkly things on it.

"Thank you. I love it," I say.

That is one hundred percent *taarof.*

Pooya and Pooyan smile. They don't care.

What am I going to do with a traditional Persian village costume in Newport Beach?

Possible scenario:

Person handing out full-size Butterfinger bars on Halloween: "And what are you dressed as, young lady?"

Me: "Oh, this is just a traditional costume from the Rasht region of Iran."

Person handing out full-size Butterfinger bars to everyone but me: "I don't know where that is, but I assume you'd prefer a piece of fruit for your camel?"

As I'm putting away the useless costume, I wonder if Pooya and Pooyan know that their names are totally rude in English. When you learn English in another country, you don't learn words like "poo." You learn polite things like, "Excuse me, sir. When does the bus arrive?" or "Could you, madam, kindly guide me to the main directory?" You learn things that no one actually says in America. That's why even though my dad knows English, he can't talk to any Americans. He knows the English in books, not the English that comes out of people's mouths.

My mom started cooking for the Poo brothers days before they arrived. She washed, dried, chopped, and fried cilantro, parsley, onions, eggplants, and scallions. I had to help her peel and clean the vegetables and herbs, and then wash and dry all the extra dishes. There were *a lot*.

After we thank them for the gifts, my mother says that the food is ready. We all go to the dining room. My mom has set up the table. The boys *ooh* and *aah*.

"*Daste-h shoma dard nakoneh,*" they say. *May your hand not hurt.*

That's a Persian expression you say when someone has done a lot for you.

"No," my mom says. "This is nothing."

We sit down and my mom passes the plates of food around. "I wish I could have made more, but it's so hard to find ingredients here," she says.

I wish she didn't say that, but that's *taarof.*

"Oh, no, this is wonderful," the brothers say, echoing each other.

"This doesn't even count," my mom responds.

It counts for me! I was the one stuck helping her clean all those herbs and dishes. I hate *taarof.*

The Poo brothers take some rice, two kinds of stew, and some chicken. We all start eating and my dad asks them about their plans. They tell him how excited they are to see schools here. Then they take seconds. Less conversation this time. Just my dad lecturing them about useful college majors. The Poo brothers are not listening. Then they take thirds, cleaning out the rice platter, both stew containers, and the rest of the chicken. My mom is so happy. I'm not. It's like watching vultures eat an entire zebra on a National Geographic special.

I have so much to tell Carolyn.

AN AFTERNOON WITH
JOHN WAYNE AND ELVIS PRESLEY

The next day, after the Poo brothers finally wake up, my mom tells me to take them to the pool. We're not allowed to let guests go by themselves. That's in chapter four: "Pool Rules." *All guests must be accompanied by a resident.*

It's Saturday afternoon and the last thing I want to do is spend the day with these two. Just my luck, they actually want to go. I think about asking Carolyn to come with me, but decide not to. I'm just too embarrassed. I have been in Newport Beach for less than six months and now I have the two biggest weirdos in the world staying with me.

The Poo brothers go to their room to change and come out a minute later. I think I am going to barf! Their bathing suits are like teeny, tiny bikini bottoms. I have never seen a man in America wear such a thing. To make things worse, the brothers are way hairier than any man I have ever seen. It's like King Kong and his brother, Ding Dong, are visiting us, for the sole purpose of ruining my new life.

The brothers keep saying how they are so excited to go to the pool to meet Ka-lee-for-nee-ya girls. I pray that no one I know is there, especially Original Cindy. Pooya says that he is going to call himself El-veeeees. He thinks Ka-lee-for-nee-ya girls really liked Elvis Presley, so this will help him meet them. I don't think anything will help him. Pooyan says he is going to tell the girls his name is John, like John Vayne.

When we get there, I sit by the barbecues to do my math homework, acting as if I came by myself. Chapter four, "Pool Rules," just says we have to accompany our guests to the pool. It does not say we have to hang out with them or admit to knowing them.

I glance at the brothers, who are setting up their towels next to a group of girls. Ew.

I take out my math worksheets and my eraser and sharpen two pencils. I take another quick peek at the brothers.

The girls have moved to the other side of the pool.

At dinner, Pooya says that the girls at our pool are too young and do not appreciate men. He asks me if any of my friends have older sisters. I pretend I don't hear him.

When he asks again, I try changing the topic. "Tell me about your necklace," I say.

The brothers wear identical huge gold charms shaped like Iran, with a turquoise stone where Tehran is.

"My mom gave us these so we never forget where we're from," Pooya says.

"That's lovely," my mom says.

I don't think it's lovely at all. What kind of person forgets where he's from?

I could live in America for the rest of my life and I would never forget my aunts, uncles, and cousins in Iran. I could never forget Persian food, or the Caspian Sea. The Caspian Sea is the most beautiful place I have ever seen. We used to go there every summer for a week with my cousins. It was a two-day drive but that was part of the fun. The closer we got, the greener it got. We'd roll down the window and sniff the air, which smelled completely different from Abadan. Abadan did not smell nice. You know when your mom or dad spills gasoline on their clothes when they're pumping gas and then gets back in the car? That's what Abadan smells like. During lunch one day, Howie told me the scent of oatmeal raisin cookies reminds her of home. I told her that for me, it will always be the scent of gasoline.

When we first moved to California, we couldn't wait to see the beach. The first weekend after we moved in, we took the freeway to Long Beach, got out, and ran to touch the water. It was so cold! We stood there looking around. There were no seashells and it didn't smell like the Caspian Sea. We only stayed about fifteen minutes. There was something missing.

On the drive home, my dad said, "Isn't it strange how you can actually miss a place, not just people?"

MOUNT LAUNDRY

It's day four of the Poo Brothers invasion. I'm at my desk doing homework. My mom comes in and dumps a huge pile of clothes on my bed. "Fold these," she says, walking out of my room.

None of it is ours.*

I start folding and putting everything in piles. Shirts, pants, socks (gross!), undershirts, and underwear (super gross!). Their shirts *still* smell like them. That industrial-strength cologne they use does not come out with hot water.

At school the next day, I tell Carolyn about Mount Laundry.

"You wash and fold their clothes?" she asks, stunned.

"They're our guests," I remind her.

"We wouldn't do that," she answers.

"We have this expression in Persian, *ghadam ru cheshm.* It literally means you can step on my eye. It's our way of telling our guests that we will do whatever to make them happy."

---

* Note to future me: Never make your daughter fold someone else's clothes.

"They're stepping all over you, not just your eye!" Carolyn says, laughing.

On Friday, the brothers ask my father if he can take them to car dealerships on Saturday and Sunday. They are particularly interested in Camaros.

My dad tells them they should get a large, solid car instead of a speedster like a Camaro.

They are not listening but my dad keeps talking. I know they are going to buy a Camaro no matter what. And their car will smell like them.

At least this gives me a chance to go to Carolyn's, finally. I haven't been there since the brothers arrived.

"Zomorod," my mother says, "I need your help in the kitchen both days."

There goes my happiness.

I know that if I don't help my mom, she will stay mad for a long time. That's how she is. It's easier to do what she wants than to fight her. I never win anyway.

On Saturday, I'm sitting in the kitchen, taking leaves off the stems of a huge pile of cilantro. My mom is frying onions.

"So what do the brothers do while I'm at school?" I ask.

"They wake up late and go to Fashion Island Mall," she says.

"Do you like having them here?" I ask.

"They're Mr. Shooshtari's sons," she replies.

"That doesn't answer my question."

My mother ignores me. We're definitely not the Brady Bunch.

I spend the entire weekend in the kitchen. To top off this festival of joy, I also have to fold their laundry again. Why do they have so many dirty clothes?

On Monday, Carolyn says, "How come you didn't call me all weekend?"

"Don't ask," I say. "But if I ever see another herb, onion, or men's underwear again, I will barf."

Carolyn laughs.

AT LAST

The big day is finally here. The Poo Brothers are leaving. *Thank you, God.* I won't have to go to the pool with them anymore, or fold their laundry. They've decided to apply to UCLA. I don't care where they go, as long as I never have to see them in their bathing suits again.

Before they leave, Pooyan says, "Hey, Zomorod, make friends with all the pretty girls."

Pooya adds, "So you can introduce us to them in a few years, okay?" Then they both laugh, as if they're clever.

I really can't stand these two.

They thank my mom and tell her that she cleaned their clothes better than anyone else. My mother tells them they are welcome to stay with us whenever they want.*

After they leave, I tell my mom that they were just saying that about the clothes because they knew they were a pain to have in our house. My mom says I should really try harder to be a nicer person.

---

* Note to the Poo brothers: That's just *taarof*. Please, never come back.

The day after the brothers leave, my mom asks me to take a plate of *fesenjoon,* decorated with radish roses, next door to the Kleins. She says that Pooya and Pooyan were noisy late at night for these past two weeks and the Kleins were very nice and did not complain even though we share a wall with them. I tell her that Americans would probably not like *fesenjoon* because it looks like mud. I don't even say anything about the radish roses, which also look muddy.

My mom says that *fesenjoon* is one of the most delicious and exotic Iranian foods and I should never say such a terrible thing. I should also try to be a nicer person.

As soon as Mrs. Klein opens the door, I say, "Hello, Mrs. Klein. My mom has sent this plate of *fesenjoon.*" Before I can tell her that it has pomegranate syrup in it from my country, David says, "Ooh, that looks like mud!"

I want to say, *But it tastes good,* because it really does, and my mom would want me to say that.

Instead I say, "It does not taste like mud at all."

David looks skeptical, but I just shrug and turn to

leave. I don't think they're going to try it. Mrs. Klein says, "This looks wonderful and exotic. Please thank your mother for it."

"I will," I say.

SOME OF THE TRIMMINGS

With the Poo Brothers finally gone, I can concentrate on the most important event happening soon in America: Thanksgiving.

According to the all the magazines I have read at the supermarket, there are three things you need at Thanksgiving: a big family, a long table, and a turkey with all the trimmings. This is a huge problem. My mom doesn't know how to make any of the required foods. We also do not have family, or a long table. Our Thanksgivings so far have been just like any other meal.

This year, though, with a little help from El Rancho market, I have solved the problem.

"We just have to order it at least two days before Thanksgiving," I explain, showing my mom the advertising flyer. "And we get a complete meal already cooked. It's so easy! Can we please do this?"

"A turkey is too big for three people," she replies.

"According to *Good Housekeeping* magazine, there are dozens of meals we can make with leftover turkey: turkey sandwiches, turkey soup, turkey casserole, turkey—"

"No." My mom cuts me off. "And why would you want a meal cooked by strangers?"

"Because I want to try turkey with the official stuff that goes with it."

"Persian food is better," she insists.

When my dad comes home, I ask him if we can at least buy a pumpkin pie at El Rancho. "How am I supposed to do well in school if I don't experience such an important part of America?" I plead, making a particularly sad face.

"Okay," he says. "Let's go."

My mom rolls her eyes.

My dad and I drive to El Rancho and buy not only a pumpkin pie but also cranberry sauce. I knew that linking Thanksgiving with school would put him in a generous mood.

A few days later, we sit at our kitchen table to eat our holiday meal. My mom has made lamb shanks with rice, dill, and lima beans. My dad grabs the can opener for the cranberry sauce. I watch him turn the handle until the lid pops off. This is our best Thanksgiving yet! He turns the can upside down. Nothing comes out. He turns the can back over and peers inside, then turns it upside down again, taps it on the bottom, and gives it a good shake. A purple, shiny tube with ridges slides out and makes a popping sound as it lands, wiggling, on the plate. It looks like a newborn alien.

"What is that?" my mom asks. "That's not a sauce."

"I don't know," my dad answers, carefully touching the wobbly mass with the tip of his finger.

It doesn't look like any of the pictures in *Good Housekeeping* magazine.

"It's gone bad," my mom announces.

At least we have pie.

We eat our dinner quickly, like we always do. I don't have seconds because I want to leave room for a slice of America, which is what pumpkin pie really is.

My mom brings the dessert to the table and places a slice on each of our now-empty dinner plates. I taste it. It's absolutely delicious. I quickly take another bite.

"It's too sweet," my mom says. She puckers her face and takes another bite.

"Too sweet," my dad agrees, with his mouth full.

A few minutes later, our plates are empty. I reach for another helping.

"I'll have more too," says my dad, holding out his plate.

"Give me a small piece," my mom adds. "Just a little."

I give her a slice.

"That's too small," she says.

I give her more. I serve my dad a big slice.

"Too sweet," they both say, digging in.

We eat in silence. A few minutes later, my mom gets up to put away the dirty dishes. My dad grabs the pie tin. "Let's just finish the rest, Zomorod."

This time, we eat the pie directly out of the pan. "You just have to get used to the flavor," he says, tilting the empty tin to slide the remaining crumbs directly into his mouth.

"Don't get any on the floor," my mom reminds him.

It's too late for that. I go to get the vacuum cleaner. It was worth every crumb.

Christmas in Newport Beach is much fancier than in Compton. *Much*. Everything is decorated: store windows, lampposts, even dogs. In the evening, our street looks like a giant present, with all the twinkling lights on the houses. One of our neighbors even has a life-size reindeer with a flashing red nose—*on the roof!*

Of course there's one home with no decorations, inside or out. Welcome to Dullsville, USA, otherwise known as my house. This is a very sad part of my life in America. We don't celebrate Christmas: no tree, no presents, no stockings, no gingerbread men fresh out of the oven.

In third grade, I asked my mom to take me to the mall so I could ask Santa for an Easy Bake Oven.

My mom was in the kitchen, rolling meatballs in the palms of her hands.

"Santa Claus is not at the mall," she said.

"I've seen him!" I replied. "He's right next to J. C. Penney."

"That's just a guy in a costume," she said, putting the first batch in the oven.

"That's not true! He's visiting from the North Pole, but only for two more weeks."

"Listen, Zomorod. The guy at the mall is just a man who didn't do well in school, like your uncle Bahbak. He's probably a smoker. And being Santa is just his job. The rest of the year, he probably asks relatives for money, like your uncle Bahbak."

I started to cry.

"When you're done crying, can you help me with the cilantro?" my mom asked, holding up a bunch of herbs.

That was a few years ago. Now I'm used to being part of the audience, just watching, while everyone else celebrates. I don't like it, but what can I do? This year, my mom is making some kind of rice dish, no surprise there, and we're going to watch all the Christmas specials on TV. I'm really excited about the *Donny & Marie Christmas Show*. But I still wish I had an Easy Bake Oven. That would be nice.

I wake up to the sound of my dad talking loudly to my mom. The news is blasting on the radio.

I jump out of bed.

"Chee shodeh?" I ask.

What's happened?

"The shah has left!" my dad says. "He's been the shah for thirty-eight years and now he's left!"

"Left for where?"

"Egypt."

"Forever?"

"I don't know."

"Is this a revolution?"

"They say he left for a vacation or some kind of medical treatment."

"What's going to happen now?"

Before my dad can answer, the phone rings.

It's my uncle Kourosh from Iran. He's talking fast and loudly but not loud enough for my mom and me to hear. My dad has a worried look on his face. I wish I knew what my uncle was saying.

"Bavaram nemeesheh."

I can't believe it, my dad keeps repeating. After a few minutes, he hangs up.

"Chee goft?"

What did he say? my mom and I ask at the same time.

"The shah has left but no one knows for how long. He has appointed Shapour Bakhtiar to form a new government."

"Who's that?" I ask.

"He's a well-respected fan of democracy who spent six years in prison because he opposed the shah," my dad explains.

"And now the shah appointed him?" my mom asks, sounding puzzled.

"Bakhtiar does not want Iran to have a religious government. Neither does the shah. He's already made some important announcements. Your uncle Kourosh says that Bakhtiar is ordering all political prisoners to be freed, is stopping censorship of newspapers, and is getting rid of the SAVAK, thank God."

"He sounds like a good guy," my mom says.

"You want to hear something interesting about him? When he was young, he fought with the Spanish against Franco and with the French against Nazi Germany."

"Whoa! A Nazi fighter?" I say.

"Yes," my father answers. "Now let's see what he can do for this mess. He has asked everyone to give him three months to hold elections for an assembly that will determine the future government of Iran."

"But what does that mean?" I ask.

"Just get ready for school and we'll talk later. You're going to be late."

I hate that I have to go to school today. I put on my clothes, brush my teeth, and grab my backpack. I'm not hungry for breakfast.

When I go downstairs, I see my parents are now watching TV. There is a special news report about Iran that is interrupting the regular program. Bakhtiar is mentioned briefly, but the news keeps showing people burning effigies of the shah and chanting "Ayatollah Khomeini." I have never heard of Khomeini, but he is suddenly like a rock star at a huge concert—except there is no music, there are no T-shirts to buy, and there are no answers to our questions.

I have a math test today. I am so anxious—not about the test, but about my whole life! What is going to happen to us? What is going to happen to Iran?

As I walk past the football field, I see the cheerleaders working on a routine to "Boogie Oogie Oogie." That's one of those songs that stick in your head all day. It's an ordinary Wednesday, just another sunny day in California. I'm pretty sure that none of the cheerleaders are thinking about the shah. They're so lucky to have such easy lives.

AYATOLLAH KHOMEINI

After roll call in English, Miss DeAngelo says, "Cindy, can you tell us a little bit about what's going on in Iran? Who is this Ayatollah Khomeini who is suddenly all over the news?"

"I'm not really sure," I say. "I had never heard of him until now."

"Really?" Miss DeAngelo sounds surprised. "He certainly seems to be a key player in all this. Maybe you can get back to us next week? For an extra-credit project. Wouldn't that be interesting?" she says, looking to the class.

Nobody says anything.

"That would be interesting," one lone voice speaks up.

"Thank you, Carolyn," Miss DeAngelo says. "All righty, then. Do you want to do this, Cindy?"

"Well . . ."

"I would love to hear it," she adds.

"Okay."

I am not looking forward to this. I appreciate that Carolyn is interested, but that brings the grand total of interested people to two, maybe three. I don't want to stand up in front of the class and talk about my country that I don't even understand anymore. Why do I have to be from a country that is suddenly all over the news?

That night, our phone keeps ringing. We receive more calls from Iran than we have in all the years we've been in America. No one has anything new to say. It's the same conversation over and over, followed by "I can't believe it."

Right when the phone finally stops, someone knocks on our door. My dad and I open it. It's Dr. Klein.

"Hi, Mo. Hi, Cindy. Hey, are you going to the meet-and-greet tomorrow night?"

"No, thank you," my father says.

I could've guessed that one.

"That's too bad. Since I'm not going to see you there, do you have a minute? I have a couple questions about Iran."

I hate this sudden popularity. I don't want to answer questions about Iran all the time.

"Yes, yes," my father says. "Please come in. Would you like something to eat or drink?"

Dr. Klein keeps talking as he enters. "I'm fine, thank you." Lucky for him, my mom is in the shower. Otherwise, the food and drink part of the conversation would not end so quickly and easily. "So, as I understand it, the ayatollah is the man behind the revolution. He's managed to get millions of people protesting in the street and now the shah gets the heck out of Dodge. What is going on?"

I know my father is wondering where "Dodge" is.

"This is a very good question, Davood," my dad says, sitting on the sofa. I sit down next to him, across from Dr. Klein.

"Iran's history is long and complicated. What is happening now cannot be explained quickly, so I give you a very short answer. I can explain more later when we have more time."

"It's a deal," Dr. Klein says, crossing his legs.

"Between 1951 and 1953, we had a democratically elected prime minister, Mohammad Mossadegh. He was very popular and very good for Iran. The U.S. and the British overthrew him in a secret operation."

"*We* did that?" asks Dr. Klein.

"Not you, but your government."

"Why?"

"Oil profits."

"Jeez, I never knew that," says Dr. Klein.

"The U.S. and the British put the shah in power because he was willing to do whatever they wanted. So the shah was already unpopular with Iranians, who felt like he was just a puppet of Western powers. He symbolized the loss of democracy."

"I see." Dr. Klein is nodding.

"Now I skip ahead to fourteen years ago. The shah kicked Ayatollah Khomeini out of Iran."

"Why?" Dr. Klein asks.

"Again, the answer is long, so I give the short version." My dad takes a deep breath. I want to hear this too.

"The shah wanted to modernize Iran. He used some of the oil money to invest in the country, like for transportation, water, and power. He called this his White Revolution."

"Sounds good," Dr. Klein says.

"He created more educational opportunities for everyone. He gave women more freedom. There were female ministers, congresswomen, and women in other important roles in the government. This part was true progress."

I have a lot to say for Miss DeAngelo's class now.

"But there was also a bad side. The White Revolution was supposed to spread the oil money; instead, it ended up in the hands of very few, who got richer and richer. Friends of the shah were all very, very wealthy. The money did not trickle down. Even though the shah made some improvements to the country, the rich got richer and the poor got poorer. The difference between the rich and the poor became bigger and bigger."

"That seems to happen often in history," Dr. Klein comments.

My dad nods. "What the shah called progress, many devout Muslims called corruption. Although the clergy in Iran were not happy about many aspects of the White Revolution, the clergy as a whole were not actively protesting. There was one member, however, who often spoke against the shah and his reforms. His name was Khomeini. Opposing the leader is normal for countries with freedom of speech, but this was Iran. We don't have freedom of speech. In order to silence him, the shah eventually forced Khomeini into exile in 1964."

"I bet he regrets that now," adds Dr. Klein.

"Fourteen years ago, the shah kicked Ayatollah Khomeini out of Iran, and now Ayatollah Khomeini's followers kicked the shah out of Iran. The shah didn't want to hear what his critics had to say, no matter how they said it. The shah also had secret police who arrested, tortured, and imprisoned those who opposed him. And of course there was so much corruption! Iranians of all backgrounds were angry at the corruption, except those who benefited from it. And now here we are. Waiting to see what will happen next."

Dr. Klein stands up. "Thank you, Mo. I hope things work out for the people of Iran." He shakes my dad's hand. "I appreciate the history lesson, and let me know about that round of golf."

"Davood, I don't know how to play golf," my dad confesses.

"I'll teach you," Dr. Klein replies.

"Yes, yes," my dad answers.

SPEECH

It's Tuesday and I'm standing in front of Miss DeAngelo's class, looking at a sea of uninterested faces. My heart is pounding. I have practiced my speech five times at home, but it's very different standing here. I wasn't nervous in my room. I now realize that was because I was alone. I look over at Carolyn, who smiles at me.

I take a deep breath.

"I know some of you have been wondering about what is going on in Iran," I say. My voice is shaking.

"Not really!" Mike McSummit yells.

"Excuse me," says Miss DeAngelo, standing up behind her desk. "Mike, can we please show some respect for our speaker?

"Please go ahead, Cindy." She sits back down.

"Okay. First, I'm going to show you Iran on this globe, since a lot of people don't know where it is. And this is Abadan, where I'm from. Abadan is, like, the polar opposite of Newport Beach. It's known for its huge oil refinery. Everyone we knew in Abadan worked for the National Iranian Oil Company. Otherwise, I'm not sure anyone would live there. It's too hot. I guess I was born where I was born because of gasoline."

"She's got gas!" someone shouts.

I turn red. Miss DeAngelo stands up again. "Who said that?"

Total silence.

"Please go on, Cindy. I apologize for that interruption. It won't happen again." She glares at the class.

"Now I'm going to tell you a really short version of what is happening over there right now, and then I will explain more. In America, you have a democracy. In Iran, we have a monarchy, which is a type of government where the leadership is passed down in a family. So we don't have elections like you have here—"

Before I can finish my sentence, Steffie St. Clair's hand shoots up in the air. "Oh, oh, oh, so it's like a daisy chain of shahs."

I'm confused.

Steffie continues. "When you make a daisy chain, it's a bunch of daisies that are attached. So in I-ran, the ruler is the king, and then his son, and then *his* son. It's all attached in the same family."

"I see. I never thought of it that way. Also, the country's name is pronounced 'ee-ron.' 'I ran' is a sentence. For example, 'I ran to Iran.'"

Steffie smiles. I glance at Carolyn, who looks like she is trying not to laugh.

"Let's see," I say. "Where was I? The shah did not allow freedom of speech, so people were never allowed to disagree with him, so no rallies or petitions or things like that. Ayatollah Khomeini, who was a cleric, did not agree with a lot of what the shah was doing and he and his followers protested rather loudly, so the shah kicked him out years ago. And now Khomeini's followers kicked out the shah and Khomeini is coming back."

Before I can say anything else, Flynn Mitchell raises his hand. "Yes," I say, pointing to him.

"It's like those movies where one cowboy goes, 'This town just ain't big enough for the both of us,' so the other one has to leave. Except that, like, instead of cowboy hats, the dude's wearing a turban," he says.

Everyone laughs.

"Settle down," Miss DeAngelo warns.

Someone else raises his hand.

"Yes," I say, pointing to a boy whose name I do not know.

"The ayatollah is Muslim, right? So is, like, Allah his God?"

"Allah is the Arabic word for God," I say. "It's the same God."

Sherman Dorfman raises his hand. At least I know this will be an intelligent question.

Before he can say anything, Mike McSummit yells, "Sherman DORKman!"

Mike's equally stupid friends start to laugh.

"Mike," Miss DeAngelo says, "go to the principal's office right now. That is the second time you have interrupted this class today."

"But—"

"No buts." She points to the door. "Go *now!*"

As Mike shuffles out, I'm desperately trying to think of what I was going to say next. I guess it's good that people are asking questions, but I hadn't planned for that. I'm getting even more nervous now.

"Go ahead, Sherman," Miss DeAngelo says wearily.

"I just want to point out that Jews, Christians, and Muslims all believe in one God, and they all trace their roots to Abraham," he says.

"Thank you, Sherman. And who can tell me the word that means the belief that there is only one God?"

Sherman and Carolyn raise their hands.

"Anybody else?" asks Miss DeAngelo. The class is very quiet now.

"All right, then. Carolyn, what is the word?"

"*Monotheism.*"

"That's right," Miss DeAngelo says. "And for the rest of you, we will be adding *monotheism* to your vocabulary list this week."

"Isn't that the kissing disease?" Weston Hunt blurts.

The class bursts out laughing again.

This speech experience is a thousand times worse than anything I could have imagined.

"That's mononucleosis, or 'mono,' as you call it," Miss DeAngelo says. "And for that, I am adding *mononucleosis* to the vocabulary list also. Anybody else want to make a stupid comment? Shall I also add *monopoly, monogamy,* and *monocle*?"

"That's not fair," Steffie protests.

"You know what's not fair?" says Miss DeAngelo, standing up again. "What's not fair is that because of the rude behavior in this class, we now don't have time to hear the rest of Cindy's fascinating speech."

Miss DeAngelo turns to me. "I'm so sorry, Cindy. If you want to share the rest of your speech with us, we can do this again next week."

Is she serious? I would rather die.

"That's okay," I say. "I'm pretty much done."

I am not done, but I do not want to stand in front of those kids ever again.

I go back to my seat and look over at Carolyn. She gives me an enthusiastic two thumbs up. I give her an enthusiastic two thumbs down. We both try not to laugh.

On Saturday, Rachel calls to invite me to her bat mitzvah. "It's a Jewish coming-of-age ceremony," she explains.

"I'll be there," I say, before she even tells me the date.

"I'm nervous," she adds. "I've been studying for a whole year and I have to stand up in front of everybody and read from the Torah."

"You'll do great," I tell her. "You get A's on everything. Plus, you won't have Mike McSummit there to ruin it." We both laugh. I had told her about my nightmare of a presentation for Miss DeAngelo's class.

After I hang up, I go in the kitchen to find my mom. "I just got invited to Rachel's bat mitzvah. It's a very important event in the Jewish religion, and I need to take a very nice gift."

My mom doesn't say anything but goes upstairs and comes down five minutes later holding a gold and turquoise bracelet from Iran. "You're right," she says, giving me the bracelet. "It is a very big deal. Your uncle went to many bar mitzvahs in Tehran."

"Thanks!" I say. "This is perfect."

"You need to wrap it nicely. We have that pretty blue paper in the cupboard."

I am not going use the "It's a Boy!" wrapping paper, but I don't say that to my mom.

I think I will use the Sunday comics. I saw that once on TV when a lady showed how to reuse things that we normally throw away. She even made jewelry out of bottle caps.

I've gone to Rachel's house a few times to do homework, and I really like her family. Her dad is a history professor at University of California, Irvine. He taught me to say *shalom,* which means "peace" in Hebrew, but you use it to say hello or goodbye. I taught him *salam,* which means "peace" in Arabic. It's also how we say hello in Persian. Turns out he already knew that.

One time he asked me if I knew about the history of the Polish people and Iran. He said that during World War II, 116,000 Polish refugees, including 5,000–6,000 Jews, were relocated to Iran from the Soviet Union. Among them were thousands of children who ended up living in the city of Isfahan. "Did you know," he asked me, "that Isfahan is often called the City of Polish Children?"

I had no idea.

My mom, dad, and I are sitting on their bed, listening to the news on the radio. Khomeini has come back to Iran from France. The reporter says that millions of people are cheering for him in the streets of Tehran. We hear the crowd chanting in the background.

We rush downstairs to see if we can see any news reports on TV. Channel 7 is showing the frenzied masses and we watch in stunned silence. We have never seen anything like this.

"Bavaram nemeesheh."

I can't believe it, my parents keep saying over and over again once the news report is finished.

Later that night, my dad tells me that Khomeini made a speech rejecting the government of Bakhtiar.

"But I thought Bakhtiar is a good guy," I say.

"He is," my dad answers, sounding hopeless.

After dinner, our phone rings. I jump up to answer it.

"I'm so confused. So Khomeini does not like—how do you pronounce his name?—Bokteer?" Carolyn starts right in without even saying hello.

"My dad says Khomeini doesn't like him because he was appointed by the shah," I explain.

"Wow, Khomeini must really hate the shah. That's called throwing the baby out with the bath water," Carolyn says.

"And my dad says that Bakhtiar believes in democracy that is separate from religion," I add.

"That's what we have here. Separation of church and state. That's a good thing."

"I'm not sure Khomeini agrees," I say.

Sure enough, a week and a half later, we hear on the radio that Khomeini and his followers have forced Bakhtiar out. He was only in office for thirty-seven days.

I wake up to noises coming from down the hall. I look at my clock. It's barely five in the morning. I have a feeling something big has happened.

I get out of bed and rush to my parents' room. The light is on and they are both listening to the radio. They don't even look up at me.

"No more shah," my dad says. "The monarchy is over."

My mother looks exhausted. "I'm so worried about my family." She wipes her eyes with a tissue.

My dad does not try to comfort her. I don't think he knows how.

I don't know what to say either. I have absolutely no idea what any of this means. All I hear on the radio is that Iran has officially had a revolution. We also hear that the fifty thousand Americans living there are leaving the country because the U.S. government feels that they are no longer safe.

It is the first time in my *entire* life that the shah is no longer the ruler. I have a huge science test today, but I feel like my brain has just frozen. I wish my dad could write a note: *Please excuse Cindy from the test today. Our country just had a revolution.*

It's not like in America, where the president changes but everything else stays the same. No one knows what is going to happen. There is no rulebook; whoever has power makes up the rules, and it's clear who has the power now. People are claiming they see his face on the moon.* Iranians are in a frenzy over Khomeini!

---

* Note to Khomeini: There is no way your face is on the moon. That's ridiculous.

A SLICE OF KEY LiME PiE WITH A SCOOP OF DiGNITY, PLEASE

Our friends and neighbors seem to think we have become experts on the revolution. "What's going to happen?" the Kleins ask. So does Miss DeAngelo, the Williamses, and our dentist. We always say the same thing. "We don't know. We hope everything turns out well."

The truth is, we worry all the time. Everything is changing and we don't know if things are going to get better or worse.

All *I* can say is thank goodness for Girl Scouts. I'm volunteering at the Goodwill factory this Saturday, and I know we're going to be busy. I'm hoping there will be no time to talk about revolutions.

Carolyn can't make it because it's her aunt's birthday. Rachel and Howie are coming, but my house is not on their way, so I get a ride from Mrs. Woods, one of our troop leaders.

As soon as we all gather at the factory, a guide meets us in the lobby and starts showing us around. She keeps telling us to remember that everyone deserves dignity. I'm not sure what she means. I've never really thought much about dignity in my life.

The guide explains that the Goodwill factory hires people with Down syndrome and gives them simple jobs. One man is in charge of putting the hooks onto IV bags for hospitals. Another assembles boxes. They show up for work every day, earn a paycheck, and have a chance to be a part of society. All of a sudden, I get it. That's the dignity part.

We have lunch in the cafeteria, where all the cooks and servers also have Down syndrome. Some of the other Scouts say they aren't hungry and don't eat anything. I hear two girls from another troop whispering about how grossed out they are. That's really mean. I eat a cheeseburger, fries, and a slice of key lime pie. I keep saying, "Yum, this is delicious," loud enough for the workers to hear.* They all smile at this. I give them a thumbs-up too, and keep nodding my head with approval while chewing.

I'm not being entirely honest. The key lime pie tastes nothing like limes. In America, there are so many things with lime in the name that don't even remotely taste like limes. They're just green. But I eat the pie anyway, to be polite. The workers keep thanking us for coming, and one of them tells us that we are prettier than flowers. Most of the girls smile or say thank you, but some of them snicker. They are the same ones who didn't touch their food.

The fries were really good. That is the truth.

---

* Note to Saint Anthony: I'm thinking of you!

· · ·

On the ride home, I think about a time in Iran when I went with my mom and my aunts to a fortuneteller's house. In the middle of her reading my mother's fortune, a boy barged into the room. The fortuneteller had never even mentioned she had a son. He was huge and grunting. She got all flustered and took him back to wherever he had been. When she returned, she pretended like nothing had happened.

At the time, I was only six and I didn't understand why the boy and his mother were acting that way. But I realize now that the fortuneteller's son had Down syndrome and she probably just kept him at home, hidden away in a room.

I don't know who thought of the Goodwill and the idea of giving jobs to people with Down syndrome, but I wish there was something like that in Iran.

"Why are you being so quiet, Cindy?" Mrs. Woods asks, and the bright, palm-lined streets of Newport Beach outside the car windows snap back into focus.

I don't want to tell that whole story to her, so I just say that I am not feeling well because I ate too many french fries. That's true too.

When I get home, I tell my parents about the Goodwill and dignity. They listen quietly. I can tell that they're impressed. I think it's the first time in a while that they have thought of something other than the current events in Iran. When I get to the end of the story, my dad shakes his head a few times. "Only in America, Zomorod. Only in America."

GiRLS RULE! (NOT ANYMORE)

That's it. I am officially *not* a fan of Khomeini. He has decided that women can no longer be judges.* I grew up proud that Iran was so modern while women in many other countries in the Middle East had almost no rights. A few days later, Khomeini declares that women have to wear a hijab—a headscarf that covers all hair—*plus* long coats that cover the body. I absolutely one hundred percent hate this revolution. Why is the new government so mean to women? If all the mothers, daughters, sisters, and aunts in the country are unhappy, how is this good for Iran?

As we're taking the groceries in from the car that afternoon, Dr. Klein comes out to say hello.

"Hi, Cindy," he says, patting my head. He always does that.

"Hi, Dr. Klein."

"Hey, Mo, I've been watching the news. Not good, huh?"

My dad puts the grocery bags on the hood of the car. I'm still holding mine.

* Note to Khomeini: I would be a great judge. This is a stupid rule.

"Davood, I am very worried."

"Didn't you say that women in Iran have more rights than other countries in the Middle East? It doesn't seem that way anymore," Dr. Klein observes.

My father shakes his head. "I don't know what to say, Davood. I am watching my country go backwards."

It makes me so sad to hear my father say this. It somehow makes it even more real.

"I'd say so." Dr. Klein shakes his head in sympathy. "Do your wife and Cindy have to wear those cover-ups if you go back?"

"Yes, and I cannot believe this. When we lived in Iran, my wife, my sisters, all the women I knew wore Western clothes. No tennis clothes like you see here, but regular clothes. Only religious women chose to wear hijab. When you saw a woman wearing a hijab, it meant something. Imagine if everybody in America had to wear a cross around their neck or a Star of David—what would those symbols mean? Nothing. If you *have* to wear it, it means nothing. If you *choose* to wear it, it means something."

"I feel truly bad for the women of Iran." Dr. Klein is looking at me as he speaks. "And what's with all the killings? Is it true that the new government is killing anyone who worked with the shah?"

This is the first time I have heard about this.

"Anyone rich and successful is considered suspect," my

dad says. "I am very worried for two of my brothers, who are successful doctors. People are escaping out of Iran with just the clothes on their backs. I hear stories of people leaving their homes, their photos, everything they own, just to get out alive."

I had no idea my uncles were in danger! My parents had not told me.

"It seems like Iranians have traded one set of problems for another." Dr. Klein shakes his head again.

"Things don't look so good right now." My father looks down at the ground. "And now please excuse me. I must take these groceries to Nastaran."

Now I know why my parents are so worried. Is there something else they're not telling me? Will *our* lives be in danger when we go back?

Iranian New Year, or Nowruz, is going to arrive right before spring break. I am dreading this Nowruz. It was such a fun holiday in Iran, but not here—and not this year.

We celebrated Nowruz three times in Compton. The highlight for my mom was calling her family and talking to her sisters. We have to get up in the middle of night to do this because of the time difference. It always takes a bunch of tries before the call goes through. Then as soon as she hears an *allo* on the other end, she bursts into tears. Long-distance calls are very expensive, so my dad always says, "Why don't you cry *before* the call, so we don't have to pay for it?"

That makes sense to me, but it's definitely the wrong thing to say to my mom. The problem is that we don't know what the *right* thing to say is. My dad and I used to think that talking to her sisters would make my mom happy, but it doesn't. Not talking to them makes her sad too.

So for all three Nowruzes in America, my dad and I ended up having cereal for dinner while my mom cried in her room. No matter what my dad and I say or do, we cannot make it better.

At lunch, I'm sitting with Carolyn, Rachel, and Howie in our usual spot. I mention that the Iranian New Year is coming. "What is that?" Carolyn asks, her mouth full of sandwich.

"What do you do for it?" Rachel chimes in.

"We celebrate the new year, or Nowruz, the exact moment that spring begins. It's called spring . . . something."

"Spring equinox," Carolyn says after she swallows.

"Yeah, that's it. So the exact hour, minute, and second are different every year but it's around March twenty-first. In Iran, everything closes for weeks before Nowruz while people sew or buy new clothes, bake sweets, and clean their houses."

"I like the new clothes part," comments Howie. "Hey, anybody want an oatmeal raisin cookie?" She holds out her plastic container full of homemade treats.

"Thanks!" Rachel, Carolyn, and I each take one. No one refuses Mrs. Howard's baked goods.

As soon as I finish chewing, I continue. "In the weeks leading up to Nowruz, you can just feel the excitement. Since it is not a religious holiday, everybody celebrates."

"Like Thanksgiving," Rachel notes.

I nod.

"At the exact time that the new year begins, everyone hugs and kisses, then eats homemade sweets. We don't have oatmeal raisin cookies, but I think you would like Persian treats."

Howie offers me her last cookie.

"Are you sure?"

"Sure," she insists.

I take a big, delicious bite and chew quickly. "In the days after the new year, we visit relatives, in order of oldest to youngest. It's good to be old in Iran."

"Sounds like a great holiday," Carolyn says. Howie and Rachel nod in agreement.

"Not this year. All my relatives say that people are scared, especially women. Can you imagine being arrested for not wearing the right clothes? It's nuts."

"You're never going back. That's for sure," Carolyn declares.

I can't believe she just said that.

"But my entire family is in Iran. My cousins are like brothers and sisters to me. I miss them *so* much."

"You want to go back?" she asks.

"I've never thought about *not* going back. I wish you guys and my family were all in the same place. That would be perfect!"

Carolyn looks surprised. I don't even want to think

about never seeing my cousins again, so I change the subject.

"Guess what else? We've heard that the government is now listening to long-distance phone calls, so my relatives tell my parents not to ask too many questions."

"How often do you talk to your relatives in Iran?" Howie asks.

"Normally twice a year, or if someone is sick or getting married. But these days, my dad's been calling his family a lot."

"I can't believe you guys are going through all this." Carolyn gives me a sympathetic look.

I'm beginning to get really sad. Talking about Nowruz with my American friends reminds me of my old life. I want to remember the good parts. I'm wondering if there's anything good left. I think hard.

"Did I mention we get gifts?" I add.

"Cool!" they all say.

"I'm hoping for a pair of those skirt pants you guys have."

"You mean gauchos," says Carolyn.

"Yeah, those. Plus a pompom belt and a puka shell necklace."

"Sounds like a very Newport Beach gift list," says Rachel.

I chuckle. I had never thought of it that way, but it's true.

On Nowruz, my dad comes home from work and hands me a brand-new five-dollar bill. "Don't spend it all at once!" he warns.

"I'm going to save it for college," I say.

My dad looks pleased to hear this.

Later that evening, while we are sitting on the sofa waiting for the news to start, my mom gives me a small box wrapped in the "It's a Boy" gift paper.

"I thought of you when I saw this at the Sav-On drugstore. I want you to put it on your desk so you can always look at it and think of me," she says.

I start to open the gift. "Don't rip the paper," my dad warns. "We can reuse it."

Between the three rolls in the cabinet and the recycled pieces, my grandchildren's grandchildren will be stuck with this giftwrap.

I open the box. It's a small porcelain cat.

"Merci, Maman," I say, kissing her on both cheeks. "I'll put it next to my stapler."

This way, every time I look at it, I will think of all the gifts I did not get. I don't say that part out loud.

LAST CHANCE CLEARANCE

Our Girl Scout troop is finally going camping for two nights at Big Bear. At the first meeting back in the fall, Mrs. Woods and Mrs. Stahr gave us a list of camping equipment we would need for overnights. My family doesn't own a single item on it. That's why my dad and I are on our way to Woolworth's—or as he calls it, Voolvort's. My mom stayed home to watch TV. I don't think she's happy that I'm going on a camping trip. Lucky for me, my dad says that any camping trip that the Girl Scouts organize is fine with him. For once, *he's* not worried.

As usual, we spend twenty minutes looking for the closest parking spot.

"We don't have to park right in front of the store. We can walk for, like, three minutes, you know."

"Shhh," my dad says. He turns into a hunter when it's time to park the Impala. We drive round and round and round slowly until he sees someone walking to a prime parking spot. Then we sit and wait while my dad complains about how the person is taking so long. "We could have been in the store by now if you had just taken any of the other twelve spots we already saw," I tell him.

"You don't get it, Zomorod," he says. He's right about that.

We finally park and go into the huge store, past the bins of neatly organized plastic ladles, fake flowers, rows of tape dispensers, and refrigerator magnets. Finally, we arrive at the Last Chance Clearance aisle, home to the cheapest of the cheap, the last exit on Bargain Highway. Need a tea-kettle without a lid? You'll find it there, and it's an extra forty percent off. The whole aisle is unorganized and messy, but judging from the enthusiasm of the shoppers going through the bins, no one cares.

That is where we find the first item on the list, a sleep-ing bag. It's big and bulky and is missing the straps to tie it together and the bag to carry it in. "Not a problem," my dad insists. "You can tie it with a rope and put it in a trash bag." Then he adds, "Zomorod, when you're an engineer, you solve problems."

I know all the other girls will have one of the smaller sleeping bags that roll up into a tiny drawstring sack, but of course they are not on sale.

I also buy a mesh bag, a flashlight, and a metal bowl that can be turned into a skillet by attaching a handle. The handle by itself can be used as a spoon or a fork. It is the cleverest gadget I have ever seen. I feel like an explorer get-ting ready for the jungles of Africa—not that I would ever go there, with the tsetse flies and all.

My dad refuses to buy an air mattress even though it's on the list, because he says people don't go camping to be comfortable.

The air mattress is not on sale.

He also refuses to buy the folding knife because he says we have plenty of regular knives at home.

"But they don't fold," I tell him.

"You have to unfold them anyway to use them, so you might as well save time and take a regular knife. Just wrap it in a towel, put it in a plastic bag, then tie the bag so it's safe," says my father, the engineer.

The folding knives are not on sale either.

We walk out of the store, our arms full of bargains. I am trying not to trip on anything, since I can't see in front of me. The unfolded sleeping bag is *huge.* No matter how I try to hold it, some portion of it drags on the ground.

"This parking spot is so good that I feel like leaving the car here and walking home," my dad says. He always makes that same joke, which no one thinks is funny except him. I roll my eyes and fold a dragging corner of the bag back in. Another corner falls down. It's like trying to hold an enormous water balloon.

At the last two meetings, Mrs. Woods and Mrs. Stahr taught us about camping, wilderness, and first aid. I learned a lot of important survival skills. For instance, if I see a snake, I should stand still or walk backwards slowly, never run. I am one hundred percent sure I will not do that. But now, while running as fast as I can, I will be thinking, *I shouldn't be running.*

I also learned how to apply pressure to stop bleeding, how to give mouth-to-mouth resuscitation, and how to save someone from choking. So far, camping sounds way more dangerous than I expected. I can't believe they encourage eleven-year-old girls to do this in America!

No one in my family has ever gone camping. My dad says that since he grew up poor, he can imagine what it's like. I don't think so. Official camping is different from being poor. For one, poor people don't have all-in-one bowl/spoon/skillet sets. At least I have that.

WHERE THE MILD THINGS ARE

Carolyn, Rachel, Howie, Kris, Colleen, and I are sharing a tent at Big Bear Lake. Kris and Colleen are twins who are in a couple of my classes. They're very smart and quiet and neither of them has ever gotten a grade lower than an A on anything. Carolyn told me that the twins' mother had bragged about that to Mrs. Williams in the vegetable aisle of the supermarket last week. Apparently, Mrs. Williams was very impressed. Carolyn seemed a little annoyed.

There's no television or radio at the campsite, which is a gift. There are no flushing toilets, which is not a gift. But at least I will be away from all reminders of revolutions for an entire three days and two nights.

The first night we grill hot dogs, make s'mores, and sing songs around the campfire. It's really dark, since there are no streetlights. There are so many stars in the sky! Mrs. Woods points out the Big Dipper and the North Star.

After the campfire, we go near the outhouses and take turns holding flashlights to brush our teeth. We use water from the canteen to rinse our mouths.

We set up our sleeping bags three in a row on each side

of the tent, with our heads in the middle. I'm the only one without an air mattress. The leaders are sleeping five whole tents away. Mrs. Stahr is pretty strict, so I'm glad that we can talk without bothering her.

Once we're all in our sleeping bags, we turn off the flashlights. It's pitch-black. Carolyn suggests we take turns describing our first kiss. I am horrified! I have a feeling this is going to be a repeat of the turtle episode, where saying the truth—"I have never kissed anyone"—is going to be weird. But it's not as if I can lie. What if they ask questions?

"Since I've never been kissed, someone else has to start," Carolyn says.

I am so relieved to hear this!

There's total silence. That game goes nowhere fast. Turns out none of us has ever kissed a boy. I could not be happier! No one here can say I'm weird.

"We're such losers," sighs Kris.

"Not really," Carolyn insists. "My mom says we're late bloomers and that smart kids are usually like that."

"Are you sure?" asks Rachel. "Maybe we're just ugly."

We all laugh, a little nervously.

"The girls our age who have boyfriends are the ones who are willing to do stuff in the back parking lot," Colleen says, sounding like an expert. "That's why we don't have boyfriends. We're not wild."

"We're mild," says Carolyn, laughing.

"But it's true," chimes in Kris. "If you go to the back parking lot during lunch, you can smell the pot. Who knows what else is going on behind the trash bins?"

"I don't know why people smoke pot," says Rachel. "It kills your brain cells, and I'm pretty sure my brain cells are my best quality."

"I know what you mean," Howie agrees. Even though it's completely dark, I imagine everyone nodding.

When we finally decide to go to sleep, we say good night to each other. Then Colleen says, "Good night, stars."

Kris adds, "Good night, nobody; good night, mush."

"What is this?" I interrupt.

"You know that book *Goodnight Moon*?" Carolyn asks.

"No."

"Sometimes I forget you're not American." She sighs. "I'll lend you my copy."

In the morning, Mrs. Woods makes eggs, cinnamon rolls, and hot chocolate over the campfire. It is the most delicious breakfast I have ever had. "Food always tastes better in the outdoors," she tells us. That is the first important thing I learn about camping.

After breakfast, we attend workshops to earn badges.

"Leaves of three, let it be" is the second thing I learn: how to identify poison ivy.

Everything is going surprisingly well. I haven't choked

on anything or seen any snakes. But then during the fire safety workshop, Mrs. Stahr sees my knife and takes it away so no one will be hurt. I'm so embarrassed! That stupid knife was already giving me trouble. On the drive over, it had managed to slip out of the protective towel and made a big hole in my trash bag (a.k.a. my sleeping-bag pouch).

That morning, everyone had quickly rolled her sleeping bag into a tight little ball and put it in the corner of the tent. I tried with all my strength. It compressed an inch and then bounced right back to its normal size. Carolyn and Howie tried to help me, but even the three of us together couldn't roll it up. It just kept popping open like a life raft. We finally gave up and left it.

And that was the third thing I learned on my first-ever camping trip: avoid the Last Chance Clearance aisle at all costs.

NAME CHANGE, GAME CHANGE

It's another sunny Saturday morning in Newport Beach, and my mom and dad and I turn on the TV to watch the news. The first report is about Iran, of course. Khomeini has announced that the country is now called the Islamic Republic of Iran. The news keeps showing images of him waving to the adoring masses.

My dad turns off the TV and says, "You know, Zomorod, I watched Iranians from all backgrounds march in the streets against the shah, hoping for honest government, democracy, and freedom of speech. Communist groups, student activists, human rights supporters, and men and women who were just tired of the shah's corruption—they were all there. Sure, Khomeini played a key role in the revolution, but I did not expect him to end up as the new leader of Iran. I hope this is going to be better, but something tells me it won't. It doesn't seem like we're moving closer to a democracy."

I don't like to hear my dad saying this. Maybe it's because a part of me knows it's true too. I glance at my mom, who is sitting quietly, looking worried.

• • •

On Sunday, I go to Carolyn's again for taco night. When I walk in the door, the heavenly smell of spices and onions greets me like an old friend.

This time, I do not have any questions about taco shells. Instead, the Williamses have all the questions.

"So what does it feel like to have your country change its name?" asks Matt as soon as we sit down to the table.

"It worries my dad," I say. "He doesn't feel like we're getting closer to a democracy."

"And what's up with the 'Islamic' part? That sounds like more than just a name change," Matt says, helping himself to the grated cheese.

Up to now, I have been really good at explaining Iranian things to Americans. When someone asks me what a kebab is, I tell them, "It's like a hamburger in a different shape, and instead of a bun, there's rice." Easy. But what's happening now in Iran is really hard to explain. Plus, things keep changing so fast!

"People in Iran are mostly Muslim, but the government was not religious when I lived there . . ." I begin slowly, but Matt interrupts me.

"Yeah, but you don't seem very religious."

"Let her eat," Mrs. Williams says gently, biting into her taco.

"Being Muslim means different things to different people," I say. "My family doesn't do anything officially religious. My dad says religion is kindness and that's what everyone should practice."

"It's the same thing with us," Mrs. Williams says. "We're Christian, but we don't go to church every Sunday."

"But we eat chocolate every Easter," Matt chimes in, adding more hot sauce.

I laugh, then wonder if maybe I shouldn't have.

"As I was saying before I was interrupted," Mrs. Williams continues, giving Matt a stern look, "everyone defines religion differently. But I agree with your father. Bottom line, it's about kindness."

"We buy chocolate eggs too, but the day *after* Easter, when they're half price," I offer.

The Williamses all laugh.

"So is every single person in Iran a Muslim now?" Carolyn asks, in between bites.

"Most are, but no. Did you know that there are more Jews in Iran than there are in any other country in the Middle East outside of Israel? Rachel's dad told me that."

"Really?" Carolyn sounds surprised.

"Yes, and there are Christians, Baha'i, and Zoroastrians, too," I say.

"What are those last two?" Carolyn asks. "I've never heard of them."

"Baha'is are known for a being a peaceful, gentle religious group, and Zoroastrianism was Iran's religion before the Arabs invaded in the seventh century and brought Islam with them," I explain.

"Wow, it makes you realize how young the U.S. is compared to Iran," Mrs. Williams comments. "We just celebrated the bicentennial, our two hundredth birthday, and here we are talking about Iran being invaded in the seventh century. That's thirteen hundred years ago!" she exclaims. "Would anyone like more guacamole?"

"Yes, please!" I have discovered I love guacamole.

Mr. Williams, who has been listening quietly to the conversation, finally speaks up. "What's most worrying about the new government in Iran is that they're killing the people who worked with the shah. They're trying to ensure that there won't be another revolution."

"Killing people doesn't seem like something a religious government would do," Matt observes.

"I know." I shake my head and look down at my plate, suddenly saddened by what is happening in my country.

"In America, if a Republican wins an election, he doesn't get to kill the Democrats," Matt adds. "Although I'm sure some of them would like that option."

"I bet some of them would," Mr. Williams agrees with a chuckle.

On Monday, Miss DeAngelo pulls me aside after class. "Cindy, can I ask you something?"

"Sure," I say cautiously. Did I do something wrong?

"Is your family going back to Iran?" she asks.

"Oh. My father is here on assignment, so when the project ends, yes, we'll be going back."

"But will you be safe?"

I think about this for a moment. Watching the events on TV and being able to turn off the news and go back to my own life makes it feel like they have nothing to do with *me*. But suddenly I realize that it *is* about me, and about every other Iranian whose life will never be the same.

"Well, we weren't rich. My dad's an engineer and he had nothing to do with the shah."

"That's good. But what about the headscarf—what's it called? Will you have to wear that?" she asks.

"All women and girls have to now."

"I just can't imagine that," she says. "I mean, look at you. You're wearing shorts, sandals, and a T-shirt. You are so all-American! And I know you and Carolyn are in Girl Scouts. I guess I just can't see you in Iran with all those rules about what girls can and can't do."

"I can't see myself there either." This is the first time I've really thought about going back, and what it might mean for me. I feel shaky and my heart speeds up. I do not want to wear a headscarf. I'll be afraid every time I leave my house. All that meanness toward girls! That's not religion!

I mumble something about getting to my next class

on time and walk down the hall in a daze, trying to picture myself and my female relatives all covered up with hijab. I think of my cousin Fariba, famous in my family for her long, thick hair, and for spending an hour each day with rollers and a can of hairspray so it looks "just right." What is she going to do now?

ARE YOU THERE, ALLAH?
IT'S ME, ZOMOROD

Khomeini has declared that alcohol, night-clubs, and gambling are now illegal. My parents do not drink, go to nightclubs, or gamble, but still my dad says that it's not the government's job to tell people what they can and can't do with their private lives. "It's a bad sign," he keeps saying. The government has also declared that kids have to pray in school, and all music on the radio and television is banned. People are actually being arrested for listening to Western music in their own homes. Disco is a crime!

At the same time that Western music is being banned in Iran, the sixth grade student government at Lincoln Junior High is busy planning the end-of-the-year dance. All sixth-graders voted on the theme and "Aloha, Friends!" won. This is going to be my first dance, and I am super excited!

"*Aloha* means both 'hello' and 'goodbye' in Hawaiian," Carolyn tells me. She's been to Waikiki twice with her family.

"Just like *shalom*," I say knowingly.

Carolyn, Rachel, Howie, and I decide to go to the dance together. We meet at Rachel's, and all three of them are wearing puka shell necklaces and look very tropical. I wish

I had a necklace like that. Rachel's mom also gives us leis made of plastic flowers. Mine looks particularly nice against my yellow sundress with the matching yellow corduroy vest. Rachel's mom says so too as she takes our picture.

We all pile into their station wagon, trying to hide our excitement. But we can't!

As soon as we arrive at Lincoln, I start to feel nervous. I have never danced with a boy before. It didn't seem like a big deal an hour ago, but now it does. There's something about seeing the other kids that makes me really anxious. As we walk to the gym, I notice the other sixth grade girls, who are all dressed up. Some of them are wearing makeup and high heels. How are they going to dance in high heels?

The gym is decorated with inflatable palm trees and a slightly leaning papier-mâché volcano that spews steam. The four of us quickly take places against the back wall. The DJ plays three or four fast songs, then a slow one.

Couples start to form on the dance floor. We scan the remaining boys and try not to look too interested. I wish we didn't have to wait for a boy to ask us to dance, but that's how it is.

"We look like Mount Rushmore," says Rachel.

"I hope not," I say. "Those guys on Mount Rushmore never dance."

After eight more fast songs and two more slow ones,

Carolyn suggests we stand somewhere else. "THE STEAM FROM THE VOLCANO IS MAKING IT HARD FOR GUYS TO SEE US!" she yells over the music. We move next to the snack hut, which has a sign that says LUAU PARTY! spelled out in seashells. There's a table full of popcorn and cotton candy inside. I don't want to eat anything yet. I brushed my teeth before I left the house.

I begin to notice that the same girls are asked to dance over and over again while the rest of us are about as popular as the inflatable palm trees. Brock has been dancing the whole time. He's a really good dancer. And when he flips his hair in between moves, it's not annoying at all. He's a jerk, but I wish he would ask me to dance. I keep watching him, pretending that I'm looking at something else. I would *die* if he saw me looking at him.

"I hate this," I tell Rachel.

"What?" she asks.

"I HATE THIS," I yell.

She points to her ears and shakes her head. We stand, shifting our weight from one leg to the other. They really should have chairs at these events. It seems like all the girls with high heels are dancing while the rest of us, like members of some sensible shoe club, are just watching.

All of a sudden, I hear the unmistakable opening to Gloria Gaynor's "I Will Survive." *Dear God, please have a boy, any boy, ask me to dance.* I've given up trying to look cool and have a big smile on my face that I hope says, *Ask me!* Not only have I practiced dancing to this song many times, but I know all the words.

A few lines in, I know this entire dance is a lost cause. Why do they call it a dance? They should call it a stand, 'cause that's all we're doing.

"I DON'T THINK I WILL SURVIVE THIS," I say to Carolyn.

"KEEP SMILING," Carolyn says. "THERE'S STILL HOPE. THERE ARE LIKE TEN MORE VERSES LEFT. AND LOOK! FREDDIE ARNOLD IS WALKING TOWARD YOU."

I smile extra hard at Freddie Arnold, who is indeed walking toward me. We are now face-to-face.

"Excuse me," he says, reaching for a bag of popcorn behind me.*

I feel like an idiot. An idiot standing in front of the snack hut.

The DJ announces that he will be taking a break.

"I WILL NEVER GO TO ANOTHER DANCE." Rachel is still yelling, even though the music has stopped.

* Note to Freddie Arnold: You missed out on some *awesome* dance moves. Now you will never see them. Too bad.

"If you lived in Iran, you wouldn't have to," I tell her.

"What?"

"Never mind."

"There's a name for us, you know. Wallflowers," Carolyn says glumly.

I usually like it when Carolyn teaches me new words, but not this time.

If you are a wallflower at one dance, will you also be a wallflower at the next dance? Is it a permanent condition? I wonder.

"Did you see Brock?" Carolyn asks me.

"Yeah."

"He's such a jerk."

"Totally."

"And he dances like one," she adds.

"I know."

When the DJ starts playing music again, Howie and I decide we've had enough. We go outside to the Shark Attack Snack Shack, which consists of two card tables filled with cookies and chips. Two inflatable sharks are attached with duct tape to either side of the tables.

"Boys never ask me to dance. I'm too tall." Howie sighs. "I just pray the Lord delivers me a tall husband one day."

I don't know what to say. I've never heard an American friend talk about her future husband. I assumed only Iranian girls thought about marriage.

We stand next to a shark, scooping onion dip with potato chips.

"In Iran, my Aunt Zohreh finds husbands for all the girls because she knows everyone."

"Maybe the Lord works through your aunt," Howie says.

I've never considered the Lord working through anyone. "I always figured God is busy dealing with starvations and floods," I say. "But I did pray one time to Saint Anthony about a lost key, and one of our neighbors found it."

"There you go," she says, wiping potato chip crumbs off her dress. "That's definitely the Lord working through your neighbor."

I think of Skip, wearing bright plaid pants, walking his tiny bulldog every morning in the greenbelt. I always pictured someone working for the Lord to be wearing a loose white gown, with a thick rope tied around his waist, followed by a goat or two.

But maybe I'm wrong.

"If you ever want an Iranian husband, I'm sure my Aunt Zohreh can find you one," I offer. I smile, just thinking of Howie with an Iranian husband. I could marry an American because I love American food, but Howie doesn't even like feta cheese. One time I offered her a piece at lunch and she said, "No, but it looks interesting." I know what that means. How can you marry someone if you don't like his food?

"Thanks," says Howie, smiling back. "That's very nice of you."

"You're welcome."

And we both move on to the chocolate chip cookies.

For my twelfth birthday, I decide to have a pool party with Carolyn, Rachel, Kris, Colleen, and Howie.

I contact the person in charge of events for the condo association. Chapter four, "Pool Rules": *All parties of six or more must obtain permission to use facilities.*

Then I plan the menu: hamburgers with lots of toppings to choose from, inspired by all-you-can-eat buffets. I even buy American sliced cheese in plastic wrap because Carolyn and Rachel like cheeseburgers. My uncle Fattolah tried that kind of cheese once and said it tasted like plastic even after you take the plastic wrap off. But he ate it anyway. My uncle often says something's disgusting but next thing you know, he's eaten the whole thing.

We also get ketchup, mustard, pickles, and lemonade (powdered) from El Rancho Market. I want a homemade moist and delicious deluxe classic yellow cake mix with easy-to-spread rich and creamy chocolate frosting, like in the commercials. I tell my mom that I will translate the directions for her on the box.

"I don't have the right kind of pan," she says.

"I'll get one from Carolyn's mom," I offer.

"No," she says, shaking her head firmly. I can tell by the look in her eyes that there's no point in arguing further.

She also wants to make kebabs. This is where I draw the line. I *insist* on a kebab-and-rice-free party. "The last time we grilled lamb kebabs at the pool, all the neighborhood cats came begging."

"Smart cats," she says.

"It's *my* party," I remind her.

My parents end up getting a pre-made chocolate cake from the bakery section. It has a rainbow on it and the word CONGRATULATIONS!

"This is not a birthday cake!" I say when they show it to me.

"Of course it is!" my father insists. "It means 'Congratulations on your birthday.'"

"Where is the 'on your birthday' part?"

"Not enough room," he explains.

Despite the weird cake and my mother's chronic bad mood, I know the party will be a total blast. My friends all arrive on time and we immediately jump in the pool. After seven rounds of Marco Polo, I announce the balloon fight. I hand out two balloons to each person. (My dad and I filled them with water that morning.)

"Ready, set, throw!" I yell. There's lots of squealing and ducking. None of the balloons burst. We pick them up quickly and throw them again. They remain intact.

"What kind of balloons are these?" Howie asks, examining hers closely.

"They're really thick," says Kris, stretching one out.

"I guess I bought the wrong kind," I admit sheepishly.

"Who cares?" says Carolyn. "Let's keep throwing them at each other."

After another few rounds of pelting each other with unbreakable balloons, we sit down to eat. My parents have set out the food on the picnic tables by the grills. They're both smiling as they watch us put toppings on the hamburgers. I really don't want them to sit and eat with us and say embarrassing things. Thankfully, there is no room. They eat by themselves on the other side of the pool. Every time I look, they're peering over toward us. That's okay.

After dinner, they bring out the cake. My friends take one look at it and start singing, "Congratulations to you" instead of "Happy birthday to you." We all laugh. I have to admit, I have pretty funny friends. I'm so lucky.

"Open the gifts now!" they insist as soon as we finish eating the cake.

I look at the huge pile and take the one with the fanciest ribbon. It's from Carolyn. I carefully remove the paper and ribbon and set them aside to be used again later, because my parents are watching and I don't want them to say something and embarrass me. It's a pompom belt! Howie gives me a banana-flavored Bonne Bell Lip Smacker, the big one that comes on a rope that you can wear as a necklace. We pass it around so everyone can smell it, then I hang it around my neck. It's the coolest thing. Kris and Colleen give me a huge paint-by-numbers set of a mountain scene with a waterfall. I know exactly where in my room I will hang it after I finish it. Rachel gives me a Clue game, which I always play at her house.

"Thank you, everyone! You guys are the best!" I hug each one of them and we decide to jump back in the pool. I take my banana-flavored Bonne Bell Lip Smacker off first, of course.

After the party, I ask my parents if I am getting the gift that I asked for, one session at Camp White's Landing, the Girl Scout camp on Catalina Island. "It sounds dangerous," my mom insists. She's been watching the news too much and is convinced that there are kidnappers and murderers hiding behind every tree in America.

"It's not dangerous, *Maman*! It's Girl Scouts! Pleeeeease," I beg. "Carolyn and Rachel and I have already decided to share a tent, and if I don't go, they will be stuck with some random stranger. I promise that I will be extra, extra careful. I will never go anywhere alone or in the dark. Even if I have to go to the bathroom in the middle of the night, I will wake up Carolyn or Rachel, or maybe both, to go with me."

That's a lie but I had to say it. My mother is so unreasonable.

"Will there be any horseback riding?" my dad asks.

"No."

"That's good, because horses can kick you in the head and leave you blind, just like that," he says, snapping his fingers to show the speed of the tragedy. "Just ask my friend Mehdi, who wishes he had stayed home that fateful day instead of trying to pet a horse."

"Can I pleeeeease go?" I beg again.

They look at each other and then back at me.

"Okay," they say together.

"Yay!" I jump and clap for joy around the living room.

"You're getting the carpet wet," my mother points out.

TWENTY-SiX MiLES
ACROSS THE SEA

Carolyn, Rachel, and I, along with two dozen other campers, are standing on the upper deck of a huge boat in Long Beach Harbor, waving goodbye to our parents. We're surrounded by tourists taking too many pictures.

It's my first time on a boat. It's my first time away from my parents. It's my first time going to summer camp. I'll be there for two weeks. And I'm not scared, not even a little! In fact, I have never been so excited in my entire life!

"I can't wait to get there!" Rachel declares.

"Did you guys have to make a million promises to your parents about things you wouldn't do at camp?" I ask them.

"I had to promise to have a good time," says Carolyn.

"That's it? What kind of promise is that?"

"Isn't the point of going to camp *to do* stuff?" asks Rachel.

"Yeah," I say, taking the cap off my Bonne Bell banana-flavored Lip Smacker, which is conveniently hanging around my neck. I apply another coat. I love the stuff.

I'm wearing the floppy hat my mom gave me. The extra wide rim goes all the way around, practically touching my shoulders. I look like a stumpy mushroom. But my mom doesn't want my face to get sunburned. She made me promise to wear it the whole time. I'm pretty sure I'm going to have to break that promise.

As soon as the ferry leaves the dock and we can't see our parents anymore, we decide to check out the lower deck. The boat moves with the waves and we hold on to the railings tightly as we go downstairs. There's a snack shop, tables full of people, and lots of outdoorsy types with their huge backpacks. The smell of greasy food fills the room. "You better hurry up, little mushroom," says Carolyn, "before someone decides to make you a side dish."

We all start laughing and cannot stop. I can barely see beyond the front rim of this ridiculous hat. I notice that a bunch of tourists, with their dorky clothes and cameras around their necks, are staring at us. We don't care. We're not tourists. We live in Newport Beach. As they continue to stare, I apply another layer of Bonne Bell banana-flavored Lip Smacker.

"Let's go back to the upper deck," Carolyn suggests.

The wind in the stairwell almost blows us over as we climb. It's a good thing my hat's tight elastic band is so secure on my head.

As soon as we get to the top, Rachel points to the water. "Look!"

I can't believe what I'm seeing. Dolphins—and not the

ones that jump through hoops at Sea World, but dolphins in the wild.

"I swear to God," I say, "this is the best day of my life."

"For sure!" says Rachel. "Plus, we're going to have *so* much fun at camp."

"Look over there," interrupts Carolyn. "Flying fish!"

"What?" I blurt. Before she can answer, I see them with my own two eyes. Fish that jump out of water, fins spreading like wings, gliding in the air. Flying fish! Fish that *actually* fly!

"I can't believe this! I wish I had a camera," I say. I keep staring at the water, wondering what other magical creatures are in it.

The hour-and-a-half boat ride goes by too quickly, and next thing I know, we are in Avalon on Catalina Island. We gather our bags and get off the boat. Howie has loaned me her sleeping bag, which actually fits in my duffel. I'm so glad I don't have to wrestle a giant black garbage bag down the stairs.

I immediately spot two tanned counselors wearing camp T-shirts, cutoff shorts, and puka shell necklaces. They're standing on the dock, carrying a big sign that reads WELCOME TO CAMP WHITE'S LANDING!

The counselors consult their list, check off all our names, and then tell us that we will be taking a bus to the camp. Ten minutes later, we're leaving touristy Avalon for the part of the island that only locals see. "Oh my God, it's like *Fantasy Island*," Rachel exclaims.

"I love that show," I say. As the bus continues its drive through the unspoiled parts of Catalina, we finally stop talking and just stare out the windows. I never knew there were so many shades of green! There are birds everywhere, and I don't know where to look.

At the campsite, we are greeted by the rest of the counselors. They're all current or former Girl Scouts who are in high school or college, except for the two CITs—counselors in training—who are only a year older than us. They all have camp names like Cricket, Blue, and Rocket, and they tell us that we each have to pick a name too. Then we gather in a huge circle in front of the "mess hall" and they teach us the camp song.

> *Camp White's Landing*
> *Oh, how I dream of thee!*
> *Camp White's Landing*
> *So much you've taught me*
> *Camp White's Landing*
> *How I love the blue sea*
> *Camp White's Landing*
> *Forever I love thee!*

The tents are already set up. All we have to do is pick one. But before the counselors let us go, they warn us that Catalina Island is full of feral pigs and bison and we are not to leave any food, or even toothpaste, in our tents, because the scent will attract them.

Carolyn, Rachel, and I look at each other, mouths open. I'm so glad my parents did not know about this.

We finally go to the tents to set up our stuff and choose camp names.

"We should be a famous threesome," I suggest. "How about Huey, Dewey, and Louie?"

"Donald Duck's nephews?" Carolyn cracks up, and Rachel joins in.

Once they stop laughing, Rachel says, "Oh my God, no."

"Fine," I say, "you guys pick something."

"How about Nina, Pinta, and Santa Maria?" Carolyn suggests.

"Columbus's ships?" says Rachel. "No."

"It makes sense, since we took a boat to get here," Carolyn argues.

"Yeah, but didn't the *Santa Maria* sink?" asks Rachel. "Like I want to be named after a sinking ship."

We ponder that for a few seconds, then Rachel says, "I know! How about Earth, Wind, and Fire?" She starts to sing "Boogie Wonderland" and dance around the tent.

"No one's gonna wanna be Wind," Carolyn says, giggling.

We realize we can't agree on a famous threesome, so we give up on that idea. Carolyn ends up calling herself Sommers, like Jaime Sommers, the Bionic Woman. Rachel chooses Cleo, short for Cleopatra, and I become Lentil, in honor of my favorite bean.

Every day is filled with crafts, games, and sports. For my three main activities, I pick sailing, snorkeling, and canoeing. My counselor, Rainy, proclaims that I'm a natural.

She doesn't believe me when I mention I've never sailed, canoed, or snorkeled before.

"But you live in Newport Beach," she says.

"I just moved there last summer," I tell her. "I'm originally from Iran."

"Really? You mean the country with the bearded guy? What's his name?"

"Khomeini."

"Why did you move here?" she asks.

"My dad's a petroleum engineer and he's helping an American company build an oil refinery," I explain.

"That's cool," Rainy says. "Hey, I heard on the news that they beat up women in Iran if they're not wearing the right kind of clothes. Is that true?"

I'm so embarrassed that this is what everyone seems to know about my country now.

"Yes, that's true, unfortunately—but it wasn't like that when I lived there." I feel it's important for her to know this.

"I hope you never go back," she proclaims. "You seem so American."

I don't know what to say. Here I am, spending the summer in my bathing suit and shorts while some poor girl in Iran—maybe even one of my friends or relatives—is getting punished for showing a strand of hair.

"I like it here" is all I come up with.

"You should try to be a counselor in training next summer," Rainy suggests. "You get to spend eight weeks at camp. You don't get paid, but then you can be a counselor when you're in high school. Then you get paid."

"I would love that!" I can hardly believe such a wonderful job exists.

The next day, we come back to our tents to discover that the feral pigs have visited. There is gooey, sticky saliva all over everything! Even though we're completely disgusted at the slime invasion, we burst out laughing—we had been *so* careful, and the boars came anyway. Luckily, none of our stuff is damaged; it just needs to be washed. My parents don't need to know.

Ever since my conversation with Rainy, I can't stop day-dreaming about being a CIT next summer. Sailing quickly becomes my favorite activity. I finally understand why everyone in Newport Beach is so into it. Out on the water, with the wind in my face, navigating the tiny vessel, I feel a happiness that I have never felt before. Even though my dad has told me all about the dangers of the ocean (sharks, jellyfish, tsunamis, lightning, drowning, and rip currents, to name a few), I feel completely safe in that little sailboat. I am far away from the daily bad news about Iran, and from my mother's sadness. I close my eyes for just a few seconds and try to hold on to that feeling.

OH HECK, IT'S OPEC

After two heavenly weeks at camp, where I tanned without even trying (take that, Original Cindy!), I am now in the back seat of the Impala, telling my parents about flying fish. They can't believe it either. Suddenly, I see about fifty cars parked in front of a gas station, with people standing all around. "What is that?" I ask.

"You've missed the big news of the summer," my dad says wearily. "Gas lines. The protests in Iran have interrupted the export of oil, and suddenly there isn't enough gas. And it costs more than one dollar per gallon!"

"Everyone is so angry," my mother adds. "You're lucky we filled up the car yesterday. Your dad waited in line for two hours."

"Less supply and more demand means that OPEC increased its prices," explains my dad.

I am the only kid in Newport Beach who already knew about OPEC, since it is, unfortunately, another branch of my father's favorite subject. I don't wait for Carolyn to call me this time. I call her as soon as I get home.

"Do you know what OPEC stands for?" I ask.

"No," she says. "But do tell, my fascinating friend." Her voice drips with sarcasm.

"Organization of Petroleum Exporting Countries," I say. "According to my dad, every American should pay attention to what OPEC does, since the American economy is tied to its decisions. OPEC decides the price of oil. When the price of oil goes up, so does the price of everything else."

"Thank you for this captivating phone call." Carolyn makes snoring sounds.

"If you're going to be a journalist, you need to know this stuff," I say. "You're welcome."

"Hey, you wanna go see *Rocky II* at Fashion Island Mall tomorrow?" she asks. "My mom says she can pick you up at eleven thirty for the matinee."

"Sounds good." I'm totally looking forward to not having to think about OPEC or see my parents' constantly worried faces, even if it's only for a couple hours.

BUTTERCUP

That weekend, I'm washing the Impala in our driveway when I hear an enthusiastic "What's up, buttercup?" I stop soaping the hubcaps and look over the hood to see Skip—dressed in a light blue plaid shirt, collar up, cheerful as ever—walking his bulldog.

"Hi," I say.

"How nice of you to be washing your dad's car. You seem like a kid who doesn't lollygag much."

Judging from the words he uses, I'm beginning to think that if I looked in Skip's garage, I'd find a covered wagon. My confused expression may have given that away.

"What I mean is you seem like a hardworking kid. Brock tells me you are very smart in school."

"He said that?"

"Sure did. You're a go-getter. I wish some of your gumption could rub off on him."

"Brock is really good at things that I'm not very good at," I offer. "I don't even know how anyone can stand up on a surfboard."

"It's all about practice," Skip says. "If he practiced math as much as he surfs, he might be a little Einstein. Brock just doesn't believe he can be good at school. Like my dad always used to say, 'Can't never did 'cause can't never tried.'"

I'm not sure how to respond to that.

"Maybe he will like math more next year."

Skip laughs. "Hope springs eternal." He starts to walk away. "And that means 'I hope so.'"

"See you later," I say, smiling.

"See you soon, raccoon," he replies with a wave.

SEVENTH GRADE

I already know seventh grade is going to be a great year because I am no longer the new kid at school. And thanks to Matt, I have inside information about most of my teachers. I have friends to eat lunch with every day, and I know where all the bathrooms are. Turns out I have three classes with Carolyn and two with Rachel. None of the subjects seems that difficult. I'm beginning to think that once you have attended school in Iran, you never think tests or assignments in America are that hard. It's like being vaccinated against difficulty.

I go to Carolyn's all the time. We always study first, then play a board game or just talk. Matt is usually holed up in his room studying. But one day he comes over and says, "Hey, Cindy, did you know that the name of your street, Vista del Oro, means 'view of gold'?"

"Who cares?" Carolyn says. "Go away."

"Have you noticed how so many streets in Newport Beach have Spanish names, but no one who lives on them speaks Spanish?" continues Matt.

"But our street has a view of a school parking lot," I say. "Where's the gold?"

"It's called marketing," Matt says. "I bet 'view of parking lot' doesn't sound so good in Spanish."

I laugh.

"Don't laugh," Carolyn tells me. "You'll only encourage him."

Matt ignores his sister. "You should take Spanish in high school. It'll help with the vocabulary on the SATs."

"The what?" I ask.

"The SATs. You take them before going to college," he explains.

This is news to me. I didn't know you have to take tests before college! "I always planned on learning French, since I've already learned English."

"Why?" Matt asks.

"That's what people do in Iran, so they can study in America or England or France. Plus, all the famous movie stars speak English or French: John Wayne, Elizabeth Taylor, Brigitte Bardot, Alain Delon."

"Who's the last guy?" Matt wants to know.

"He's a French actor. I guess he's not famous here, but in Iran, if a man is really good-looking, you call him, 'an Alain Delon.'"

"Never heard of him," says Carolyn.

"John Wayne lived in Newport Beach," Matt adds. "He just died in June."

"Really?" I had never thought of John Wayne as a real

person, but here I am, living *in the same town* where he had lived. Maybe I saw him at the grocery store but didn't recognize him. It's not like he would have been wearing a cowboy hat to buy a carton of eggs.

"I probably should take Spanish," I say, "because ever since I moved to Newport Beach, people think I'm Mexican."

"What do you mean?" asks Carolyn.

"Our neighbor across the greenbelt asked me to tell the gardeners 'in Mexican' that they keep forgetting to trim her hedge. When I said, 'I don't speak Spanish,' she was shocked."

Carolyn and Matt both laugh.

"Then I told her that I'm not from Mexico and she looked *really* confused. 'I'm from Iran,' I said, and she goes, 'Oh, that's nice.'"

"I think she probably meant, 'Oh no! Not that scary country with the bearded guy!'" says Matt.

I laugh.

"Stop feeding the beast with your laughter," Carolyn warns.

"But that *was* funny," I say. "Another time, Mrs. Harris, who lives two doors down from us, asked me if I could tell her window washer, Jesus, not to come next week. I told her that I only know how to say *lavar los manos, por favor, buenos dias,* and *muchas gracias.* Do you know what she said? 'It's a pity you have forgotten your Spanish.'" I roll my eyes.

For an extra-credit project for Social Studies, Carolyn is going to interview my dad. This is the first time she's coming over to my place for dinner. I am so happy to finally be doing something for her. I spend a lot of time at her house and her mother is always driving me places, since mine doesn't have a driver's license.

My mom has made eggplant stew, lamb shanks, and rice pudding with rose water. "Something smells good!" Carolyn says as she walks in the door. She is off to a great start. My mother's favorite thing in the whole world is when someone compliments her cooking.

Carolyn comes equipped with a tape recorder, extra batteries, a yellow notepad, and sharpened pencils. "You are already a great journalist," my dad tells her.

After dinner, she takes out her recorder and looks very official. I can tell my dad is excited. He loves to talk about Iran, but no one except Dr. Klein ever wants to listen to his long answers.

Before Carolyn can ask a question, my dad jumps in. "Let me first tell you one thing, Carroleen. Iran has about ten percent of the world's oil reserves. This has been both a blessing and a curse."

"Why?" Carolyn asks, pushing the record button.

"The history of Iran's oil industry started in 1901, when an Englishman received permission from Iranian officials to explore and develop southern Iran's oil resources," my dad says. "In 1908, the British found oil in southwest Iran."

"Near where I was born!" I add.

"Your claim to fame," says Carolyn, smiling at me.

"Yes," I say hesitantly, not sure if that is a compliment.

My dad continues. "This discovery changed Iran's history. I have worked in the oil industry my whole life, and I tell you, Carroleen, that if the investment that has been made in the oil industry had been made in educating men and women, Iran would indeed be a rich country today. The greatest resource of any country should always be its people. You see, Carroleen, when a precious resource like oil is found, it brings a lot of money quickly, and this brings out the worst in people and governments."

Then my father goes through the entire boring history of oil in Iran. I'm amazed that Carolyn manages to look genuinely interested the whole time. If being a journalist doesn't work out, she can always be an actress.

"I think about where Iran is today with all this turmoil and I wonder, *What led us here?* That is not an easy question to answer, but the greed and corruption that came with the oil have deeply damaged Iran and its people."

Carolyn is still nodding her head and writing.

My dad then shows her his favorite book, *The Petroleum Industry of Iran*. Uh-oh. We're about to take a detour deep into Boringville. "On this page, you see large pipes. On the next page, you see large pipes attached to larger pipes. On the next page, you see large pipes attached to larger pipes with steam coming out of them," he drones on. Now I am certain that Carolyn is only pretending to be interested, but she's still doing a fine job.

Once both sides of the cassette tape are used up, she says, "Thank you very much, Mr. Yousefzadeh. That was the most interesting sixty minutes I have had in a long time. I will always think of you when I go to the gas station."

I giggle, but my dad seems very pleased to hear that.

As Carolyn starts to put away her notebook, my dad says, "Carroleen, I have one more thing to say.

"If I had one son and one daughter and could only educate one of them, I would educate my daughter. You know why? A girl without an education has no power; she is always at the mercy of others."

Carolyn takes out her notebook again and writes that down.

I am the luckiest girl in the world.

My dad and I are driving to the hardware store, listening to the radio as usual. The disc jockey suddenly announces that there is breaking news. I just know it's going to be about Iran, and I'm dreading it.

He says that President Carter has allowed the shah to come to America for cancer treatment.

"Bavaram nemeesheh."

I can't believe it, my dad says.

According to the journalist, the shah has lived in Egypt, Morocco, the Bahamas, and Mexico since leaving Iran.

"Can you believe this, Zomorod? No country wants to keep him. He used to be welcomed in nations around the world with red carpets and military salutes, but now . . ." He doesn't finish his sentence, just shakes his head. "Who would have ever thought that a person could be so powerful, then so completely powerless, all in the same lifetime?"

It's my second Halloween in Newport Beach. This time, we've decided to go trick-or-treating in Howie's neighborhood. Rachel is dressing as Little Red Riding Hood. Howie is going as a cowboy, and Carolyn's costume is a surprise again. I'm going as a tourist. It's an easy costume. I'm wearing my mother's sweatshirt that says, I LUV NEWPORT BEACH! and has a drawing of a koala wearing star-shaped sunglasses, lounging at the beach, sipping a drink out of a coconut with a bendy straw. Aside from my mom, no resident in the history of Newport Beach has ever owned such a sweatshirt or sipped a drink out of a coconut. People in Newport Beach drink Tab, which has only one calorie. Rumor has it that Tab stands for Thin And Beautiful. All I know is that it tastes like liquid tin.

Halloween is even better this year. Carolyn is dressed up as a bunch of grapes. She's wearing a purple leotard with about twenty purple balloons attached to her. It's a cute costume, but she can't really sit down.

At the first house we go to, the family is making caramel apples and the dad asks us what toppings we want. There is actually a whole tray of toppings to choose from! Normally

I do not accept unwrapped candy because of possible poisoning, but this family has a fancy garden and they seem like people who plan vacations, not murders.* I decorate my apple with peanuts and chocolate sprinkles and gobble it all down. It's incredibly delicious.

We collect a lot of candy, but not as much as last year. Thanks to Howie being so tall, people keep saying, "Aren't you too old for this?" I'm thankful that I come from a short family. I figure I still have many happy years of trick-or-treating ahead of me.

* Note to the Newport Beach Police Department: In case I was wrong and it is too late for me to tell you this, the murderers live at 117 Cornelius Lane.

A few days later, I'm still enjoying my candy and thinking about how Halloween is the best holiday in the history of holidays when we see the worst news ever. A group of Iranian students, angry that President Carter has allowed the shah to come to this country, has stormed the U.S. embassy in Iran, taking American hostages. Even though most Americans have left Iran by now, some are still working there. The news program shows mobs of angry men and women marching in the streets of Tehran, pumping their fists in the air and shouting, *"Marg bar shah! Marg bar shah!"* *Death to the shah! Death to the shah!* My parents and I watch without uttering a sound. We're all thinking the same thing: *This cannot be happening.*

Carolyn calls me immediately. I pick up the phone next to the sofa. "What's going on?" she asks.

"The protesters are mad at America for supporting the shah," I tell her. My parents are staring at me with pained looks on their faces.

My dad, who hasn't even tried to hide the fact that he's been listening to my conversation, calls out, "Tell Carroleen they will release the hostages tomorrow. Iranians have never been hostage takers."

WRONG!

My dad is wrong. The hostages are not released the next day. To everyone's horror, Khomeini says he supports the hostage taking. That's like Santa Claus admitting he doesn't like children. How can anyone religious take hostages?

I come home from school and find my dad sitting on the sofa.

"What are you doing here?" I ask.

"The project has been suspended," he says, shaking his head. "No more work on the oil refinery until the hostages are released."

I know I should say something to my dad to make him feel better, but I can't think of anything. I go upstairs. My parents' door is closed but I can hear my mom sobbing. I know I need to cry too, but I can't. I feel frozen inside.

I wake up to the sound of my dad's radio. I figure he is shaving and listening to the news like he does every morning. But then I remember. He does not have a job. How can this be? He has *always* worked. Maybe he still has a job. Maybe I misunderstood him.

I get ready and grab my backpack. I'm not hungry. I leave early. I don't see my parents or even say goodbye to them. I just want to get to school and forget my life.

I come home after school and my dad is sitting on the sofa, listening to the radio. I don't know what he did all day, but he and my mom are both in a very bad mood. Yesterday really did happen.

I go to my room and decide to stay there until morning.

I lie on my bed and realize that this yellow, frilly décor—especially the froufrou canopy with all the lace—is really bothering me. Why did I ever buy this?

I go downstairs. "*Baba,* can I sell my furniture? It's so ugly."

"Do what you want," he says, barely looking up at me.

I find a copy of the *PennySaver* and look at the furniture sets for sale to get an idea of the price. Two hundred dollars for the whole set seems right. I dial the free number and place my ad.

The next day, a girl calls about the bedroom set. I give her our address and she tells me they will come tomorrow evening, as soon as her dad gets home from work. *Her* dad has a job.

Four more people call. I take their names and numbers and tell them that I will call them back if the furniture is still available.

I clean up my room, and the next evening, they show up right on time. As soon as I open the door, the dad starts talking to me in Spanish. I must really look Mexican if actual Mexicans think I'm Mexican.

"*No hablo español,*" I say. I learned that from Matt.

The parents don't speak English. Their daughter is the translator for her family, like a Mexican version of me.

We go upstairs to my room and I can tell right away they like the bedroom set. They start talking in really fast Spanish. "You can try out the bed if you want," I say. They all get on the bed, and a minute later the girl says, "We will buy it." My dad tells them that the sheets and frilly pillows are a gift. As soon as we get downstairs, I see my mom holding a tray of hot tea and cake. "Please, tea and cake," she says.

"*Maman,* I asked you not to do this. They don't do this kind of stuff in America," I remind her.

She ignores me.

I roll my eyes.

We all sit in the living room in awkward silence, drinking tea. My mother also offers them a bowl of fruit, decorated with pickling cucumbers. They smile. I can tell they're confused. They came to buy a bedroom set and now they probably think they've been taken hostage.

"What is your name?" I ask the girl.

"Maria."

"How old are you?"

"I am eight."

She is so happy. She loves the bedroom set and can't stop smiling. I hope she doesn't hate it in a few years, but I'm pretty sure she will.

That night, I sleep on the floor on a pile of blankets. It kind of reminds me of camping. But instead of giggling before bedtime with my friends, I go to sleep worrying alone.

CiRCLE TiME

On Monday during lunch, a tomato lands splat in my lap, making a huge stain on my dress. Before I can figure out what happened, another one hits me on the head. Carolyn and Rachel stand up, trying to see who's responsible.

"It's Brock!" says Rachel. "Why was he throwing tomatoes at us?"

"Because he's a loser," Carolyn huffs. "And look! He's being congratulated by his idiot friends."

I don't think the tomatoes were aimed at *us*. I have a feeling *I* am the target.

We all go in the bathroom so I can rinse the tomato juice out of my hair and clothes.

"You know what, Cindy?" Carolyn says. "Last night, on the news, they said that some Iranians in America were getting beat up."

"I didn't know that," I say.

"What's the purpose of beating up Iranians in America? They're not the ones who have taken the hostages," observes Carolyn.

"So let me see," says Rachel, thinking for a moment. "A

group in Iran has taken American hostages because they're mad at President Carter for letting the shah into the U.S."

"That's right," says Carolyn.

"And now some Americans are beating up Iranians in America because they're mad at the hostage takers in Iran, who are mad at Carter for letting the shah come to the U.S.?"

"You got it," says Carolyn. "It's a circle."

"How is this going to end?" asks Rachel.

I shrug and look down at the giant wet spot on my dress. I wish I could stay in the bathroom for the rest of the day.

TRASHY DRAMA

A few days later, my dad goes out to bring the empty trash cans back into the garage, like he always does. He comes back in and yells, "Zomorod, come to the garage, quickly!"

As soon as I get there, my dad hands me a note. It's from the Newport Beach Sanitation Company. "Due to overflowing bins, your receptacles could not be emptied." The note also says that "further violations will lead to fines." I look at our trash can. It is indeed overflowing, but not with our trash. Empty pork rind bags, beer cans, ribs with gooey barbecue sauce, and cereal boxes are spilling all over the place.

"Zomorod," my dad says. "Call someone at the association and ask what to do. And don't mention this to your mother."

I turn to chapter three in *Rules for Condominium Living*, "Waste Management," and look up the person in charge. It turns out to be Darleen Linden, Original Cindy's mom. I have never met her, and Cindy never mentioned anything about her, except that she sells insurance.

I dial the number. When Mrs. Linden picks up the phone, I introduce myself and explain what has happened.

"If it's in your trash can, it's your trash. Maybe you forgot what you ate," she says.

"I am one hundred percent sure that no one in our house has ever eaten pork rinds or Dinky Donuts cereal. And my dad tried beer one time in Compton and it gave him a terrible stomachache and he hasn't had any since," I add.

"I am sorry, but nobody in the condo association has ever made such a claim. I suggest you buy another container and clean it up. Of course, you will have to pay a fee, since you will have an extra trash bin next week."

"Can we not pay the fee this one time since it isn't our fault?" I ask.

"There are rules for living in America and they need to be followed. If I make an exception for you, I will have to make an exception for everyone else, too," Mrs. Linden says, sounding very angry.

I thank her and hang up. I can see why Cindy spends so much time with animals.

I tell my dad what Darleen Linden said, but I leave out the last part. If there is anyone who follows rules, it's us.

"Don't mention any of this to your mom," he repeats, glancing at the door to the kitchen and sounding very worried.

I wish he would yell or scream, but instead he quietly goes outside to clean up. I follow and help him put the overflowing trash in plastic bags. Then we hose down the driveway, since the ribs have attracted an entire ant colony. We don't say a word the entire time.

I can't stand the silence anymore. "Why would anyone do this?" I ask.

"Zomorod, at least this can be cleaned up in fifteen minutes. There are far worse things happening in the world, things that will take years and years to clean up, if ever. This is not so bad, really." He shakes his head slowly and rinses the barbecue sauce off the bottom of his shoes. Then he walks back into the house, staring at the ground the whole time.

A week has gone by since my dad's job was suspended. It's been the most miserable seven days for all three of us. Once again we're sitting on the sofa, waiting for the news to start, when the phone rings. I assume it's either Carolyn or a relative from Iran. My dad answers. He's listening carefully, then smiling. He hangs up after a minute.

"Great news!" he announces. "I must be at the office tomorrow at nine o'clock for a meeting."

"What kind of meeting?" my mom asks.

"The secretary didn't say, but the company has lost a lot of time and money and I'm sure we're going to start the project again."

For the first time in what feels like forever, a smile appears on my mother's face. I hug my dad and he gives me a kiss on the cheek.

The next day, he shaves while listening to the radio, puts on his suit and tie, then eats a bowl of Sugar Corn Pops, just like he used to. I hear him whistling all the way out to the garage.

When I come home from school, my dad is sitting on the sofa, still wearing his suit. He looks exhausted. There's a cardboard box on the floor next to him containing the nameplate from his desk, his Sea World coffee mug with a picture of Shamu jumping through a hoop, and a half-dead red fern.

"What happened?" I ask, trying not to sound too alarmed.

"America and Iran are no longer doing business together, so the company fired me." He's not even trying to hide his anguish. "But they gave me this," he says sadly, holding up a book, *How to Write a Resume.*

This can't be real. How can my father get fired? He is a *great* engineer.

I don't know what to say. I go to my room and lie down on my pile of blankets.

That night, after dinner, my dad takes all the credit cards and spreads them across the kitchen table. He picks up the scissors and starts cutting the cards into tiny pieces. "That's it," he says. "No more trips to Fashion Island. No more going to restaurants or movies. The clothes we have, that's what we use. We're living off our savings now, and there isn't a lot."

My mom starts to cry and runs up to her room. I know she won't be coming out for the rest of the night.

Saturday morning, I wake up to the sound of click-clacking. I go downstairs. My dad is at the kitchen table, typing with his right hand. He's holding a book open with his left hand.

"What are you doing, *Baba*?" I ask.

"In America, you have to write a resume to get a job," he explains.

I look over his shoulder. He has typed his name, address, and phone number at the top, then listed his degrees from the Abadan Institute of Technology.

I run back upstairs and get my bottle of Wite-Out from my desk drawer.

"Here," I say, handing it to him.

"What's this?"

"See those two mistakes?" I point to an extra *o* in his name and a missing *s* in our address. I unscrew the cap of the Wite-Out with its attached brush. "You just take this little brush, cover the mistakes, wait for it to dry, then retype. It's magic!"

"Amazing!" my dad exclaims.

I'm so glad I've been taking typing at school.

"What are you going to do with the resume?" I ask.

"I'm sending one to every engineering company in the phone book. And here, look in the back of this paper. See if there are any job listings that mention engineering."

He hands me the *L.A. Times*. I flip to the back, the classified section. I scan the want ads. "Here's one!" I say.

"Circle it." My dad hands me a pen.

I find three more and circle them, too.

My father's resume is not very long. He has worked for two companies. The sample resume in the book shows people who have changed jobs many times. I wonder if that is better, but I don't say anything to my dad.

"I have to write a cover letter now," he says, removing the resume from the typewriter.

He opens the book to the chapter "How to Write an Effective Cover Letter."

He starts to type:

Dear Sir or Madam:

My name is Mohsen Yousefzadeh. I am a Petroleum Engineer with 31 years of experience with the National Iranian Oil Company and five years with AMP Gas.

He pauses. "What else should I say, Zomorod?"

I look at the sample cover letters in the book for a few

minutes. "You should also mention something that you've done in those jobs. You need two more sentences."

> *I have been involved in building two refineries in*
> *Iran. I was part of the team from the National Iranian*
> *Oil Company helping AMP Gas Company build*
> *a refinery in Tabriz, but I lost my job because of the*
> *recent and very unfortunate events between Iran and*
> *the United States. I do not agree with these events and*
> *hope they are resolved soon.*

"I don't think you should mention the events between Iran and the U.S.," I suggest.

"Why not?"

He does not realize how unpopular Iran is these days. "Because I don't see anything like it in the sample letters."

"Give me that white stuff," he says.

When the Wite-Out finally dries, my dad adds another sentence.

> *I can start working immediately.*

He removes the cover letter and reads it again, looking pleased. "I am going to the pharmacy to make ten copies. Zomorod, since you are a better typist, can you address the envelopes?"

So that's how I spend my Saturday morning. But I don't mind.

"GiVE ME YOUR TiRED, YOUR POOR, YOUR HUDDLED MASSES YEARNiNG TO BREATHE FREE"

Iranians are arriving in America in droves—especially the upper classes, who are afraid of being killed by the new government. Some have enough money to buy homes and set up small businesses, like dry cleaners. But a lot of people are escaping with only their lives. Many are given political asylum, which means they are allowed to come to America because their lives are in danger. We hear stories about generals in the shah's army who are now scrubbing toilets in Los Angeles.

As we're eating dinner, Pooya calls to say hello. The minute I hear my dad say his name, I go upstairs and pick up the phone on the table in the hallway. I cover the receiver so my father doesn't know that I'm listening. Pooya says that his father took money out of Iran before the revolution, and his parents are now living in London. But his uncle, who owned a shoe factory, was murdered by the new regime and all his belongings were taken away from his family. His house, his car, his wife's jewelry—everything disappeared. His wife and kids fled to Turkey.

"I am so sorry," my father says. "I hope you two are okay."

"We're both studying business at UCLA," Pooya says. "It's hard being Iranian right now with the hostages, but we tell everyone we're Italian. Pooyan is now Giovanni and I'm Antonio."*

"Just study hard," my dad reminds them. "And remember that in America, you can become the best version of yourself. Only in America."

* Note to Italy: Your reputation is about to be ruined.

Every night we wait for "The Iran Crisis: America Held Hostage" to come on Channel 7 so we can hear the update on the hostages. The show always starts with a count of how many days it's been since the hostages were taken. We cannot believe that it has now been *two weeks*. Even though we're not responsible for this terrible event, it's happening in our country, so we feel a connection. We feel *horrible*.

After Social Studies class on Monday, Mrs. Thompson pulls me aside.

"During the faculty meeting on Friday, Miss DeAngelo mentioned you are from Iran. Would you like to give a presentation about the current events there?" she asks.

It's hard for me to say no to a teacher, but I can't think of anything I would like to do less. I don't want everyone at school to associate me with the events in Iran. School is where I go to get a break from all that stuff.

"No, thank you," I say.

"May I ask why not?"

I don't want to admit that I'm embarrassed because

of the hostage situation, so instead I say, "I'm really busy right now."

"I see. But keep in mind that if at the end of the semester your grade is between an A and a B, a report like this would bump it up to an A."

"Can I do it after the hostages are released?" I ask.

"Of course," she says.

A NOTE, NOT FROM HALLMARK

The next morning, I open the front door to go to school and there's something on the doormat. It looks like a stuffed animal. I bend down to pick it up, then jerk my hand away. It's not a toy. It's a dead hamster. There's a handwritten note next to it: *Iranians go home!* If the note hadn't been there, I might have thought a hamster had escaped his cage, crawled to our welcome mat, and died there. But the note . . . Somebody actually placed a dead hamster on our doorstep, on purpose.

I immediately shut the door so my mom and dad don't see it.

I definitely do not want my parents to know about this. They are already upset enough about everything else in the world going wrong. They worry every day about my aunts and uncles. Unlike Pooya and Pooyan's parents, my relatives were not clever enough to take money out of Iran before the revolution. I don't know if they're trying to leave the country, but I do know that as more and more Iranians try to leave, the government tries even harder to prevent them.

I have to get rid of the hamster fast, but I know you're not supposed to touch dead animals because they carry diseases. I lean against the door and think, then take my brown lunch bag out of my backpack. I dump my sandwich and apple slices out of their Ziploc bags and into the brown bag. Then, using one Ziploc as a glove, I put the hamster in the other Ziploc. It feels limp and helpless and I feel so sorry for it. I hope it didn't die a painful death. I go to the greenbelt trash can and dump it in there, looking back over my shoulder to make sure my parents aren't watching. I rip up the note and throw it away too. I keep thinking, *Who would do such a thing?*

As soon as I get to school, I tell Carolyn the whole story. I also tell her about the overflowing trash can, which I haven't mentioned yet.

"Why didn't you tell me about the trash earlier?" she asks, sounding insulted.

"I just thought it was one incident. I didn't want to make a big deal out of it and I didn't realize there would be other weird stuff happening."

Carolyn reacts exactly like I thought she would. "We must find out who did this!" she declares. "I'm coming to your house after school."

I can barely concentrate on classes that day. Who would do such a thing? Does someone hate my parents? They hardly speak enough to make friends, let alone enemies.

Carolyn distracts me by asking questions all the way home.

"Does your father owe anyone money?"

"No."

"Do any of your relatives work for the government?"

"No."

"Have your parents ever paid any bribes?"

"No. And you're confusing my parents with people you've seen in movies. My parents have a glass of warm non-fat milk before they go to bed at nine thirty. Nobody would ever make an action movie about them."

"I have a method," Carolyn insists.

Right when we turn the corner to my house, I start to panic. Carolyn has come over for dinner, but never right after school. My name may be Cindy and my English may be without an accent, but the contents of my kitchen are entirely Iranian. There are no snack foods at my house.

Whenever I go to Carolyn's or Rachel's, there are so many snacks to choose from. I usually have ice cream—any flavor is fine with me.

This is what we have in our freezer: ice.

As we walk up the driveway, I warn her. "You should know that the closest thing we have to a snack that you might recognize is apples and cucumbers."

"That's fine," she says, sounding surprised that I would even say that.

"And there is no peanut butter or cheddar cheese to go with it," I continue.

"We have an important job ahead of us, more important than snacks," she says firmly.

"Right," I say, and try to ignore my growling stomach.

Carolyn and I are sitting cross-legged on the blankets in my room, where my bed once was. The door is closed.

"What do you remember about the note?" she asks. "I wish you'd kept it."

"It was just a plain white piece of paper."

"What was the writing like?" Carolyn asks.

"I don't know how to describe it."

"Was it neat? Did it look like a kid's writing? Was it cursive?"

"It was cursive and pretty neat," I recall.

"It sounds like a female. We already know it's someone who knows where you live," Carolyn says, crunching on a pickling cucumber. "You're in the Girl Scout directory, so it could be someone in the troop."

"No way!" I exclaim.

"Listen, Cindy, you can't eliminate anyone. It could be *anybody*," Carolyn insists.

We go through the Girl Scout directory, page by page. Carolyn circles some names, underlines a few, and puts question marks next to others. I am not clear on her method, but I trust her.

"What about Cindy, your next-door neighbor?" Carolyn asks.

"Nope," I reply.

"But you don't hang out anymore. Maybe she has a vendetta against you."

"What's a vendetta?"

"A gripe," Carolyn explains. "It's when someone's mad at you and they want revenge."

"I know she doesn't like me, but why would she want revenge?" I ask.

Carolyn looks thoughtful but doesn't reply. Suddenly she says, "I know who it is! Brock Vitter. He lives around the corner and he's a jerk. Remember how he threw tomatoes at us during lunch? Plus he teased you about camels. It has to be him."

"But I thought you said it's a female," I remind her.

"He probably had someone else write the note. Criminals often work in pairs. Think of bank robbers—one person goes in the bank, the other drives the getaway car," she explains.

"You're right. It's Brock," I say.

I suddenly feel let down. Would Brock really do something so horrible? I know he threw tomatoes at me, but part of me had hoped maybe there was a sweet person hidden underneath those overgrown bangs.

"What do we do about it?" I ask.

Carolyn decides that we need to go to Brock's right away and catch him off-guard. I don't want to, but I can't say that to Carolyn.

We start walking to his house. I hope it's not Brock. I feel like throwing up. This is my first foray into detective work, and I am not cut out for this.

We ring the doorbell. Brock answers immediately. It's almost as if he's expecting us.

"Hey," he grunts.

"Hi, Brock," Carolyn says.

I keep quiet. I'm afraid that I might say something wrong and give the plan away. I don't even know what the plan is.

Carolyn continues, "We're doing a book report on surfing and we were wondering if we can ask you a few questions. It'll just take a few minutes."

"I guess," Brock says, flipping his hair out of his face.

"So what do you like about surfing?" Carolyn asks.

"I don't know. I just like it." He leans against the door.

"Do surfers usually like animals?" Carolyn asks.

"I guess," Brock answers, looking at us suspiciously.

"Which animals?" She presses on.

"What does this have to do with surfing?" he asks, uttering his longest sentence yet.

"The report is about surfers and the animals they like," Carolyn says, thinking fast.

He seems to buy it. "I like dolphins, I guess, and dogs."

"What about hamsters?"

"Hamsters are cool," Brock says, in a neutral tone of voice. I can't read the expression in his eyes, since I can only see one of them.

"Do you have any?" Carolyn asks calmly.

My heart is beating so fast that I think Brock must hear it.

"I did, but it died."

"Do you still have it?" she asks.

"You mean the dead hamster? Do I still have the dead hamster?"

"Yes."

"What are you? A sicko?"

I want to turn around and run home.

"We know what you did, Brock!" Carolyn exclaims suddenly. "There are witnesses."

"I don't know what you're talking about," he says, taking a step back.

"Did you or did you not, Brock Vitter, leave a dead hamster on Cindy's doorstep on the morning of November twentieth, 1979?" Carolyn asks.

"What?" he says, looking back and forth between us as if we are completely crazy.

"I don't think he did it," I whisper.

"Whatever. I'm outta here," he says, and starts to close the door.

"Wait," Carolyn says, catching it before he slams it shut. "Someone left a dead hamster on Cindy's doorstep and we thought it was you."

"Why?" Brock asks, looking genuinely puzzled.

"You've teased Cindy about camels, and you threw tomatoes at us last week," Carolyn says.

"I happen to be a fan of dromedaries, or as you might call them, 'a one-humped camel.' And I enjoy throwing tomatoes," he adds, as if hurling vegetables is a legitimate hobby. "Okay, I shouldn't have thrown the tomatoes. It was a dare. I'm sorry, Cindy," he says, looking at me.

Even though I can still see only one of his eyes, it's enough for me.

"I accept your apology."

He starts to close the door again, then stops. "Hey, what did the hamster look like?" he suddenly asks.

"Now, that is a gross question," Carolyn says.

"No. I mean, I know all the pets in the neighborhood. Haven't you seen my flyers everywhere?"

I suddenly realize that the flyers all over the greenbelt that say GO ON VACATION WITHOUT THE JITTERS, LEAVE YOUR PETS WITH VITTER'S CRITTERS are his. I didn't know he could rhyme.

"So what did the hamster look like?" he asks again.

"It was light brown with white spots all over and one of its ears was white," I say, recalling the poor creature.

"It's Darleen Linden's. She called me last week all frantic. She was all, 'Brock, what do I do? J. Edgar Hoover just ate a whole bar of baking chocolate.' And I was like, 'Chocolate is so killer for hamsters. Go to the vet *muy rapido* and just give it as much lettuce as you can.' I never heard back, but I didn't know J. Edgar croaked. That's a gnarly way to go. Death by chocolate. Not good."

Carolyn and I look at each other.

"Thanks, Brock," we say at the same time. "Please don't mention this to anyone," adds Carolyn.

"No problemo." He shrugs, and we let him close the door this time.

Carolyn practically drags me back down Brock's driveway, and as soon as we reach the sidewalk, she yells, "I told you it was Cindy! I knew it! I knew it!"

"I can't believe it," I say. "She was a jerk to me, but she

doesn't seem like someone who would do something so cruel."

"Who knows what evil lurks in the hearts of men?" asks Carolyn, ominously.

"Whoa, did you just make that up?"

"Of course not," she says. "It's from *The Shadow,* an old radio show."

"Never heard of it," I say.

"You know, Cindy, sometimes I forget you're not American."

"Except that none of this would be happening to me if I *were* American," I point out.

We walk in silence for a minute.

"But why didn't you recognize the hamster?" Carolyn asks.

"I haven't gone over to Cindy's in a long time. The last time I was there, she didn't have a hamster."

"We have to think about what our next move should be," Carolyn says. "Give me a few days. I gotta go home now, but To Be Continued."

LOVE MAKES THIS HOUSE
A HOME

I can't wait. As soon as Carolyn's mom picks her up, I walk next door and ring the doorbell. A few seconds later, Original Cindy is standing in front of me. My heart is racing and my palms are sweating. I'm not sure I should've done this, but it's too late.

"Hi, Cindy," I say, trying to sound calm.

"Hi, Cindy," she says. "Listen, it's not a good time right now."

"Can I say something for a minute? I know it's been a while, but I wanted to apologize for calling Magic a unicorn."

Original Cindy looks a little surprised.

"Thank you. I'm sure Magic will appreciate that, but I'm still kinda busy."

"This will just take a minute," I insist, taking a deep breath.

I decide to copy the method of detective work used by Carolyn, who, I'm pretty sure, copied Nancy Drew. "This is about what happened on November twentieth."

"November twentieth?" she repeats. "You mean today?"

"Correct."

"You noticed?" she asks.

"Noticed what?"

"That I haven't been at school?"

I'm so confused. Nancy Drew would know what to say. I don't.

"Hold on. Let me show you something," Original Cindy says, running up the stairs.

I wait outside her front door, staring down at her welcome mat. LOVE MAKES THIS HOUSE A HOME it says, with a cheery apple border. I wonder what she's going to show me. I hope it's not a dead animal.

"Here it is!" she says as she returns, holding up a yellow ribbon. "Third place. Best finish yet!"

"What is this?" I ask.

"Third-place ribbon," she says, handing me the prize. "Look!"

"You were at a horse show today?" I ask, reading the inscription.

"Yes, in Carmel," she says. "I just got back an hour ago. That's why I haven't been at school the past two days. It's sweet of you to notice and come over."

"Congratulations," I say quietly.

"All those hours at the stable *finally* paid off," she adds. "And you know something? I kinda knew you were still my friend even though we don't hang out anymore."

"Sure," I say, handing back the ribbon. "I just wanted to congratulate you — and Magic, of course."

"Thanks," she says.

TO THINK DEEPLY ABOUT
SOMETHING

I *have* **to call** Carolyn, even though it's dinnertime.

Mrs. Williams answers right away. "Is everything okay?" she asks, when she hears the urgency in my voice.

"Yes, I just have to tell Carolyn something. It'll be quick."

"Hold on," Mrs. Williams says.

A few seconds later, Carolyn is on the phone.

"It's not her. Cindy was at a horse show in Carmel."

"Are you sure?" she asks.

"Positive. She has the ribbon to prove it."

Silence on the other end of the line. Just as I'm about to ask Carolyn if she's still there, she says, "Didn't you mention that she has a brother?"

"Yes, but he's at a boarding school in Hawaii."

"What about her parents?"

"I've never met them. Her mom is a member of our condo association board," I reply. "She wasn't very nice when I called to ask about the trash situation. But she's a grownup. Adults don't do stuff like this."

"Hmmm. I have to ruminate," Carolyn says.

"Wait, what does that mean?" I ask.

But she's already hung up. I need to look up *ruminate* in the dictionary.

DAY 16

On the news that night, we learn that thirteen of the sixty-five hostages are released. We are so happy! My dad says he's certain the rest will be freed soon too. I can't wait.

It's Thanksgiving. Instead of turkey and all the trimmings, we're having cereal. My dad isn't himself since he lost his job. He just listens to the radio all day like a zombie, and my mom is more depressed than ever. And they don't even know about the dead hamster!

After "dinner," I go in the living room, where my parents are listening to the radio in silence. The reporter is interviewing some of the families of the hostages. We'd been hoping they would all be released before Thanksgiving. My mom keeps saying that she feels especially sorry for the two women. My dad keeps saying he never imagined that Iran would be the enemy of the world.

I wish we could just be like everyone else in Newport Beach, worrying whether or not we're going to have time to buy all the gifts on our Christmas list, wrap them, *and* bake cookies shaped like candy canes. I'd gladly trade unemployment and dead hamsters for those worries any day.

Eventually, my parents turn off the radio. We watch happy people eating Thanksgiving feasts on TV and go to bed early.

The Sunday after Thanksgiving, I go over to Carolyn's house. We hurry to her room and close the door.

"I have made a list of possible suspects in our Girl Scout troop," Carolyn announces. "Suspect number one is Mary Elizabeth Crenshaw. Do you remember how she wanted to share a tent with us at Big Bear and you said there wasn't room?"

"But there *wasn't* room."

"That's beside the point," says Carolyn. "Criminals do not need logic."

I consider this in silence.

"Then we have the O'Shaughnessey twins, Kris and Colleen," she continues.

"Are you kidding?" I ask. "They're my friends."

"They're very competitive in math and they want to go to Harvard. You're the best student in math class. It's possible they want to get you out of the picture."

"That's ridiculous. I think you've been ruminating too much," I add, smiling at my own cleverness.

"Fine." She sounds a little miffed but she crosses their names off the list with great flourish.

"Let's go back to Cindy," she continues. "It was, after all, their hamster that ended up at your house. Let's assume Cindy's *mom*, Darleen Linden, is the perpetrator. Let's also assume she's the one who put the extra trash on your driveway. We need proof. You're going to have to hang out with Cindy at her house, then check her pantry."

"No way!" I reply. "There is no way I can do that. I would be so nervous. Not possible at all. No way. Uh-uh."

Carolyn continues as if she didn't hear me. "You mentioned beer and pork rinds. Do you remember the brands?"

I do remember, since I helped clean it up. "It was Budweiser beer and El Rancho pork rinds. And Dinky Donuts cereal."

Carolyn writes that down. "We have to talk with Brock. I know what to do!"

Before I can ask any questions, she's rushing to Matt's room. I follow.

"Hey, Matt, can you please drive me to Cindy's, wait for ten minutes, then drive me back? In exchange, I'll walk Sam for a whole week."

Matt looks up from his desk where he's doing homework. "You'll walk Sam *and* clean up after him for one month."

"One whole month?" Carolyn protests.

"Take it or leave it. As I see it, you have no bargaining power," Matt confidently states.

"Fine," she says.

The three of us go to the garage. Carolyn gets in the front seat of the Pinto. I get in the back.

As soon as we get to my house, Carolyn says, "Okay, Matt. Can you wait for us here? Ten minutes, max."

"Can do. I'll just be sitting here thinking about how nice it will be *not* to clean up after Sam for a whole month."

I laugh.

"Don't laugh at his stupid jokes!" she says.

We go to the back of my house so it looks like we're going inside. But instead we take the side street to Brock's.

We ring the doorbell. Brock answers.

"What's up?" he says.

Carolyn wastes no time. "Listen, Brock, we have a really important job for you. We need you to go look for something in Darleen Linden's pantry."

"Whoa," he says, taking a step back. "That's like breaking and entering. I don't do that stuff anymore."

"That's not what we mean! You have to find an excuse, maybe something having to do with pet-sitting."

"No can do," Brock replies, shaking his head.

"Cindy will help you with your math homework," Carolyn says, pointing to me.

Brock considers this while I focus every ounce of my willpower on keeping a straight face and not kicking my best friend in the shins.

"Deal," he finally says. "What do I have to do?"

Carolyn hands him the list. "Let us know if she has these items in her pantry. We'll explain later. And do not tell anyone about this!"

"Okey-dokey," Brock says. "My lips are sealed."

As we walk down the driveway, I turn to Carolyn. "What was that about me helping him with math homework? Did you just throw me under the car?"

She smiles smugly. "The correct expression is 'throwing someone under the *bus*.' And yes, I did."

PLEASE ASK ME ABOUT CAMELS INSTEAD

My dad's daily routine: wake up, start arguing with my mom, look at the want ads for jobs, ask me to address more envelopes (if there are any new ads), continue arguing with my mom, ask me to put stamps on the envelopes, ask me to put letters in the mailbox (I say a little prayer before I drop them in), go to bed. Repeat the next day.

The bickering usually starts because my mom tells my dad that he shouldn't listen to the radio so much. She is right, but my dad has nothing else to do. He says he wants to know the minute the hostages are released. On weekdays, the world news on TV doesn't come on until the evening, but the radio has news all the time. That's why it's on all day.

My dad hasn't heard back from any of the employers we've sent resumes to.

Things were so much better before, when no one knew where Iran was and everyone asked us if we rode camels.

GO, BROCK

During lunch on Monday, we look for Brock. We find him in his usual spot by the flagpole, surrounded by his jerky friends. "Hey, Brock," Carolyn yells. "Come here a second."

His friends stop talking and stare at us. Brock starts walking over.

"Come here, Brockie-boo," one of the guys says in a high voice. "We love you, Brock."

"Smoochy smoochy, kissy kissy," another calls out.

Brock ignores them. "What is it?" he asks when he reaches us.

"First of all, your friends are idiots. Second, the time has come for us to put the Lindens' pantry plan into action. Meet us tonight in front of your house at eight p.m."

"Okey-dokey." He turns around and heads back to the flagpole. His friends start making loud kissing noises.

"It's a loser convention," Carolyn says to me.

"Totally."

That night, Carolyn and I go to Brock's. My parents wanted to know why we were going out so late, so I told them we had a science project about stars. It's not like telling the truth was an option.

Brock is already waiting for us on his porch. Alone in the dark, he looks different from when he's surrounded by his posse of nitwits.

"Hey," he says.

"Hey, you ready?" Carolyn asks.

Brock nods and joins us in the driveway. We start walking toward Cindy's house. The darkness is interrupted by the glow of the streetlamps. There's no one out but us. People seem to go to bed very early in my neighborhood.

"So, Brock, what exactly are you going to say?" Carolyn asks.

"Just chill and trust me. There's a method to my madness."

"You don't even know what that means." Carolyn laughs.

"Do too," Brock responds. "It's from *Hamlet*. And I don't mean the chill part, although Shakespeare was definitely chill."*

"There is no way you have read *Hamlet*," Carolyn insists.

"Didn't say I did. It's on my mom's coffee mug," Brock replies with a flip of his hair.

---

* Note to Shakespeare: You are very chill in Iran, too.

When we arrive at the Lindens', Carolyn and I hide behind the hedge near my house, while Brock goes up and knocks on the door. I feel nervous and excited, but mostly nervous. I have only seen Cindy's parents in the pictures in their house, and now here I am, spying on them.

Cindy's mom opens the door and Brock says, "Hello, Mrs. Linden. Let me first say how sorry I am about the passing of J. Edgar Hoover. He was a fine hamster."

"How did you know he died?" she asks, putting her hands on her hips.

Carolyn and I look at each other. "I knew we couldn't trust him," Carolyn whispers. "He's an idiot."

But Brock continues calmly. "I assumed the worst, since you didn't call me after the chocolate tragedy."

As soon she hears the word "tragedy," Mrs. Linden's expression softens. "Oh, honey, you have no idea! It was the most painful thing. Poor J. Edgar. Now of course Dotty is all alone in her cage. She's just sitting by the hamster wheel, waiting. It's like *Romeo and Juliet* but worse."

"That's why I'm here," Brock says. "I would like to offer you one free hour of playing with Dotty the next time you go out. It's my way of helping you both move on."

"That is just so darn sweet of you, Brock," Mrs. Linden says. "How about tomorrow after school? Cindy will be at the stables and I have a hair appointment."

"Deal," Brock says with a grin.

"Maybe his brain isn't so waterlogged after all," Carolyn whispers.

We sneak around the back of my house and meet Brock on the sidewalk in front of the Kleins', where Mrs. Linden won't see us. He holds up his hand triumphantly, and Carolyn and I both give him a high-five.

"I'll have a full report for you on Wednesday morning at school, Mr. Holmes," he says to Carolyn. Then he turns to me.

"And I'll see you in the library Wednesday at lunch, Watson. I have a math test on Friday."

COWBOYS AND IRANIANS

On my walk to school the next morning, I see a car with a bumper sticker that says IRANIANS: GO HOME! I read it twice, because I'm sure I must be wrong. I have never seen such a thing. I want to see what the driver looks like. What kind of a person puts such a hateful bumper sticker on his car? Two minutes later, I see one that says, I PLAY COWBOYS AND IRANIANS. My heart starts racing. *What is going on? Is this allowed in America?*

"Where are all of these anti-Iranian bumper stickers coming from?" I ask Mrs. Williams as I'm studying at Carolyn's that afternoon. Mrs. Williams is reading the newspaper at the dining room table while we do our math.

"Some people are just out to make a buck, and this is a horrible way to do it. Try not to take it personally," she replies, looking up from the paper.

"It's hard," I admit.

"Believe me, the day after the last day of the world, there will be someone selling bumper stickers that say I SUR-VIVED THE LAST DAY OF THE WORLD," Mrs. Williams tells me.

"People will put anything on a bumper sticker if they think someone will buy it."

"I just hope the hostages are freed soon." I sigh. "I don't like everyone hating Iranians."

"Not everyone hates Iranians," she assures me, putting down the paper. "People who hate just happen to be the loudest."

IF ONLY YOUR ACCENT WERE FRENCH, OR ENGLISH, OR ANYTHING ELSE

My dad still has not gotten any responses to the resumes he sent out. He telephoned a bunch of the companies to follow up, and they all said, "Don't call us, we'll call you."

I don't think anyone is going to hire him. Who in the U.S. is going to hire an Iranian now, especially one with a thick accent? I can never say this to him, though. I don't think he gets how bad it is.

Dr. Klein came over last week and asked my dad if there was anything he could do to help him find a job. My dad gave him five copies of his resume.

BROCK ROCKS

Wednesday morning before the bell rings, Brock comes looking for us. "So, I went to Mrs. Linden's yesterday, and guess what? She has the stuff on your list. It's all in her pantry." Before we can say anything, he continues, "Hey, Cindy, instead of math, can you help me with my essay on *Of Mice and Men*? I haven't finished the book yet. There aren't a lot of mice in it so far."

"Sure," I say, glancing sideways at Carolyn.

"Stupendous! I'll see you at the library at lunch," he says.

"This is your fault," I whisper to Carolyn as Brock turns around to leave.

"I know," she replies, smiling as she hurries away to her homeroom.

So Darleen Linden is the culprit. It's hard to wrap my mind around this. How could an adult do something like that? Though her behavior explains a lot about Original Cindy. I'm unsure what to do next. During our next class together, I tell Carolyn I have to think about it for a few days.

At lunchtime, Brock is already in the library when I

arrive. For some reason, I'm really nervous. I rub my sweaty palms on my pants.

"Hi, Brock." I sit down across from him.

"Hey, thanks a lot for writing my essay."

"Wait a second. I didn't say that I would write your essay. I'm going to *help* you. When is it due?"

"Friday."

"Finish the book today and I'll come to your house tomorrow after school. I'm not writing your essay for you."

"Whatever," he says, looking disappointed.

"And let me give you one hint: It's not about mice."

"I was beginning to think so. Is it a metaphor?" he asks.

I'm stunned. "You know what that means?"

"Yeah."

I'm not sure if I should say what I'm thinking. I decide to go for it.

"You know something? You are so much smarter than you act."

Brock just stares at me with a funny look on his face. He doesn't say anything.

"I gotta go," I mumble. I push my chair away from the table and hurry out of the library. I shouldn't have said that.

OF MICE AND MEN
AND METAPHORS

The first thing that pops into my head when I wake up the next morning is that I'm going to Brock's after school. I have butterflies in my stomach. Maybe it's because this is the first time I'm going to a boy's house alone. I'm not telling my parents. There's no way they would let me go.

I come home after school, drop off my stuff, and tell my mom I'm going for a bike ride.

"Good," she says. "It'll make you taller."

Whatever.

I ride to Brock's, which takes less than three minutes. I lean my bike next to his gate and ring the doorbell.

Skip answers. "Hi there, Cindy!" he says enthusiastically. "I hear you're helping the Brockmeister with his essay. That's awfully nice of you."

"Sure thing." I don't mention that I am doing this because Brock helped us solve the mystery of the dead hamster.

Skip leads me to the dining room. The first thing I see is a huge clock in a shape of a boat's helm on the wall. On either side there is an oar. Just as I notice the huge marlin on another wall, Skip yells, "Brock, your teacher's here!"

I blush.

Brock comes down the stairs. "Hey, Cindy."

"Hey."

"I'm gonna leave you two to work here in the dining room," Skip announces. "Cindy, let me know if you want something to drink." He turns around to leave, then stops. "You know, if someone had told me that Brock would have such a smart friend, I would have said, 'That'll happen when pigs fly.' I guess pigs are flying now!" He laughs as he leaves the room.

"My dad's so weird," whispers Brock. "He calls all my friends blockheads."

"So how come your dad's home at this time of the day?" I ask, wondering if Skip has also lost his job.

"He owns the golf shop at Fashion Island, Bye-Bye Birdie, so he's home a lot."

"You're lucky."

Brock shrugs.

"Okay, let's get started. Did you finish the book?"

"Yup."

"What did you think?"

"Most depressing book ever. I had to go surfing this morning to get it out of my system."

"You went surfing *this* morning? *Before* school?"

"Yeah. Best time to go."

"What do you mean, 'to get it out of my system'?"

"You just get on a wave. Sadness goes away. I mean, you

can't be sad and surfing at the same time. You just wanna hold on to that, but you can't. You gotta keep going back."

I pause for a moment, thinking of sailing at Camp White's Landing. It seems like so long ago now. "I know exactly what you mean."

We sit in awkward silence. There are sides to Brock that are just as hidden as his eye.

"Okay, now the essay," I say, trying to change the mood. "Which essay question did you choose to write about?"

"I picked the metaphor theme. I went with how Steinbeck uses the dead mouse and the dead puppy as metaphors for George and Lennie's dreams dying."

"Wow. That's great." I hadn't even thought of that myself. "So what do you need help with?"

"I don't know. I guess I just wanted to run this by you—you being a brainiac and all." He hands me a piece of paper with neat writing covering both sides.

I read his essay. It's really good.

"I wouldn't change a thing. You're smarter than you think, Brock. I mean, you picked a harder essay question than I did."

"I don't know."

"It's true. You just hang out with a crowd that thinks being smart is not cool."

"So I should hang out with you and Carolyn?" he asks, smiling. I can't tell if he's joking.

"Yeah. You should." As soon as the words come out of my mouth, I think I shouldn't have said them. Why does this keep happening to me when I talk to Brock? "I gotta go," I say, standing up quickly.

"Thanks, Cindy," he says, following me to the entryway.

I open the door. Before I leave, I pause. "I didn't even help you. Your essay's really good," I say, without looking back. I need to avoid another awkward moment. There have already been too many.

I walk my bike back home so I have a few extra minutes to think. If Steinbeck's dead animals are a metaphor for dead dreams, what is the meaning of the dead hamster in my life?

A REAL DRIP

Saturday morning, my mom wakes me up in a panic. "Zomorod! Help! Come!" I run downstairs. There's a small pond in our kitchen. "Your dad is out putting air in his tires. Call the plumber!"

Since I'm the only person in my house who knows how to use the yellow pages, it's always my job to look up phone numbers. I find the plumber who advertises for emergency repairs on weekends and call him. He says he can come right away. I help my mom put towels on the kitchen floor, then get dressed.

Twenty minutes later, someone rings the bell. I open the door. It's the plumber. He's wearing a T-shirt that says WANTED: IRANIANS FOR TARGET PRACTICE.

I freeze. I don't know what to do. Is he going to hurt us? Should I call the police? Why is my dad inflating the tires today?

"Are y'all gonna let me in?" he asks.

"Yes, yes," I say automatically.

I show him to the kitchen. My mom has gotten off the couch and is following us. I need to warn her not to talk. I know she can't read his T-shirt.

The plumber pushes the fridge away from the wall, looking for the source of the leak.

"*Maman, goosh kon,*" I whisper.

Mom, listen.

"*Chera enghadar yavash harf meezani?*" she asks loudly.

Why are you talking so softly?

The repairman pokes his head out from behind the fridge.

"Hey, where you folks from?"

My mom and I say nothing for what seems like an entire minute. Then my mother breaks the silence.

"Tore-key."

The repairman goes back to his work. I breathe again.

I can't believe what just happened. My mother, who's never learned English, said the right thing. I'm pretty sure she saved us.

I keep quiet because the man is still in our house and he is way bigger than we are and he's wearing a toolbelt.

He replaces the leaky pipe and my mother pays him. He leaves. I've never been so relieved in my life.

I don't ask my mom why she lied and said we were from Turkey. I'm just glad she did.

None of this will be mentioned to my father. He doesn't need to know.

THE PLAN

Neither Carolyn nor I have said anything to anyone about Mrs. Linden. For once, Carolyn's not sure what to do either. She has not been her usual self lately. At lunch, she usually laughs and jokes, but now if we're with Rachel and Howie, Carolyn barely says anything. If we're alone, she talks nonstop about prejudice in America.

I assume Mrs. Linden is one of those people who can't find Iran on a map and who thinks we live in tents with no running water and like to take hostages as a hobby. My dad says that people like that are not truly horrible; they just need a geography class, a passport, and a few foreign friends.

Carolyn keeps talking about a program she saw on public television about Irish immigrants in the 1920s. She tells me that some American businesses put up signs in store windows saying NINA, which meant "No Irish Need Apply." "Your dad not being able to find a job, plus Mrs. Linden's actions, make me think that there is something bigger going on here. We need to do something about it. It's like those horrible signs are being recycled sixty years later, but now it's 'No Iranians Need Apply.'"

"So I guess people from countries starting with *I*

shouldn't come here," I joke, trying to distract her from her mission.

"That's not something to joke about," she says. "We must *do* something."

All of a sudden I remember that Carolyn had, for her first Halloween costume in elementary school, dressed up as Eleanor Roosevelt. I hadn't thought about it much when she told me, but now it makes perfect sense. Even as a little kid, she wanted to change the world for the better.

"Look, Carolyn, Darleen Linden is on the board of our condo association, *and* she's our next-door neighbor. She might get my family kicked out. My dad's already without a job. Please, please don't say anything," I beg.

"She can't get your family kicked out, and we need to report her," Carolyn insists.

"If she does one more thing, we'll report her, okay?"

"You're not reacting like an American," she says.

"Maybe it's because I'm *not* American," I remind her. "I grew up in a country with a secret police and a monarchy."

"Fine," Carolyn says with a sigh, "but you are making a big mistake."

A HAM FOR A TURKEY

Hansen's Supermarket is where all the rich and beautiful people buy their groceries in Newport Beach. The store and parking lot are decorated with huge planters that are regularly changed before a single flower wilts. The people who shop there make an equal effort to stay forever young.

Before every holiday, Hansen's has drawings for free gifts: a heart-shaped box of chocolates for Valentine's Day, a turkey for Thanksgiving, and the famous Hansen's Honey and Nutmeg Ham for Christmas. You don't have to buy anything to enter the drawing, and everyone I know signs up for every contest. It was a shock to realize that even people who can afford to valet-park their cars at the supermarket sign up for a chance to win a free turkey.

That weekend, lying on the floor in my room, I start thinking about Cindy's mom and how horrible she has been to us. I try to imagine what it might feel like to be her, to be someone who lives in fear of anyone who doesn't look like her or dress like her or eat the same foods. Then, as I'm thinking about food, I get an idea. But not just any idea. Like the Grinch's, it's a wonderful, awful idea.

I find the *Rules for Condominium Living* binder and take the phone from the hallway into my bedroom. I shut the door and dial the Lindens' number. I figure Cindy is at the stables, so chances are her mom will answer.

She picks up. I take a deep breath and say, in my most enthusiastic game-show-host voice, "May I please speak to Darleen Linden?"

"This is she."

"Congratulations, Darleen Linden! You are the lucky winner of this year's Hansen's Honey and Nutmeg Ham, featuring our own secret recipe that's been in the Hansen family for three generations." I had read that on their advertising flyers.

"But I didn't enter this year," she says.

"Well, Ms. Linden," I continue, trying to think quickly, "we keep all the names and numbers from previous years, so I assume you entered for something at some time."

"Well, come to think of it, yes, I have." She sounds quite excited. "This year alone, I entered the giveaway for the Fourth of July Stick-It-to-Me Rib Basket, the fall I'll-Have-Another-Butter-Cookie Extravaganza, the Halloween Death-by-Chocolate Candy Coffin, and of course the Thanksgiving Turkey with All the Trimmings. I meant to enter for the Honey and Nutmeg Ham as well, but I forgot. I never thought I would win! I guess good things do happen to good people."

I can't believe she's falling for this.

"Please come by tomorrow between three and four and ask for the manager," I say quickly, before I lose my nerve. "And thank you for shopping at Hansen's."

"Thank *you!*" she says. "I can't wait!"

The next day, I'm at Hansen's Market at two forty-five, pretending to be looking at the magazines in the front of the store. I didn't tell Carolyn about this. I know what she would say. "This is a terrible idea and you shouldn't do it." And she's right. I'm nauseated and sweaty. Mrs. Linden and I have never met, but what if she recognizes me somehow? This is the absolute worst thing I have ever done in my entire life. Right when I start thinking about how awful it would be if I get caught, she walks into the store, her hair in a towering bouffant. I recognize her instantly from the photos in Original Cindy's living room.

She click-clacks in her high heels to the customer service station and asks for the manager. While she's waiting, she tucks in a few strands of hair that have somehow escaped her unmoving helmet of a coif.

"May I help you?" asks the manager.

"Well, yes, I'm Darleen Linden and I'm here to pick up my ham," she says, flashing a big smile.

"If you ordered a ham, you may pick it up at the deli counter," the manager informs her.

"No, I'm the winner of the Christmas ham drawing," Mrs. Linden says, still smiling.

The manager looks confused. "But, ma'am, that's not until next week."

Mrs. Linden shifts her weight from one high-heeled shoe to another. "Well, I received a phone call from the store yesterday saying that I had won a ham and that I should pick it up today."

The manager's brow furrows. "Well, let me see what I can do. Can you please wait a moment?" she asks, and disappears into the back.

While she's waiting, Darleen glances around the store, as if looking to see if anyone she knows is watching.

The manager comes back with an older man, who looks flustered. Mrs. Linden's smile fades. He says, "Ma'am, I'm sorry about this, but there must have been some kind of mistake. I assure you, as general manager of Hansen's, that no one called you from this store yesterday. Our drawing is not until next week."

"This is unacceptable!" Mrs. Linden shouts, definitely no longer smiling. "One of your employees called me yesterday and told me to come today between three and four to pick up my ham. I will not leave without my ham."

The managers look at each other. "Please allow us to offer you a free cake from our bakery," the general manager says, pointing to the display case in the back of the store.

"I don't *want* a cake," she says, raising her voice even more. "Any half-brained dimwit knows how to bake a cake. I want my ham."

A small crowd starts to gather around her, drawn by all the yelling. I put down the magazine I have been pretending to read and join the onlookers.

"Ma'am, we're so sorry, but we cannot give a ham to everyone who claims to have received a phone call from us," the general manager says. "Would you like me to walk you to our bakery, where you can select any one of our—"

"Are you calling me a LIAR?"

"No, ma'am. We are merely trying to—"

Mrs. Linden takes one step closer to him. Waving her long, manicured finger in his face, she says, "Listen to me and listen to me good—"

But before she can finish, a security guard grabs her arm.

"This way, please," the guard says. Judging by the look of excitement on his face, it is fair to assume that this is the most action the Hansen's security team, which consists of one elderly gentleman, has ever seen.

"Let me go!" screams Mrs. Linden at the top of her voice. By then, the entire store is watching the drama unfold.

"Not without my ham!" she shrieks as she is led out of the store.

The crowd stays by the door for a while, everyone talking about the "crazy lady demanding a ham."

I go to the deli section and buy a turkey sandwich with cheddar cheese, lettuce, and tomato, along with a bag of barbecue potato chips. I owe it to Hansen's. I feel bad that the managers had to go through that, and I actually feel bad for Darleen Linden, too. She seems like such a sad person.

I'm walking to school thinking about my upcoming math test when I hear someone calling my name. I turn around and see Brock waving to me from his bike. I wave back. As soon as he catches up, he gets off his bike and walks next to me.

"Hey, I just wanted to tell you that I got an A on my English paper," he said.

"That's great! But I'm not surprised."

"Yeah, so thanks a lot for your help," Brock adds.

"I didn't do anything."

"Yeah, but you said something about me not acting as smart as I am, and, I don't know . . . My dad always says that too."

"Your dad's right," I say. "You understood that book better than I did. Do you like to read?"

"Sometimes."

"I can recommend some books to you, if you want."

Brock says nothing. Why did I say that? I'm such a *Dorkus maximus*.

"Maybe," he finally answers.

"You don't have to," I add.

"Well, I gotta go." He climbs back on his bike and starts pedaling quickly.

"Okay, bye!" I yell.

Brock rides without his hands on the handlebars. I never learned how to do that.

Everyone who can leave Iran is now leaving. The government does not allow Iranians to take money or jewelry out of the country, so we hear all kinds of crazy stories about people sewing their gold coins and jewelry in their children's stuffed animals, or even hiding them in fake casts. Some people get away with it; others are caught and punished. Those who succeed in bringing their jewelry sell it in America and use the money to rebuild their lives.

Even though we're living here, our family, home, and belongings are still in Iran. My dad keeps telling me that we're safe, but I'm not sure I believe him. My dad doesn't always tell me the truth if the truth is scary.

Two of my uncles are trying to come to America. They don't feel safe anymore. Like most doctors in Iran, they are rich—not because they were dishonest, but because they worked hard their entire lives. But the new Iranian government thinks that anyone who got rich under the shah's regime is corrupt and must be punished. Bank accounts and homes are still being taken away, and hundreds of high-ranking Iranians who had worked with the shah continue to be arrested and killed without trial. One of my uncles told my dad that names of streets and institutions are being changed to honor the Islamic Revolution. Farah Pahlavi University, named after the shah's wife, is now Al Zahra University, after the Prophet Mohammad's daughter. My dad says that the new government is trying to erase history. But he didn't say that on the phone with my uncle; someone from the government could have been listening and he didn't want to get my uncle in trouble. My uncle didn't seem to care if anyone was listening on the line. He even said that the fire at the Cinema Rex in Abadan, the one that killed about five hundred people last summer, was actually set by Khomeini's supporters. He said they blamed it on the shah so they could get the revolution going. Then he swore at Khomeini. My dad told him to be quiet and not to say stuff like that on the phone.

The Iranians who come to America have plenty of worries too. Our phone rings all the time with calls from newly arrived families who have questions about living in this foreign country.

The mothers want to know about American kids and drugs and alcohol. My mom tells them that there are many good, kind families here, and that I have all sorts of friends who do well in school and who would never use drugs and alcohol. "You just don't see the good American kids on TV," she assures them.

I can't believe this is my mom talking, the same one

who's been depressed forever. If you didn't know her, you'd think she's the most well-adjusted foreigner in America. Maybe it's because everyone seems to think she's an expert on something now. Or maybe it's because she has people to speak Persian with again.

Listening to her tell yet another newly arrived Iranian that it's really not so bad here, I know I have done the right thing by not telling my mom about the hamster and the note. It would have ruined America for her.

I'm doing my homework at the kitchen table when I hear someone knock. I answer the door. It's Brock.

"Hi," I say, hoping I don't sound as surprised as I feel. I wish I weren't wearing sweatpants.

"Hi, Cindy. Hey, I'm going to Mexico with my dad and he told me to bring a book. Remember when you said you had some to recommend?"

"Yeah, but . . ." I suddenly can't think of a single book I have ever read. "Can you wait a minute?"

"Sure," he says.

I run upstairs and scan the two piles of books stacked on the floor. I grab the one on top and run back down.

"Here you go." I hand him my dog-eared copy of *Roll of Thunder, Hear My Cry.* "You'll love it."

Brock examines the front and back cover. "Looks good. Thanks." He turns around and leaves.

I was hoping he would ask me to tell him something about the book. It would have been nice to chat a little longer.

We're sitting on the sofa, watching the news, as usual. The shah has been kicked out of the U.S. to Panama. We are sure the hostages will be freed now. After all, the shah's coming to the U.S. was the excuse the kidnappers gave for taking hostages in the first place.

My dad, shoulders hunched, mumbles something to himself. I lean closer. "I never, in my whole life, thought I would be without a job," he mutters.

I've never been so sad for my father. I want to say something to make him feel better, like he's always tried to do with me.

"Are you afraid of never having a job again?" I ask him.

"Afraid? No, no. Everything is fine," he says, sitting up straight.

We both know he's lying. No one has called him yet for an interview. He's sent out forty-eight resumes. I have said forty-eight prayers.

Then, maybe to prove that he isn't worried, he suddenly insists we go to Sears to buy a new bedroom set. My mom says she doesn't feel like going. Neither do I.

"I am perfectly fine sleeping on the floor," I say.

"It's not right," he insists. "Let's go."

Shopping at Sears is not as much fun this time. I end up buying a bed made of fake wood that looks real from far away. Up close, I can see some of the veneer peeling away on the floor model, but I don't say anything. The bed has three drawers under it, so I don't need a dresser. My dad says he's really sorry that we can't buy the whole bedroom set, but since he's not working anymore, we can only spend what I made when I sold my old furniture. I assure him that I don't want the whole set because it would make my room seem smaller. That is a lie, but technically, it doesn't count as one because I said it to make my dad feel better.

Then he starts swearing at the hostage takers and the revolution, right there in the Sears showroom. He's just standing there, surrounded by bedroom sets, swearing in Persian. The salesman is staring at him. So is a couple standing nearby with their two children. I've never seen my dad act this way, and it scares me. I start to cry. I want all these people to know that my dad doesn't usually act like this. He's a really good human being. He's honest and he's always worked hard, ever since he was fourteen. He is the most generous and kind person I have ever known. But his life has been ruined now. And it's not his fault.

My dad sees me crying and comes over and puts his arm around me. "Let's go," he says.

We don't say anything on the way home. We drive in silence and pretend none of that just happened. That's how we are.

Christmas vacation at our house is always a dud because we don't celebrate the holiday or exchange gifts or bake cookies. But this Christmas makes the other years look like explosions of joy. My home is possibly the most depressing place on earth. All the programs on television are about the hostages and their families. My dad spends the entire day in front of the TV, swearing. My mom cries every morning, saying she is embarrassed to be Iranian. My dad says that at least when the shah was in power, Iranians were not hostage takers.

I want my dad to have a job *so* badly. That is my Christmas wish, even though technically I can't make a Christmas wish because I'm not Christian. But it's not like there is a huge difference between me, Rachel, and Carolyn, even though we belong to three different religions. We are alike in so many more ways than we are different.

Even though the shah is no longer in the U.S., the hostages are not released. Current footage of some of them is shown on TV. Their families in the United States are also shown, praying for their safe return. They all look like average families you see at the grocery store. There is a little girl named Marci who looks just like me. Her brother is one of the hostages and she says how much she misses him. Then the family shows his photo. He looks so young. My mom and I both start to cry. My dad swears and turns off the TV.

ROLL OF THUNDER, HEAR MY THANKS

We're in the middle of dinner when the doorbell rings. I'm almost done eating, so I get up to answer. It's Brock.

"Hi, Cindy. Thanks." He hands me back the book I loaned him.

"So you liked it?"

"Oh, yeah. The Logans are kind of amazing."

"Yeah, they are."

"Oh, and I brought you this." He reaches in his pocket and hands me a seashell. "It's from the beach I went surfing at in Mexico."

I hold the shell with both hands. "Wow, thank you."

Right then, my father shows up.

"Hello, young man," he says, glaring at Brock.

"Oh, hello." Then he turns to me. "Well, I should go."

"Bye," I say.

My dad shuts the door quickly. "That boy needs a haircut."

"I don't think so," I mumble, holding the seashell carefully in my hand.

I can't believe the hostages have not been released yet. Every single evening on *Nightline,* I hear that count and I hate it. It tells us how many days the hostages have been held captive. I want to hear Ted Koppel say, "Today, the hostages were freed. No more tally."

Before we know it, it is Day 67.

Day 67! I remember when it was Day 14 and my parents and I kept saying, "Two *weeks!*" And now it's been three *months.*

Tonight, *Nightline* is showing the two female hostages, Ann Swift and Kathryn Koob. The hostage takers think all the Americans are spies. These two, with their big glasses and gentle voices, look and sound like librarians—sweet librarians who help children find the right book.

Kathryn Koob looks straight in the camera, smiles, and says, "And the only reason I'm losing weight, Mother, is because I decided that was one thing I could do while I was here."

What a practical person! Most of the women in Newport

Beach are constantly trying to lose weight, and here is this hostage, finding humor in a horrible situation and trying to keep her family from worrying. I imagine she must be funny and practical in real life, too.

The program also shows some Christian religious leaders who have visited the hostages. The Iranian government is allowing the visits so the world can see that the Americans are in good shape and have not been mistreated. They also show a table full of fruit and sweets the government has provided to give the impression that the hostages are being treated like guests. My dad says, "If those hostage takers are so humane, why don't they release them?" Once more, my mom and I start to cry. He swears and turns off the TV again.

Since it doesn't look like my father will be finding a job anytime soon, I decide to get one myself. I had hoped to work as a CIT at Camp White's Landing this summer, but since that doesn't pay, I have to look elsewhere. I still babysit once in a while but not as much as I used to. David has a bunch of after-school activities that will continue into the summer, so Mrs. Klein doesn't need me as often. Plus, a dollar an hour doesn't add up to much. Carolyn was right.

Carolyn tells me that the only place that hires twelve-year-olds is the *Daily Lighthouse,* the local free paper that is delivered three times a week. It covers groundbreaking neighborhood news ranging from "It's Not Just a Rumor! New Flavor at Sorrenson's Ice Cream Shoppe!" to "Local Man Shares Memories from Car Trip Through Iowa." There are classified ads for everything from boats for sale to people looking for pet sitters. All the area restaurants print coupons in it. For example, "Free soda with purchase of three tacos." We used that one a lot when my dad had a job and we ate out once a week. The *Daily Lighthouse* is also very popular with cat owners. It's the perfect size for lining litter boxes.

• • •

Carolyn gives me the number I'm supposed to call for the job. A guy named Chuck answers.

"Good afternoon. My name is Cindy and I would like to apply for a job delivering the paper."

"Do you have a bike?" Chuck wants to know.

"Yes."

"What's your address?"

"12514 Vista del Oro, Newport Beach."

"Hot diggity dog! We need someone in that neighborhood. The job is yours."

"Is that it?" I ask.

"Listen, Sandy, the turnover is very high in this job."

"My name's Cindy," I remind him.

"Cindy, Sandy, Mindy, Mandy. Same difference. All I need to know is that you're at least twelve and have a bike and two legs to pedal with. You make two ninety an hour, plus one cent for every advertising insert per paper. We deliver the papers and inserts to you. You fold 'em. You deliver 'em. It'll take you about two to three hours total. You keep track. It's not brain surgery. If you want the job, we'll deliver the papers to you tomorrow. You *can* start tomorrow, can't you?"

"Yes, yes."

Two ninety per hour is almost three times what I make babysitting, and that doesn't even include the inserts!

• • •

The piles of papers are already there when I get home from school. My mom doesn't like that they are taking up half the garage.

As soon as I finish my homework, I go into the garage to fold. There are four huge stacks of papers and eight stacks of inserts. I sit on the floor and put one of each insert (there are two today, an ad for El Rancho Market and coupons for Hot Dog Heaven) inside the newspaper, fold it, and stretch a rubber band around it. The bands are tight and thin and keep snapping on my fingers—and it hurts.

When it's finally time to deliver the papers, I put on the special vinyl delivery apron with the wrap-around pocket. It came with an instruction sheet on how to wear it, which says that the weight of the papers must be distributed evenly in the pocket. Since Chuck knows that he's not dealing with brain surgeons, there are also drawings illustrating the right and wrong way. The right way shows a kid smiling, as if there is nothing else he'd rather be doing than wearing a weird wrap-around apron and sitting on his bike. The wrong way shows a kid lying on his back on the sidewalk, arms stretched wide, with newspapers strewn everywhere. He looks like Humpty Dumpty.

I want to make sure I do this right, so I go inside to ask my dad for help. He's on the sofa listening to the radio.

He brings the radio with him to the garage, as if something important might happen in the next five minutes. I put on the apron and he stuffs as many papers as he can into the pocket. I try to get on my bike, but I'm feeling very wobbly. "This apron is too heavy," I say.

"Let me help you." My dad holds my bike steady while I climb on. "Just make sure you deliver an equal number from the front, back, and both sides. You need to maintain equilibrium," he advises. Suddenly, this seems way more complicated than I thought.

My dad pushes me down the driveway, and I'm off! I am now a paid employee, part of the American work force!

I grab the first paper from the front of the apron and throw it. No problem. I pull the second from the right side. This is easy. I reach for a paper in the back. It's packed in tight. I pull and pull real hard, steering with my left hand. The bike goes wobbly and I veer directly into Mrs. Harris's garden gnomes. Next thing I know, I'm on the ground, with papers all around me.

I am the second illustration.

My dad, who had been watching, runs to help. He pulls me up and we stuff the papers back in the apron. My elbow and hip hurt. But more than that, I am *so* embarrassed.

It takes me three hours to deliver all the papers. I'm exhausted, sweaty, and scraped up. I fell four times.

I know one thing now. Folding and delivering newspapers is a horrible job. When I get home after finally delivering the last pile, my dad says he will help me next time.

"Do you want me to drive you?" he offers.

"No, *Baba*. No one does that," I say. That would be even more embarrassing.

Two days later, my dad and I are back in the garage, determined to fold and deliver before dark. I look at him, wearing sweatpants, sitting on a box, folding newspapers as fast as he can. He should be at work, wearing a suit, sitting behind his desk, doing something that matters.

We're almost done when my mom appears in the doorway.

"Thank God you're finally not listening to the radio," she says to my dad.

"I can listen to the radio all day if I want," he snaps back.

In the same way that some animals can tell when a storm is coming, I can tell when a fight is about to happen.

A fight is about to happen.

Sure enough, a minute later, they're both yelling and screaming at each other. The garage door is wide open. They're arguing in Persian, but you don't need to understand a single word to know when people are fighting. Yelling is pretty universal. I hope the Lindens and the Kleins can't hear them.

I think the Kleins must have heard the fight, because the next day, Dr. and Mrs. Klein both come over. I answer the door with my parents.

They exchange hellos, and then Mrs. Klein gives my mom a fern.

"Thank you," she says. My parents do not invite them in like they usually do.

"Please let us know if there's anything we can do for you," Dr. Klein says. "We're very sorry that some Americans are treating Iranians poorly, and we hope that no one has mistreated you."

"Thank you, Davood," my father says. "Americans have always been good to us."

As soon as the neighbors leave, my parents start fighting again, this time about whether or not the Kleins heard their fight the day before. My home is like those stores that play background music, but instead of music, we have arguing.

I sneak upstairs to my room and shut the door. I can still hear them.

AiN'T IT AWFUL, FALAFEL?

I receive my first paycheck after two weeks: $49.00. It's in an envelope taped to the top of one of the stacks of newspapers.

I give it to my dad. He says he can't take it. I insist, and he finally accepts. I'm no longer saving for college. When you can't afford to eat out once a week, even with a free drink coupon, how are you going to pay for college? My parents and I haven't discussed this, but what's the point? My dad already had a meltdown in Sears when he couldn't afford to buy the nightstand that goes with my fake wooden bed. I can't imagine how he'd react if we talked about college tuition. It might kill him.

That evening, I'm delivering papers when I see Skip watering the plants outside his house. I've gotten much better at riding with the apron. I've only fallen two more times. I also know to avoid Mrs. Harris's garden gnomes and the Stuhlbargs' cactus plants, although some challenges remain.*

"Hi, Cindy," he says. "What's up, partner?"

---

* Note to the Nathans: I am truly sorry about the koi pond incident. I tried to fish the paper out. It sank really fast.

I stop. "Not much. Just delivering the paper."

"Hey, I think Brock mentioned that your family is from I-ran? Is that right?" he asks.

"Yes," I answer warily. I wish I hadn't stopped.

"I knew a guy in my dorm at USC who was from I-ran. I can't remember his name but he was real nice. He went back home after he graduated to run his dad's business. I wonder how he is now."

"I don't know," I say.

"I hope things are okay for your family."

"It's a scary time. We don't know what's going to happen," I admit.

"Ain't it awful, falafel?" Skip says, shaking his head. "We can only hope for the best."

I have never heard that expression. "What's a falafel?" I ask.

"I thought they were I-raynian! They're those little fried bean balls. I used to have them all the time at USC. Really good."

"They might have them in Iran, but I've never had one. It's not an Iranian food. Maybe it's originally from one of the Arab countries. Kinda like tacos in America are really from Mexico."

"I'll be darned!" Skip exclaims. "I thought I-ran *is* an Arab country."

"A lot of people think that, but it's not." I smile and start pedaling to the next house. "I gotta go deliver the papers now. See you soon, raccoon!"

I can hear Skip laughing as I wobble away.

GRAY SKIES

One morning during breakfast, we hear on the radio that President Carter had sent a secret rescue mission to Iran but the mission was unsuccessful. One of the helicopters crashed and eight American servicemen died. We are horrified.

I do not want to go to school.

At lunch, a group of eighth-graders come up to Carolyn, Rachel, and me in the cafeteria, surrounding us like vultures. They're huge. One of them points at me. "Hey, you need to free the hostages *now* or we're nuking I-ran."

I freeze.

I don't know what's going to happen next, but I'm hoping there's a grownup nearby who can help us, just in case.

"We should just nuke 'em now anyway," another one says, leaning in close to my face. I start to shake. They laugh and walk away, singing "Bomb, bomb, bomb, bomb I-ran." "Bomb Iran" is a really popular song on the radio these days. It sounds like the Beach Boys' "Barbara Ann," a song that I used to love.

"We need to tell the principal," Carolyn insists when they're gone.

"Let's not," I plead, still shaking.

"I agree with Cindy," says Rachel. "Even if those guys get detention, they'll just bug her more afterward."

"They don't even pronounce the name of the country correctly," Carolyn huffs. But thankfully, she lets it drop.

"Why did some idiot have to ruin that Beach Boys song?" says Rachel. "What do you think, Cindy?"

"I don't know."

What I really want to say is that I am *so* angry—at Khomeini and his stupid hostage takers, at the person who wrote that stupid song, and at all the Americans who can't even find Iran on a map but are so quick to declare everyone who's from there the enemy. But I'm afraid that if I start saying all this, I won't be able to stop and I'll end up like my dad in the Sears showroom. So I say nothing.

VALEDICTORIAN

I get an invitation in the mail to Matt's high school graduation party. He's the valedictorian, which means he got the highest grades out of everyone in his senior class and gets to give a speech at the commencement ceremony.

"I want to be valedictorian too," Carolyn announces.

I would also like to be valedictorian, but what's the point if I'm not going to go to college?

My parents buy a fancy pen for Matt. I think it's a terrible gift. What is the purpose of a fancy pen? A cheap one works just as well. "Every graduate needs a nice pen," my dad insists. Thankfully, the store had complimentary gift-wrap; otherwise, Matt would have been the lucky recipient of a present wrapped in "It's a Boy!" paper. I'm sure my dad would have said, *What's wrong with that? He* is *a boy.*

Carolyn's parents have decorated their house with appropriate streamers and balloons that have pictures of graduation caps on them. The paper plates and napkins have diplomas on them, and the balloons are gold and blue—the colors of UCLA, which Matt will be attending. There's a huge cake that says CONGRATULATIONS, MATT! on it. The house is filled with friends and neighbors who have known him since he was a little boy. This is what happens when you live in one place for more than a couple years; there are people in your life who have seen you grow up.

At the party, Matt thanks me for the gift. I'm not sure if he really likes it or is just being polite. In any case, I appreciate his manners.

"Even though you pestered me for the past two years, I'm glad you're Carolyn's friend," he says.

"Thanks." I suddenly feel shy and awkward with him, which is weird.

"And hang in there. Guys will eventually appreciate smart girls like you."

I blush and mumble something about having to go help Carolyn clean up.

That is the nicest thing a boy has ever said to me.

SUMMER OF '80

The summer before eighth grade is supposed to be one of the best times in a kid's life. I have heard people say this many times, both in real life and on TV. If this is the best time in my life, I'm doomed. My mom wears her pink terry-cloth robe morning to night, and my parents keep the curtains closed all day. Our house is like a tomb, and I'm trapped inside it.

I do not feel like hanging out with my friends at all this summer. Thankfully, Rachel is going away to attend music camp soon, Carolyn is taking tennis lessons five days a week at UC Irvine, and Howie is at church camp.

I look forward to delivering papers so I can spend time alone away from my parents. Other than that, I watch TV. I try to avoid the news as much as I can, since there is always something about Iran, and it is always depressing.

The first time Carolyn calls me, I tell her I'm sick.

The second time she calls, I say that I have to help my parents clean the house.

The third time, I tell her we're going on a road trip. She finally gives up.

THIRTEEN

It's my thirteenth birthday. I'm pretty sure my parents have forgotten, which is fine with me. I'm glad I didn't plan a party. Having to pretend that we're happy about something requires more energy than we have. We're sitting on the sofa watching TV when someone rings the bell. My parents are riveted to the screen, so I jump up and open the door.

"Surprise!" It's Carolyn and Rachel. Carolyn is holding a big bunch of red balloons that bob happily in the breeze, and Rachel has a fancy plate with strawberry shortcake, my favorite.

I know this should make me happy, but I regret having opened the door. I don't feel like celebrating. I wish they hadn't dropped by like this.

Before I can say anything, they hand me the balloons and a gift-wrapped box that Carolyn pulls from her back pocket. I know that I should ask them to come in and have a piece of cake with me, but my mom is wearing her pink terry-cloth bathrobe and our house is a mess.

"Thank you so much," I say quietly. "I'm sorry, but I have to go."

I close the door and walk back into the living room with the balloons and the gift. My mom starts crying as soon as she sees them. I usually ask what is wrong when she cries, but right now, I just don't feel like it. It's my birthday, and I would like one day off from worrying about my mom.

I go to my room and shut the door. I open the gift slowly.

It's a puka shell necklace. I put it back in the box and close the lid. I've wanted one for so long. I used to think that wearing a puka shell necklace would somehow mean that I was just like all the other kids. How stupid I was!

CURTAINS CLOSED

The next day, our bell rings again. I open the door.

"You wanna do something?" Carolyn asks.

"Sorry, but I'm busy."

"What are you doing?" she asks.

"Stuff."

"What kind of stuff?"

I never realized how annoying Carolyn can be.

"I'm doing Iranian stuff," I say.

"Well, I have a new Air Supply tape that you're gonna love." And with that, she lets herself into my dark home, uninvited. It's one in the afternoon and all the curtains are closed. I've gotten used to the lack of sunlight, but with the door open and Carolyn standing there, the place suddenly seems like a haunted house—a house filled with the ghosts of dead dreams.

My mom is lying on the sofa in her bathrobe, watching a soap opera. Her hair is a mess.

"Hi, Mrs. Yousefzadeh. Nice to see you again," says Carolyn.

"Hi," says my mother. She looks surprised to see another

human being. It's like I've broken an unspoken pact—no one shall enter this house—by letting Carolyn in.

I quickly take Carolyn to my room. I want her to see as little as possible of our messy downstairs. As soon as I shut the door, she says, "I know you're avoiding me. You keep saying you're busy all the time, but I know you're lying."

I'm too embarrassed to say anything. A part of me hates Carolyn at this moment. Another part of me thinks she is the best friend I have ever had.

I really do want to talk to her and tell her that we are running out of money, that I can't go to college anymore, about my mother's sadness that won't go away, about the people being killed in Iran for no reason, and about the scary stuff that my parents aren't telling me but that I know exists. I'm not sure she can understand, though. She's already heard more about me than anyone else, but I'm worried she's reached her limit. Her family is so normal. How do I explain my sad life to her?

But before I have a chance to say anything, Carolyn says, "We should totally go see *Fame* next week. It's playing at Fashion Island and it's supposed to be a really good movie."

"Yeah, totally," I say.

A part of me feels relieved that we're talking about something else. Another part of me knows I'm running away from something.

I'm folding papers with my dad a few days later, and he suddenly says, "Zomorod, remember that education can never be taken away from you." Then he wipes away a tear. It's the first time I have seen my dad cry in my whole life. I so badly want to make him feel better. I want that more than anything else in the whole world. When I go to hug him, he resists. He says something has just gotten in his eye. I know for sure that is not true.

UNCLE JAMSHiD'S
NEIGHBOR'S COUSIN

I come home from my paper route, tired as always, and go into the kitchen for a glass of water.

"Zomorod," my dad says as soon as he sees me, "I have great news."

"You got a job interview?"

"No, not that. But you know how you haven't gone shopping since I lost my job?" He pauses to swear at the hostage takers, then continues. "I just got off the phone with Bahman Mahdavi. Do you remember him? He was your uncle Jamshid's neighbor's cousin in Ahwaz. In any case, his wife, Shaghayegh—she goes by Shay-Shay now—loves to shop and is about the same size as you. She used to live in Paris. Bahman was just telling me that his wife has a closet full of clothes that she never wears, so I asked if she could give them to you. She said yes! They're coming here for dinner tomorrow night."

I have not seen my father so excited in a long time. I'm so happy to see him like this. And I'm looking forward to new clothes! I definitely need a new pair of jeans and some tops.

The Mahdavis arrive an hour late, carrying a huge baby-blue Samsonite suitcase. Shay-Shay is wearing some kind of animal print blouse with a different kind of animal print skirt, plus stacks of gold bracelets on each arm that jingle-jangle with every move she makes. I can't stop staring at her. She looks like a zebra mother and a leopard father's offspring who just robbed a jewelry store.

Mr. Mahdavi hands the suitcase to my father and tells him he wants it returned. He reminds my father two more times before dinner starts. The fourth time he mentions the suitcase, my dad takes it upstairs, dumps all the clothes in my room, and comes back down with it, saying, "Oh, Shay-Shay, you are so chic! How will we ever thank you?"

Iranians are gifted at gushing compliments. The problem is, you can never tell when they're true.

I cannot wait any longer, so I sneak upstairs for a peek at my new Parisian-inspired wardrobe. Although, having met Shay-Shay, I'm not as excited as I was before.

The first thing I pull from the pile is a sleeveless T-shirt, size XL, that says SEXY GRANDMA on it, in sequins.

I can't bear to look any further, so I go back downstairs. "Thank you, Shay-Shay. But I'm wondering about the sleeveless blue shirt that says 'Sexy Grandma' on it. You're not a grandmother, so why did you have this?"

Shay-Shay clasps her hands together and shakes them, sending her bracelets into a jingling frenzy. She lets out a booming laugh, as if the answer is so obvious. "Oh,

Zom-Zom," she says, making up a stupid nickname for me on the spot. "Those shirts were two for five dollars." She smiles magnanimously. "There's another one too, just like it, but in pink."

My life officially sucks.

That Saturday, Carolyn's mom picks me up so we can see *Fame*. She asks me how my parents are and I say fine, which really means *They're not fine but I don't want to talk about it*. I think she knows that.

"Carolyn, you have to promise me something," I say, to break the awkward silence that follows. "When you become a journalist, you have to report about normal people, too."

"What do you mean?"

"On the news, they only show the crazy Iranians, the ones who are shouting 'Death to America!' It gives the impression that *all* Iranians are like that. They don't show the normal ones. Americans don't even know we exist."

"I see. Yeah, I promise."

"There's an expression in journalism," Mrs. Williams says, looking at me in the rearview mirror. "'If it bleeds, it leads.' The more shocking a story, the more chance it has of being reported."

"But that's so wrong," I say. "Why let people only see the worst of the world? That's just upsetting and scary. It's not even the whole truth. If you're going to show bad news, show the good stuff, too. It's just as important—actually, *more* important."

"I agree. And if I ever report about Iran, I will interview you," Carolyn says.

"Only if I can wear my 'Sexy Grandma' T-shirt."

We both laugh. I'd told her about the suitcase of ugly clothes. It turned out the T-shirts were the cutest items in the entire pile. When I mentioned that Shay-Shay had lived in Paris, Carolyn said, "You know, there's a Paris in Missouri, too."

"Hey, when we get to the theater, do you want to split a jumbo popcorn?" asks Carolyn, changing the subject.

"Please don't!" Mrs. Williams exclaims.

"But, Mom, it comes with free refills."

"That's even worse," says Mrs. Williams. "If you were going to see *Fame* in Iran, you would not be buying jumbo containers of junk food, would you, Cindy?"

"We wouldn't be going to see *Fame* in Iran," I say. "That movie would be banned."

"That settles it. In honor of freedom, we shall eat popcorn!" Carolyn announces.

I laugh. Mrs. Williams gives us both a look that says, *I give up.*

JULY 27, 1980

The phone wakes me up. I look at my clock. It's four a.m. I know it's a relative from Iran. They usually get the time difference wrong and call at odd hours. I go to my parents' room.

My dad has picked up the phone. I hear him say, "Is this true, Fattolah? Is this true?"

He hangs up after only a minute. "The shah has died!"

I think I'm in shock. It sounds crazy, but you never think someone that powerful is going to die. He seemed so permanent. Maybe it's because his picture was everywhere: in all my textbooks, in all the banks, in all businesses.

My dad turns on the radio. My mom makes tea. I know none of us will be going back to bed. We're all worried. What now? We don't know and no one dares wonder out loud.

RiNG, RiNG, RiNG

Our phone is ringing, ringing, ringing. Every Iranian is talking about the same thing. If the shah had died while still in power, his memorial would have been a grand spectacle with pomp and circumstance. He would have been buried with great fanfare, in a tomb befitting a king. Kings and queens and presidents and movie stars from around the world would have flown in to pay their respects. The entire country would have shut down.

Who would have ever imagined that thousands of Iranians would be in the streets, not mourning him, but celebrating his death? And who would have believed that the shah's funeral wouldn't be in Iran?

Instead, his funeral is in Egypt, and the only head of state attending besides Anwar Sadat, the leader of Egypt, is the former and not-so-popular U.S. president Nixon.

The funeral is very fancy and Anwar Sadat says that Egypt will not turn its back on a friend.

When the shah was in power, all world leaders seemed to be his friend. But then when he lost power, everybody disappeared. I guess they weren't real friends. Maybe the shah wasn't theirs, either—who knows? I bet when you have power, a lot of people pretend to like you.

I can't imagine ever not being friends with Carolyn, Rachel, or Howie. I'm so glad none of us is rich or powerful. We're friends because we like each other and we have a lot of fun together. It must get complicated when people try to be close to you for the wrong reasons.

EiGHTH GRADE

It's the first day of eighth grade, my last year at Lincoln Junior High. My dad drops me off in the same spot he did two years ago. The sixth-graders, with their brand-new backpacks, look so tiny. I remember how scared I was of the eighth-graders back then. Now I'm one of them! I don't feel scary at all. I still feel scared. But not about school this time—about my family's future. My dad remains unemployed and I know we're running out of money. I've overheard my father say so to my uncles on the phone.

I didn't see Rachel or Howie all summer, except on my birthday when Rachel dropped by. But as soon as we got our class schedules in the mail, they called. Both said they missed me. It's true that they were busy with camp, but I also avoided them. I feel pretty bad about this. I only saw Carolyn because she wouldn't give up.

As I walk to my first class, I notice yellow ribbons have been hung all over the school. The ribbons represent the hostages. You see them all over town now; all over the country. My parents and I continue to watch *Nightline,* and Ted Koppel continues counting the days since the hostages were taken captive. It's been almost an entire year.

Carolyn, Howie, Rachel, and I are all on the advanced academic track, so we have a lot of classes together. A part of me is happy to see familiar faces, but another part of me wishes I could be like a turtle and go back in my shell.

In our Social Studies class, we talk about the upcoming presidential elections. Sherman Dorfman says that he doesn't think President Carter has a chance of winning reelection because of the hostages. I raise my hand.

Mrs. Cushner calls on me. I take a deep breath.

"My father lost his job because of the hostages." As soon as I hear my own words, I feel a huge lump in my throat.

"How so?" she asks.

"He was—" That's as far as I get. I start to cry.

"Oh, honey," Mrs. Cushner says, walking toward me.

"I'm fine," I say, wiping my nose with my sleeve. "I'm fine. My dad was working with a company that was building an oil refinery in Iran. Now that relations between America and Iran have been cut, my father has no job." I wipe my nose again on my other sleeve.

I look around the room. I'm still sniffling. I brace myself for rude comments. But the class is oddly quiet. Everyone is looking at me like they actually sympathize. I wonder if some of them have a parent who lost a job too. Maybe I'm not the only one.

"That's awful," Mrs. Cushner says. "Would you like to do a report on the current events there?"

"Can I do it after the hostages are released?" I remember that I had said the same thing to Mrs. Thompson last year. I never did the report.

"Sure," she replies.

The way things have been going, I might as well ask if I can do my report when pigs fly.

We spend the rest of class talking about Ronald Reagan, who is running against Jimmy Carter. Reagan used to be an actor, so some people don't think he's qualified. Others say anyone is better than Carter. I wonder what President Carter will do if he loses his job like my dad. I know he has a daughter that he loves too.

Carolyn's mom has suggested that instead of trick-or-treating, we can hand out candy. I don't like the idea, but Carolyn is very enthusiastic.

"I don't have a costume," I say, trying to find an excuse. I never thought the day would come that I would not be excited for Halloween.

"What about that suitcase full of clothes? How about we go as twin sexy grandmas?*

"And we can keep the leftover treats," she adds. She knows that candy works like bait for me.

"Fine," I say. "Sexy grandmas it is."

---

* Note to Shay-Shay: Sorry.

My dad drops me off at the Williamses' at five.

Carolyn opens the door. She's wearing the pink Sexy Grandma T-shirt with curlers in her hair and bright orange lipstick. I'm just wearing my shirt with jeans and tennis shoes.

"You look like a *crazy* grandma," I say, laughing. Of course she has found a way to make the costume even better!

"I'm pretty sure that any grandma who would wear this shirt would also be crazy," she says.

I go in, but before I have a chance to say hello to her parents, the doorbell rings. Carolyn grabs the huge bowl of candy and opens the door again.

"Trick or treat!" It's two angels and a cowboy, holding out their plastic pumpkins. The mom and dad are standing a few feet away, smiling.

"Here you go," says Carolyn, dropping a mini Reese's Peanut Butter Cup in each bag.

"Thank you!" they all say, and the kids turn around and run to the next house.

"Careful!" the mom yells. "Slow down!"

As soon as we shut the door, Carolyn offers me a piece of candy. "It's commission," she says. "We get to eat at least twenty percent."

We're only halfway through our third pieces of candy when the bell rings again. This time it's a group of ghosts with a grownup who's dressed as Khomeini. I stare at his mask a little too long. He notices. "Bomb I-ran!" he shouts, pumping his fist in the air. I know I should tell him something like, *That's not funny. You wouldn't laugh if someone said that about America,* but as usual, I chicken out. I say nothing.

Carolyn hands out candy to the ghosts, then says, "No candy for you!" to Khomeini and shuts the door.

"What a jerk," she says.

We give out candy for another hour, and then the older kids start to come. It seems like every fourth kid is dressed as Khomeini. I no longer feel like doing this.

"Do you think your mom can drive me home now?" I ask.

"It's only seven!" Carolyn protests.

"I'm tired."

"It's all the Khomeinis, isn't it?"

"No," I lie.

"It's just a stupid costume."

"Okay, yes. It is all the Khomeinis. It makes me sad because this is all Americans know about Iran: Khomeini and hijabs."

"I know, but I already told you. When I become a journalist, I will report on other things about Iran. I promise."

"That's a long time from now."

"Didn't your dad say that he wishes you had freedom of speech in Iran? This is what it means. People have the freedom to wear stupid costumes. There are also Nixon, Ford, and Carter masks," Carolyn adds. She always has an answer for everything, and it can be so annoying.

"I guess."

Before I can say anything else, the doorbell rings again. "Trick or treat!" the kids scream. And we're back to being two sexy grandmas, all dolled up in sequins, giving out candy to princesses and vampires.

I feel a teeny bit better. For once, I told the truth about being sad. But I still hate those Khomeini masks.

I'm supposed to babysit for David for three hours while Dr. and Mrs. Klein go out to dinner for their anniversary.

"Guess what?" David asks as soon as I walk in.

"You built a bionic eye?"

"No, not yet. I got an origami book! Here, let's make some stuff," he says, heading to the dining room. I follow him.

The dining table, which normally holds two silver candle holders and nothing else, is now strewn with papers folded into various shapes.

"I've been trying all day to make a jumping frog, but I can't get it right," David tells me. "My dad says I need to keep at it."

"That's good advice."

"He says if you want to achieve something, keep trying and you will eventually succeed," David adds.

"I hope so."

"Don't you know so?"

"Well, it's just that sometimes in life you follow instructions, but you still don't get what you want."

"Like your father not finding a job?" David asks.

"How do you know about that?"

"I heard my mom and dad saying stuff."

I can't believe the Kleins have been talking about my father being out of work. Even David knows.

"He's been trying to find a new one," I say.

"Are you going to help me with the frog or not?"

"Okay." But I can't concentrate. The directions are very complicated and my mind is elsewhere.

We spend the next hour attempting to make a jumping frog. The closest I get is a lopsided creature that doesn't jump. We finally give up and play Go Fish instead.

Ronald Reagan won the election by a landslide. He carried forty-nine of the fifty states. All the papers had predicted that Jimmy Carter would lose. People blamed him for the hostages and the failed rescue mission and the bad economy. I'm surprised they didn't blame him for the bad weather, too.

"Now the hostages will be finally released," my dad said tiredly when the results were announced.

But they're not.

The kidnappers are now asking for $24 billion! According to them, the U.S. is holding $14 billion in Iranian funds. They want that back, plus another $10 billion, which they claim the shah had in banks here.

I am beginning to wonder if this situation will ever end. It doesn't seem like it.

Christmas, 1980. Our house is the same as always. Messy. No decorations. No smells of home-cooked meals. Lots of cereal in the pantry.

We're on the sofa watching the news. It's Day 417 of the hostage crisis. Some of the hostages are shown again on TV, and Kathryn Koob, the same woman who joked with her mom about weight loss, asks her family to sing a Christmas song with her. She's wearing her glasses and looks quite slim. She starts to sing "Away in a Manger" in a soft, trembling voice. She sounds like she's trying hard not to cry, probably because she knows her family is watching. I imagine them, on the other side of the world, singing along through their own tears. How can they not be sobbing? My mom and I start to cry, and we don't even know her.

We seem to be stuck in some kind of depressing loop. Here's the recurring scene:

We watch the news.

My mom and I cry.

My dad swears.

The TV is turned off.

We all go to separate rooms.

THE FRENCH BOY

We're watching TV a couple of days later. The phone rings. It's Howie, sounding very excited.

"Hi, Cindy. Guess what? My mom got four tickets for *A Little Romance* on New Year's Eve. Do you want to go?"

"What is it?" I ask.

"It's a movie about an American girl in Paris who meets a French boy. It's supposed to be *really* good."

It's not as if I have any other plans. "Sure. I can go."

"Great! We'll pick you up at one o'clock for the matinee."

A few days later, Mrs. Howard drives me, Carolyn, Rachel, and Howie to the theater at Fashion Island. "Here's some money for snacks," she says to Howie as she drops us off. "I'll pick you up right here at three thirty."

"Your mom is so hospitable," I comment as we walk toward the snack shop.

"She's from the South," Howie says.

"Why does that make her hospitable?"

"That's what southerners are famous for. They like to feed people and take care of guests."

"Sounds like the South is the Iran of the U.S.," I say, laughing at my own joke.

We stand in line to buy snacks. Then, armed with a jumbo popcorn, two boxes of red licorice, and a package of chocolate raisins, we take our seats in the theater.

Two hours later, we walk out with our heads in the clouds.

"That was the best movie I have ever seen," Rachel declares.

"*The* best," says Howie, chewing on the last piece of licorice.

"I'm in love," announces Carolyn.

"So where in the world are there actually boys like that?" I ask.

"According to this movie, France," says Carolyn. "Or maybe there's even one here . . ." She turns to me. "Cindy, do you care to admit to your crush on Brock?"

"What?" I say, startled at the sudden turn this conversation has taken.

"Admit it. You have a thing for Brock," Carolyn insists.

"You do?" ask Howie and Rachel, in unison. "Brock Vitter?"

"No way! Carolyn's making stuff up."

"Cindy and Brock sitting in a tree, K-I-S-S-I-N-G," Carolyn chants.

"Stop it!" I beg.

"No, actually, it's more like, 'Cindy and Brock sitting in a tree, R-E-A-D-I-N-G.'" Carolyn can't stop laughing.

"It's not funny! And it's not true," I insist.

Thankfully, Rachel changes the subject. "But can you believe the part in the movie where Daniel and Lauren go to Venice alone? I mean, what thirteen-year-old is going to run away to another country?"

"Why not? What could go wrong?" asks Howie.

We all laugh, standing at the curb, waiting for Mrs. Howard to pick us up. I'm a little mad at Carolyn, though.

"Why can't there be more guys like Daniel?" Carolyn sighs. "My mom says boys mature much slower than girls, so we're doomed for now. But when they do finally catch up to us, I hope I meet one who is smart and kind and cute."

"And tall," adds Howie.

"And Jewish," says Rachel.

Right then, Mrs. Howard drives up.

"How was it?" she asks as we get in.

"Great, but now we all have to go to France to meet the perfect guy," Howie says.

Mrs. Howard laughs. "Maybe I should have bought tickets for *Rocky Two*."

"Somehow, I don't see any of us dating a boxer," Rachel jokes.

"Somehow, I don't see a boxer wanting to date any of *us*," adds Howie.

We giggle all the way home, talking about the boys at Lincoln Junior High. I'm the first to be dropped off.

"Thank you so much, Mrs. Howard," I say as I get out of the car. "And happy new year!"

"Bye!" they all call out in unison. "See you next year!"

As I walk into my house, my head is still in the clouds.

We're on the sofa again, this time watching Ronald Reagan's inauguration. He is sworn in as the fortieth president of the United States.

Right afterward, there is a special report. President Reagan is standing behind a podium. He speaks slowly. "Some thirty minutes ago, the planes bearing our prisoners left Iranian airspace and are now free of Iran." There is thunderous applause. The president looks like he's holding back tears. No one expected this!

I can't believe it. The day is finally here. There are more news reports, but I'm not listening. I look at my parents, who are staring at the TV screen. I can see that they can't believe it either. It's finally over!

"Thank God," my mother says, wiping away her tears.

During all those months of hoping and praying for the hostages to be released, I always imagined we would have a huge party to celebrate, and then the next day everything would go back to normal. But it's not turning out like that. Of course we're relieved that the nightmare is finally over, but we can't afford a party and our life is still a mess. Dad's still without a job. He's still swearing at the hostage takers under his breath. My country is still controlled by people who ban music and movies and who force women and girls to keep covered, and who still kill those who defy them. The damage they did will be with us for a long time. Our life is like a rubber band that has been stretched too many times. It can no longer snap back to normal.

That afternoon, my father calls me into the living room. He looks like someone has died. My mom is not there.

"Where's *Maman*?" I ask.

"She's upstairs. You and I need to talk." He pauses. "Zomorod, as you know, nobody called me for an interview."

My dad sent out more than eighty resumes.

"Our savings are dried up. I have no options here. We're going back."

"To Iran? We're going back to Iran?"

"I don't think things will seem as bad once you're there," he says, pretending that he believes what he's saying. He's trying to sell me something that is not sellable. I know that and so does he.

"I don't want to hear this!" I run up the stairs to my room and slam the door. My life is over.

My dad knocks on the door. "Zomorod, please let me in."

"Go away!" I yell.

"Please," he begs.

"GO AWAY!"

After a few minutes, I hear him going back down the stairs.

I lie on my bed, sobbing into my pillow. This is so unfair! Why do I have to return to a country that's become a prison, a place where I don't get to choose what to wear or become a judge or listen to music? I hate my life so much. I hate my parents. I hate being Iranian. Why is everyone else so lucky? Why did Iran go backwards?

And what am I supposed to tell Carolyn and Rachel and Howie? If there is one thing I've practiced a lot in my life, it's saying goodbye. But this time, it's different. I just want to leave without saying anything. That seems easier.

After an hour, I go back downstairs. My dad is still on the sofa. His eyes are bloodshot. I suddenly feel sorry for him, too. I know he does not want to take us back to Iran either. I sit next to him and give him a big hug. I start to cry again. My dad says nothing. What can he possibly say to make this better?

FOILED

Carolyn and I are hanging out in her room, taking a break from working on our project on the Civil War. "So what are you guys going to do now that the hostages are released? Is your dad going back to his old job?" she asks.

I hesitate for a moment, then just blurt it out.

"We're going back," I say.

"To Compton?" Carolyn's brow furrows.

"No, to Iran."

"WHAT?" she shrieks, jumping out of her chair. "Is this a joke?"

"No," I say. "We're going back to Iran."

"No way." She throws down her pencil and crosses her arms. "You can't."

"Of course we can. We've run out of money," I explain.

"Why can't *you* stay?" she asks.

Before I can reply, Carolyn yells, "Moooooooooooom, come here! Quick!"

A few seconds later, Mrs. Williams appears in the doorway, looking panicked.

"What's wrong? What is it?" she asks, all out of breath.

"Cindy's family's going back to Iran. Can she please live

351   ★

with us? She can stay in Matt's room now that he's in college. Pleeeeeeease!"

"Now, wait a second." Mrs. Williams looks at me in alarm. "Is this true, Cindy?"

"Yes." I look down at my notebook, unable to say more.

"Pleeeeeeeease," begs Carolyn.

"Calm down, Carolyn. This is a very big decision. I have to talk to your father. We have to talk to Cindy's parents," Mrs. Williams says.

Then she turns back to me. "Is this what you want, Cindy? Or is Carolyn bulldozing you?"

I have never thought of living away from my parents. In a different country halfway around the world, no less. I wouldn't even be able to talk to them more than a couple times a year. Long-distance phone calls are so expensive. I'm not sure I could stand missing them so much.

But I just can't imagine going back to Iran. Not the way it is now. There is so much I want for my life. I want to graduate from Lincoln Junior High and Corona del Mar High School. I want to go to college. I want to see Carolyn on TV when she becomes a journalist, and I want to be there when Howie finds a tall husband. I want more Halloweens. I want to learn to make oatmeal raisin cookies. More than anything, though, I want to become the best version of myself, like my dad always says. I know I can't do that in Iran.

"You don't have to answer now," Mrs. Williams says,

studying my expression, which must look conflicted. "Let's all sleep on it."

"But I do know the answer," I say emphatically. "I want to stay."

Carolyn lets out a loud cheer and starts dancing around the room.

"It's settled, then. Mom, can we get rid of Matt's stuff and paint his room?" she asks.

I can't believe what I just agreed to. I'm scared, yes, but even more excited! If you can dream it, you can be it. That's me! I get to stay here!

"I always wanted a sister!" she yells.

"Me too!"

I hug Carolyn and we jump around the room, squealing with joy.

When I get home, my dad is sitting on the couch, watching the news on TV.

"Dad," I say, before I lose my nerve, "I have to ask you and Mom something."

"Your mom's not feeling well. What is it?"

"I have to talk to both of you," I insist.

He looks concerned but says nothing, just stands up slowly and heads for the stairs, beckoning me to follow. We go to my parents' room. My mom is lying on the bed, in the dark, as usual.

My dad and I sit at the foot of the bed.

"*Maman, Baba,* I have to tell you something about moving back to Iran," I begin.

"Before you say anything," my dad interrupts, "your mom and I have been talking. We are very sad to be taking you away from all this. We see how happy you are here."

"That's what I want to talk to you about!" I exclaim, jumping to my feet.

"Please, let me finish," my dad says. I sit back down next to him. He puts his hand on my back.

"After you finish high school, we will do everything we can to send you to college in England or America," he continues. "I decided before you were born that if I ever have a daughter, she would be educated. No revolution is changing that."

My mother finally speaks up. "You are everything to us. If it weren't for you, I would not have the strength to get out of bed in the mornings. I wish we could stay in America, but your father can't find work."

"You want to stay here?" I ask my mom. "You've been wanting to go back since the day we arrived."

"Yes, but I wanted to go back to the old Iran, not the Iran our relatives are now describing to me, not the country I see on TV. How can I live in such a place?" She pauses and looks down. "But we do not have a choice."

Just when I thought I knew my mom, I realize I don't.

My dad continues. "You know, Zomorod, all these days that I have been without a job, I looked forward to one thing. Every day, I knew you would walk through the front door and remind me that despite everything, I am still a rich man."

"Me too." My mother nods in agreement, sitting up.

"When we go back to Iran, just know that our whole life is for you," he says. "No matter how difficult things may be, the three of us will be together, and that's what matters.

Family is the most important thing in the world." He hugs me tightly and then pulls back to look at my face lovingly. "So what do you want to tell us?"

"Never mind," I say. "I need to make a phone call."

I go downstairs to call Carolyn. Just a short while ago, I was jumping for joy. Not anymore.

"I'm going back," I say as soon as she picks up.

"What? I thought we decided you would stay with us. I even called my dad at work and he said it's fine with him if it's fine with your parents. We just need to work out the details, like insurance and stuff."

"Just stop," I say. "Stop bulldozing me."

"What are you talking about?" She sounds hurt and confused, and I immediately regret my words. "Don't you want to stay here?"

"I do, but it's more complicated than that."

"How?" she asks.

"You wouldn't understand."

"Try me."

I sigh, searching for the words to explain this.

"Your family is all about dreaming stuff and then having it happen," I begin. "That's not how my life is."

"I don't know what you mean," she says.

"Remember when you used to ask me how life is different in Iran?" I continue. "So here's the big difference: We don't get to dream about our future. We don't get to pursue our dreams. You know that sign you have in your kitchen, 'If You Can Dream It, You Can Be It'? That's only in America. For the rest of us, we have to take the future that comes to us, whether we like it or not."

"It sounds like you're giving up," Carolyn huffs.

"You just don't get it, do you?" I yell.

"I guess I don't!" she yells back.

And with that, we both hang up. I burst into tears.

My dad told our landlady that we will vacate the house by the end of the month. I am in the garage reassembling the boxes that we had saved from our last move. I'm sitting in the same spot I always did when I was folding the papers and putting in the inserts. When I told Chuck I was quitting, he asked me if I had found a better job. I told him no but didn't explain. I never thought I would miss that folding routine. What makes me sad is that we're moving to a country where I will never have a job like that because I'm a girl. Granted, it was a terrible career with no future. But at least *I* got to choose whether I should do that, not the government.

The garage door is open, and all of a sudden I see Original Cindy walking in. "Oh, hi," I say, a bit startled.

"Hi, Cindy. Can we talk for a minute?"

"Sure."

Original Cindy sits down on the pile of unassembled boxes across from me.

"Listen, I know you guys are moving, so I wanted to come by and say something." She takes a breath. "Um, I'm sorry."

"For what?"

"I don't know why I was so mean to you back in sixth grade. I think I was scared about starting at Lincoln. I wanted to be someone different. I just wanted to fit in."

"I can relate to that."

"And, um, of course I want to apologize for what my mom did. I'm just so embarrassed." She looks at the ground.

I had no idea that she knew! I'd assumed she'd been oblivious to it all, busy in her own world with Magic.

"It's not your fault," I say, avoiding eye contact. "But, um, just one question. Why does your mom hate us so much?"

"I don't know. I think she hates a lot of people, not that it makes it any better."

Our conversation reminds me of a poster that was in the Compton Public Library. It had a quote on it by one of my favorite writers, Madeleine L'Engle: "Hate hurts the hater more'n the hated."

"My mom is going to live in Montana with her sister," she continues.

"I'm so sorry to hear this. What are you going to do?"

"I'm staying here with my dad and Magic. We'll be fine." Original Cindy gets up. "In any case, I gotta go. Good luck with your move."

"I'll need it."

I watch my first friend in Newport Beach walk out of

the garage. I remember the first time I went to her house, and how badly I wanted her to be my friend. I tried so hard to be just like her so she would like me. It was only when I stopped pretending to be someone else that I found my real friends.

We're busy packing up the living room when our doorbell rings. "It's that man with the clown clothing," my mom says, peeking out from behind the curtains.

I open the door.

"Hey there, falafel. Is your dad home?" Skip asks. He's wearing a yellow outfit that makes the sun seem dull.

"Hold on a moment," I say. I think about inviting him inside, but our living room is full of pots and pans and half-packed boxes. It's a sad mess. I call for my dad, who is upstairs cleaning.

As soon as he appears, Skip says, "Hello, Mr. You-You—Yousef . . ."

"Please, call me Mo."

"Thank you, Mo. That's a tough name. Anyway, I'm Skip Vitter. My son, Brock, is a classmate of Cindy's, and we live around the corner. I'm sorry we haven't met yet. I must have missed you at the condo association meet-and-greets. In any case, Brock recently told me that your family was a victim of a hateful act. I wish I had known sooner, but my son doesn't always tell me everything when he should."

I immediately start to panic. Brock has spilled the beans!

My dad looks confused.

"How is Brock?" I interject, trying to detour this conversation.

"Brock is just fine, thank you. He's busy waxing his new surfboard that he just got for his birthday. That boy loves waves!"

"What hateful act?" my dad says. "Zomorod, *chee shodeh?*"
What happened?

I look at Mr. Vitter and realize that secrets are only secrets temporarily.

"Someone left a note on our doorstep a while ago, *Baba,*" I say, skipping the part about the dead hamster.

"What kind of a note?" he asks.

There is no way to avoid it now. But I realize it doesn't matter anymore if my parents find out. We're leaving in a few weeks anyway. I take a deep breath and look him in the eye.

"It said, 'Iranians go home.'"

My dad looks at the ground. He says nothing.

Skip shakes his head, then suddenly perks up, as if he can only sustain sadness for a few seconds. "But I'm here with good news," he says. "I am a member of the Rotary Club and I recently told them what happened to you, with the trash and the dead hamster and Darleen Linden—who, by the way, is no longer a board member of the condo association. And she will be sending you a letter of apology. She does not represent America, and we want you to know that."

My dad now looks utterly confused.

"I'm sorry," he says, "but I don't know what you are talking about. The trash was just an unfortunate mistake. I don't know this dead ham-whatever-it-is, and this person you mention."

My mom joins us at the door. She's wearing her bathrobe, but I don't care. We're leaving.

"Mr. Vitter," I say, desperate to cut short this painful conversation, "thank you for telling us that, and thank you for apologizing for Darleen Linden, but as you can see, we need to pack."

"Hold on. Time out." Skip makes a *T* sign with his hands. "Like I said, I come bearing good news. You see, I am a proud member of the Rotary Club, and I recently shared some of what has happened to you with the trash and the note and the dead hamster."

"Dead . . . what?" my dad asks again.

"Hamster," says Mr. Vitter. "You know, like a rat, but cuter."

"Someone also left us a dead rat?" my dad asks, turning pale. He looks at my mom, who is equally confused.

"A hamster, to be exact. *Much* cuter, but let's not dwell

on that for now." Skip forges ahead. "As I was saying, I am a Rotarian, and after I shared your story with the group, one of our members, Dr. David Klein, said that he knows you. In fact, he had apparently asked for your resume a while back and tried to help you find a job."

"Yes, yes. Davood is a good man," my dad agrees.

"Once David and I realized that we were talking about the same person, that you were unable to find a job because of the hostages and being I-raynian and all, and that you had also been treated in a very un-American way by one of our neighbors right here, well, we knew we had to do something."

"*Darleen keeyeh?*" my mom asks. *Who's Darleen?*

"*Baadan*," I say. *Later.*

Skip continues: "David and I spoke to our fellow Rotarians about your situation and it turns out that several of our members are looking to hire an engineer with your educational background and work experience. David made copies of your resume, and to make a long story short, you now have three interviews. Here are the details," he says, holding out three envelopes.

My dad is motionless, silent again. Then he reaches out slowly and takes the envelopes.

Skip opens his arms and gives him an awkward hug. It's like the sun eclipsing a little moon—a very happy little moon. My dad is smiling now, but I can tell he is also trying not to cry.

It's too late for my mom. "Tank you," she says, sobbing. "Tank you, tank you."

Then Mr. Vitter turns to me. "See? It ain't so awful, falafel. Is it?" He grins and reaches to tousle my hair.

As soon as we close the door, my mom says, "Isn't he the one who loved my stuffed grape leaves?"

"Yes," I lie, laughing.

"I knew it," she says, wiping her tears. "I will make him more right away."

HOLY MOLE

Skip has organized a potluck for us at the pool to celebrate my father's new job and our staying in America. A pool party in February—only in Southern California.

I've invited all of my friends, including Original Cindy.

My mom is upstairs putting on her new dress. It's the first one she's bought since we moved to Newport Beach. I'm wearing my new gauchos, my pompom belt, and my puka shell necklace.

Mom comes down the stairs.

"You look nice, *Maman*," I tell her.

"I forgot my lipstick," she says, and goes back up.

"Hurry!" my father yells. He's been ready for half an hour, sitting on the sofa, holding a huge pot of *fesenjoon*.

When Mom is finally ready, we set off for the pool.

As we get closer, we see that there is definitely a party going on. The association members have decorated the pool area with red, white, and blue streamers and balloons. Beach Boys music is blasting from the speakers. I'm pretty sure that, according to the *Rules for Condominium Living*, stereos are not allowed at the pool, but . . . oh well.

My parents lurk around nervously, but then Skip,

wearing a red, white, and blue plaid outfit, ushers them over to a group of smiling neighbors and makes introductions.

The Kleins arrive with a homemade chocolate cake, just like the one they gave us when we first moved in, and David jumps in the pool immediately, even though it's sweater weather.

Carolyn and her parents bring tacos, and Howie's mom has made a huge batch of oatmeal raisin cookies.

From where I'm sitting with Carolyn, Howie, and Rachel, I can see various neighbors whom we have never met trying to make small talk with my mom. Judging from the strained smiles, I know she has no idea what they're saying and they have no idea what she's saying. But for once, I don't feel the need to rescue her.

I am so happy to see Original Cindy, who joins us with a handful of flyers. Tennille now has five kittens and Cindy is trying to find them homes. I want one and I know this is the perfect moment.

I walk across to the dessert table, where my father has been hanging out pretty much the whole time. "*Baba,*" I say, "can I please have a kitten? It's free and I promise to always take care of it."

My dad puts down the bright blue cupcake he's eating and looks me in the eyes. "Zomorod, did I ever tell you about my friend Cyrus? One day he was fine, then the next day, while playing with a cat too close to his face, suddenly—boom! Blind!" He snaps his fingers, spraying bits of blue frosting in the air.

"Fine." I roll my eyes. "But just so you know, last time it was Mehdi and a horse."

I tell Cindy I won't be able to adopt a kitten, but I will help her tape flyers all over the greenbelt.

That's when I hear Skip's voice. "May I have your attention, please? May I have your attention, please?" Everyone quiets down.

"Thank you for coming to this very special event. We are here today to celebrate our neighbors. It is, after all, the people who make this such a wonderful place to live. It's easy to forget that we all came to this country from somewhere else, and we were given the opportunity to make a living and to give back. For this reason, we, the members of the condo association board, have decided to add another chapter to *Rules for Condominium Living,* which you will receive in the mail. Chapter ten, 'Our Community,' will be about some of the people who live here and their stories. When you live in a condo, you see your neighbors, you share a wall with them, you wave hello—but you don't always have a chance to hear their stories. You can live next to someone for years and years without knowing what makes them tick. We're hoping chapter ten encourages you to talk to one another. For example, did you know that the Messner family, who we all know because of the delicious apple strudels that Beatrix brings to the monthly mixers, are originally from Australia?"

"Austria!" someone yells. "They're from Austria."

"What can I say?" Skip says, laughing at his mistake. "I was too busy at USC with golf and girls to get to the other G, geography."

"At least you know it starts with a G!" someone else shouts. Everyone laughs except my parents. I am going to have to translate for them later.

Skip chuckles. Standing in front of the NO GLASS ALLOWED IN POOL AREA sign, he raises his wineglass, which I'm pretty sure is not made of plastic. "Let us all remember that everyone has a story, and everyone's story counts," he says.

"Except yours!" the same voice from the crowd heckles.

"That's what happens when you beat someone at golf three weeks in a row," Skip says, pointing to his friend.

While everyone is laughing, I see Carolyn and Howie walking to the food table. I join them. It seems like a good time for another taco.

"This party reminds me of your twelfth birthday when we had that water balloon fight that went a little wrong," Howie says.

"We were such dorks," Carolyn adds.

While we're laughing at our younger selves, Brock shows up and walks over to us.

"Hey," he says.

"Hey," I say back.

"Oh, wow, check this out," he says, pointing to the *fesenjoon*. "That looks like—"

Before he can finish, I interrupt: "Don't be rude, Brock. Just try it."

"What did you think I was gonna say?" he asks.

"You were going to say it looks like mud. I've heard it before."

"Uh, no," Brock says, "I was gonna say it looks like mole."

"What?" I ask.

"Mo-lay," he repeats, pronouncing it slowly. "It's, like, a sauce they have in Mexico. When I go surfing there, we always have it."

"Is it a sauce, or is it *like* a sauce?" teases Carolyn.

"Whatever," says Brock, ignoring her and taking a giant serving of *fesenjoon*. My mother sees this from across the pool area and smiles broadly. He is the only person so far to try the *fesenjoon*. I have a feeling I know what my dad and I will be eating for the next week.

"Yeah, whatever," I agree, knowing that at this very moment, all is right with the world. I am exactly where I want to be.*

* Note to God: Thank you.

AUTHOR'S NOTE

This book is a semi-autobiographical novel, which means that parts of it really happened in my own life, and other parts were created in my imagination. All the historical facts are true. If reading these stories has piqued your interest in the hostage crisis, there is an excellent, award-winning documentary directed by Les Harris, *The Iran Hostage Crisis: 444 Days to Freedom (What Really Happened in Iran)*. It's a great choice for classroom use. If you want to learn more about Iranian Americans, check out the PBS documentary *The Iranian Americans* directed by Andrew Goldberg. It is available on DVD and is another excellent classroom tool. (Disclaimer: I'm in it.)

My website, www.firoozehdumas.com, has many videos and links to support this book, as well as an educator's guide, which can be downloaded for free.

Also on my website, check out The Falafel Kindness Project. As readers know, kindness is a major theme in this novel, but it is also important in real life. There is so much talk about bullying these days! But realistically, who's going to stand up to a bully? Not me. However, we are all capable of acts of kindness that make a huge difference. Let's start a Falafel Kindness Project in your school! Tell me about *your* expenience. Together, we can make a difference!

I really do have a friend named Carolyn, who told me in sixth grade at Lincoln Junior High that she wanted to be a television journalist. Today, she is a news anchor at a major network, still asks a lot of questions, and wins Emmys as a result. Howie did meet a wonderful, tall husband in church and they now have two beautiful, tall daughters. (If you want to see pictures of the real Carolyn and the real Howie, go to my website.) Rachel is a composite character, made up of several friends. Carolyn, Howie, and I are still friends.

In second grade, Ms. Hensley saved my Halloween by bringing a costume for me to school, without being asked.

I did volunteer at the Goodwill, where I learned that everyone deserves dignity. I sincerely wish there were better opportunities for people with Down syndrome in Iran and other parts of the world.

And I did, at age fourteen, inherit not one but *two* shirts that said SEXY GRANDMA on them, in sequins. I could never make that up. They were donated to the Salvation Army, where perhaps an actual grandmother—one with a healthy sense of self—purchased them.

I now count Kathryn Koob, former hostage, as my friend. She is witty in real life, just like I guessed she would be when I saw her on TV. She is also an extraordinary human being and a true global citizen. (The story of our friendship is in my second book, *Laughing Without an Accent*. You can also see a picture of us on my website.)

I hope that reading this book will increase your interest in history. I used to think that history was just about memorizing dates of battles, but history is really stories about people and the battles we fight within. It's about all the stuff you don't see on the evening news. It's about hopes, dreams, and popular music. The life you are living right now will someday be history.

How will you tell it?

ACKNOWLEDGMENTS

"I have always depended on the kindness of strangers."
—Blanche DuBois, *A Streetcar Named Desire*

I would like to thank friends and their families whose kindness and hospitality shaped how my family and I feel about America. Thank you to the Sandbergs, Mrs. Popkin, the Musgroves, the Hensleys, Mrs. Batson, the Englishes, the Johnsons, the Gillards, the Howards, the Logans, the Nathans, the Gilberts, the Martins, the Stuhlbargs, the Stahrs, the Woodses, and the Jones family.

In the course of my adult life, three people told me that I should become a writer. Each time, I thought they were nuts. Hollis Veneman, Jennifer Winter, and Mary Goodspeed: What do I know? Also, if you have any other suggestions for me, I'm listening.

I would also like to thank Michael Yell, Syd Golston, Elinor Lipman, and Brigid McCarthy for reading early drafts and giving me feedback. My brother, Sean Jazayeri, proved that in addition to his many talents, he is an awesome proofreader. Debbie Duncan saved this book when I was facing writer's block and was filled with despair. (Note: I met Debbie and her mother at San Jose Airport many years ago while waiting for a flight. Turns out they were at the wrong gate. By the time they realized their mistake and ran off, we had exchanged phone numbers, and the rest is history. Sometimes strangers really are friends we have not yet met. Skip was right!)

Ever since I was first published in 2003, I have received words of support and encouragement from readers and educators all over the world. I wish I could thank each and every one of you in person. Please know that your words, spoken or by email, have impacted me.

Professionally, I have worked with some people who are not only talented at their jobs but also incredibly decent human beings. Holly Kernan (via Penny Nelson) at KALW 91.7 was the first person to ever give me a break. Thanks to her and to Sandip Roy, I was able to say, "I've been on National Public Radio." Bonnie Nadell took me as a client when I was an unknown, except for having been on National Public Radio. (See previous acknowledgment.) Bruce Tracy was my first editor and I will love him always. He read this manuscript and gave me valuable feedback. Steven Barclay and his capable and gracious staff, Kathryn Barcos, Eliza Fischer, Sara Bixler, Barry Rossnick, Susan Rolfe, Susan Durfee, and Christy Pascoe, enable me to take my message to the nooks and crannies of the United States and beyond. Because of the lecture circuit, I have been able to see parts of America that I would have otherwise never seen, and I have loved every minute of it.

Given the isolated nature of writing, I am indebted to the folks at the Sun Valley Writers' Conference and the Aspen

Institute, who enabled me to meet my peers, a detail that has changed my life immensely and has encouraged me to continue on this path, however impractical it may seem at times.

Serendipity is my favorite English word. This book came as a result of my being in New York on a particular day and having an unplanned conversation with Beverly Horowitz. I was in New York because of Justine Stamen Arrillaga and everyone at the TEAK Fellowship who had invited me to speak (still one of my favorite groups). However, I would not have been in New York on that particular day were it not for Helen Bing generously allowing me to stay in her apartment for an entire week, longer than was necessary, thereby allowing me to have that unforeseen conversation on the last day of my visit. Thank you, Helen, for that and for a thousand other kindnesses. You are truly the Queen of Good Karma.

While I was writing this book, all twenty-six versions of it, there was only one person who never tired of reading it and always giving me positive feedback. ("This is the best book ever! I *am* getting a free copy, right?") Thank you, E., for being the most enthusiastic reader ever and for comparing me to Judy Blume. That compliment alone gets you a free copy.

This book took seven long years to write and would not have happened without Lynne Polvino, who understood my intention from the get-go. Thank you, Lynne. You are a brilliant editor.

Thank you, Beverly Horowitz and Rebecca Short of Random House, for your contributions. You were part of this journey, and I appreciate your time and effort. And thank you, Mel Merger of William Morris Endeavor.

I don't think I will ever be able to write a story that is not influenced by my parents. Even though this novel is fiction, I owe my parents, Kazem and Nazireh Jazayeri, a debt of gratitude for allowing me to mine our family's history for material. And Baba, thank you for your commitment to optimism. I couldn't live without it.

Last but not least, a huge thank you to the Frenchman, with whom life has been a big adventure interspersed with great meals. And to N., S., and E., for showing me that my favorite word will always be *Mom*.